Copyrighted Material

Vampire Mage Copyright © 2018 by Joshua King
Book design and layout copyright © 2018 by Joshua King

This novel is a work of fiction. Names, characters, places, and incidents are either products of the author's imagination or used fictitiously. Any resemblance to actual events, locales, or persons, living, dead, or undead, is entirely coincidental.

All rights reserved.

No part of this publication can be reproduced or transmitted in any form or by any means, electronic or mechanical, without permission in writing from Joshua King.

1st Edition

http://joshuakingbooks.com/

SIGN UP FOR UPDATES

For updates about new releases, sign up for the mailing list below. You'll know as soon as I release new books, including my upcoming new series, as well as sequels to *Vampire Mage*.

htttps://www.subscribepage.com/joshua_king

CONTENTS

Chapter 1	1
Chapter 2	15
Chapter 3	21
Chapter 4	35
Chapter 5	45
Chapter 6	53
Chapter 7	69
Chapter 8	75
Chapter 9	89
Chapter 10	99
Chapter 11	109
Chapter 12	121
Chapter 13	131
Chapter 14	145
Chapter 15	157
Chapter 16	165
Chapter 17	173
Chapter 18	181
Chapter 19	191
Chapter 20	201
Chapter 21	209
Chapter 22	221
Chapter 23	231
Chapter 24	243
Chapter 25	257
Chapter 26	269
Chapter 27	283
Chapter 28	295

Chapter 29	309
Chapter 30	323
Chapter 31	335
Chapter 32	347
Chapter 33	361
Chapter 34	373
Epilogue	383
Sign Up For Updates	393
About the Author	395

VAMPIRE MAGE

BOOK 1 IN THE VAMPIRE MAGE SERIES

JOSHUA KING

For Laurie

1

Ten years had gone by, and I hadn't accomplished shit.

"Ugh. Fuck this madness." I paced the sidewalk in front of my old high school gym. What the hell was I doing back in New York? What exactly was I trying to prove?

That I was still *the* Hayden Taylor? Voted most likely to succeed, to get the girl, to tear a tree from the ground with my bear hands?

Yeah, yeah. And a million other things I didn't do. Nor would I ever.

The music poured from the doors, along with a sprinkle of laughter here and there. Some part of me wanted to pull my shoulders back, walk in the room, and own the fucking place. I could have. It was mine for the taking; but it was all a lie.

My best days were behind me.

"Hey, buddy," a voice called out from behind me. "You going in or what?"

I moved back and offered a cocky smile, pulling a pack of cigarettes from my pocket. "Not yet, man. Go on and get yours."

He snorted and moved past me, his beer belly leading the way. I should have recognized the guy but making friends back in high school wasn't part of the deal. Fucking girls, drinking beer, and winning the game on Friday night? All that and a little college action on the side? That was what I cared about.

But that shit hadn't served me well since leaving the dump that loomed up in front of me. I glanced around me as memories pounded inside my head. Who would have thought I'd have ended up broke, boring, and single? None of the fuckers on the other side of the gym door, that was for sure.

"Just go in. Shit. What are you waiting on?" I reached out and gripped the door handle, but I couldn't open it. Back in high school, lying to score for the night or cheat on a test was all right. Now at almost thirty, the only thing I had left was truth. No matter how much that shit hurt.

It took a minute more of fighting myself before I turned, pitched the cigarettes I wasn't planning on smoking, and walked back toward the bright city lights.

"Hey, you coming?" the taxi cab driver called out the window, his accent thick, his voice gravelly. He'd talked my fucking ear off all the way from the hotel to the school. I didn't feel like going through that again.

"Nah, I'm going to walk. Thanks, man." I waved him off. The minute I'd told the guy to sit tight while I checked the place out, I had known that I wasn't staying.

My life was a mess. I would have walked in to the reunion, and those bastards would have known right away that I'd amounted to nothing. It would just depress me, remind me that I peaked in high school. *Fuck that.*

Stars twinkled above my head, and as silly as it was, I couldn't help but glance up and wonder if there was anything beyond the tiny-ass life I was living. Something bigger had to exist.

"I sure as hell hope it does," I mumbled and zipped up my jacket. It was cold as a witch's titty up north around the holidays. A frosty wind blew through the streets, and I picked my pace up to a languid jog. I would find a place to have a beer, a conversation with an old-timer, and maybe someone to snuggle up next to later that night.

Hopefully, all three weren't one and the same. I chuckled at the thought. *That* shit would have been just the perfect shitty end to this shitty evening.

My desire to get somewhere warm had me hustling to get into the door of what looked like a club in an alleyway in downtown. I was surprised as shit that I'd made it that far. The city beamed with lights, but something about the door caught my attention.

A glow around the edges.

"Why not?" I muttered to myself and walked toward it, sliding my frozen fingers into my jacket pockets. If sex was in my future, I'd need to warm up my hands. I planned on using them, amongst other things.

"You got ID?" The big guy outside the door pressed a meaty hand into my chest. "And are you on the list?"

I pulled out my wallet. "I have an ID, and I'm thinking for a hundred bucks, you might be willing to put me on that list or let me be someone else for a night?" I offered him a weary smile.

He eyed me before plucking the bill from my fingers and moving back. "Jason Borne is your name."

I lifted an eyebrow. "Seriously?"

"No, just fucking with you." He let out a loud laugh, and his belly jiggled with mirth. "Welcome to Solomon's. Get in there, and if anyone asks who you are, just tell them you're a friend of mine."

"Your name?" I worked my license back in my wallet and slipped it in my back pocket.

"Muja." He nodded and turned back to the door as he pulled it open.

"Right." I turned and eyed the place. People filled almost every inch of the large dance floor, and the red and green lights mixed with a little too much smoke gave off a Christmas orgy vibe. I liked it, and I didn't, but the place had beer, so I walked up to the bar.

"Something to drink, handsome?" a dark-eyed gal asked from behind the bar.

"Yeah. A beer. Whatever you have imported in a bottle." I glanced at my surroundings. The bar was as busy as the rest of the place. "This place looks like a hole in the wall from the outside."

She gave me a toothy grin. "That's the point. We're busy enough without advertising or foot traffic."

"You guys should go into marketing." I slid onto the seat in front of me and took the beer she offered.

"You want a tab, Jason?" Her smile grew.

I chuckled. "Private joke around here?"

"You look like him." She shrugged and turned to wait on the next guy.

After taking a quick sip, I turned around to face the dance floor, my ass still planted on the seat. Had it not been a pussy move, I might have ordered a hot chocolate. My damn fingers were killing me. Gloves. I needed to get some gloves.

Bodies moved on the dance floor like a breathing amoeba, some of it sexy, but most of it not. Why grown men thought they could dance like they were still in their teens and get away with it was beyond me. A flash of light near the stage caught my attention, and I paused with my beer halfway to my lips.

A woman with eyes so green I could see them from twenty feet away stared my way. Her long blond hair curled around her shoulders, accentuating how perky her tits were. Red lips the color of blood turned up in a tantalizing smile.

I glanced behind me. Surely, she wasn't looking at me that way. Not the college flunky, the single, old, useless fuck wearing my jacket.

I turned back to face her and poked myself in the chest, mouthing, "Me?" It wasn't the most confident move, but I'd rather make sure before I strutted up to her like an asshole, only to get laughed at.

She nodded her head slightly.

Everything shifted. The music blasted out the next song, the natural lights dimmed, and the strobe lights raced harder and faster, making my pulse spike.

Then she was gone. I'd done nothing more than blink.

"She's waiting for you." The bartender's voice rose up from behind me.

I turned to face her, downed the rest of my beer, and offered her the bottle. "Never keep a lady waiting, right?'

She laughed. "Probably not a good idea this time."

If things didn't work out with Blondie, I wouldn't think twice about bending the bartender over a bathroom counter and making her moan a little. I shot her a quick wink, and I was off my seat and headed toward the far corner of the club where my seductress had disappeared to.

I hadn't taken more than two steps when I saw two giant meatheads square up against each other ahead of me. One was wearing a blue shirt, and one was wearing red. *It's fucking Rock 'em Sock 'em Robots*. Blue Shirt shoved a table out of the way for what looked like no other reason than to do it. Red shirt retaliated by smashing a chair with the sole of his boot.

I tried to move to the side so I could walk around them, but almost immediately, guys from both sides of the bar rushed toward the two hulks. Shouting shit I couldn't understand even from five feet away, they start wailing on each other.

Bodies were flinging around, and I couldn't tell if they were jumping at each other or being thrown. Red Shirt threw a punch that made contact with Blue Shirt's nose. It made a sickening crunching sound, and a spurt of blood shot out. It splattered on the people around them, and I expected it to at least slow down the fight. No such luck. The first blood seemed to only make the conflict, whatever the fuck it was about, worse. Suddenly, fists and feet were flying everywhere.

It was impossible to tell which people were loyal to which of the meatheads. Maybe they didn't even know. They could have just been soaked in too much liquor, pissed off at their boss, their wife, their limp dick, or just the world in general. That was enough to get people fighting, even when they didn't know what the fight was about.

I didn't feel too much like getting into the fray, but the blonde waiting for me was too delicious to pass up. My cock was already hard, and I didn't feel like going home and rubbing one out thinking about that girl's bright green eyes and luscious body. I'd much rather have the real thing. And if that meant pummeling my way through the display of stupidity in front of me, fine. I'd fuck them up and then fuck her. Maybe the adrenaline would even make it better.

Walking headlong toward the fight, I reared back and punched the first guy who got near me. He stumbled back, growling something, but it opened up some space. I pushed ahead more and felt a fist make contact with the side of my head. Stars danced around in front of my eyes. Balling up my fists, I buried one into a hard stomach and then another into something much softer I couldn't identify. Another punch knocked me back a few feet, but I rallied. Around me, I heard shouting and cursing I still didn't understand. It didn't matter. It still wasn't my fight. It was just a roadblock keeping me from the sweet body I was craving.

Suddenly, something occurred to me. I had been scared shitless to go into my ten-year high school reunion, but I was literally fighting my way through a grimy bar to fuck some ghost-like chick in the back of a club. I needed to take my brother up on getting a shrink. He was right. It was time.

Finally, I made my way out the other end of the fight. A couple of guys had started breaking up the action by that point. Oddly, I could feel the attention of the bar turning toward me. It was unnerving, and I tried not to think about it as I continued on toward where I'd seen the woman standing.

Regardless of whether it was in my head or not, eyes followed me as I passed by the dance floor and slowed my steps near the back corner. Who was this woman, and why did she feel important, not just to me, but to the rest of the fuckers staring me down?

I turned to glance over my shoulder and found them watching me, unashamed. *Fuck*.

Had I stumbled into some kind of gang bullshit? Was everyone here in a cult? Was this chick going to smoke my dick for dinner and skin the meat from my thighs by the time the sun came up?

Did it matter? I wanted inside of her. *Fuck it*.

After slamming the door shut on reason, I walked through a black door and closed it behind me. The only feature in the room was a set of stairs going up. I climbed them and emerged into a hallway with doors lining both sides. Only one of the doors was open, with dim light pouring out of it. I made my way toward it.

The room smelled like flowers and women's perfume. Blondie stood facing me, her hands gripping the counter she rested her ass against.

"Hi," I whispered, forcing the word out of my mouth. "You wanted something?"

The silky pink robe she wore was open in the front, and the thick swell of her breasts teased me with promises that her mouth would help finish.

"Cocky." She smirked. "I like it, Jason."

I laughed heartily, breaking the spell between us. "Really?"

Her smile softened, and she motioned for me to

come closer. "Just kidding. Come here. I want to taste you."

"And you should. All the girls do." I moved to her and slid my hands around her hips outside of her robe. No point in pushing too far until she invited me to.

She ran her fingers through my hair, scratching my scalp before pulling me in tightly. The warm whisper of her words across my lips had my dick growing thick. "Oh no, I'm not a girl, Hayden. I'm a woman."

I wanted to ask how she knew my name, but her lips pressed to mine, and the room grew fuzzy around me. I pressed myself to her and rested my hands on the top curve of her ass as she made quick work of my lips and tongue, her moans soliciting a deep desire I hadn't felt in a long while.

"Fuck me," she mumbled before nipping at my lips and pressing her body into mine.

My hands slid under the silk, rubbing my cold fingers along the warm wetness of her slit.

"But what if we do this, and you want more? I'm a one-night kinda guy." I teased her as she worked my dick out of my jeans. The fucker stood hard and proud, ready to take on a whole horde of hot women with loose morals.

"One night is all we need." She kissed me again before pressing her hips against mine, taking me inside of her in one long thrust.

I grabbed her hips and carried her to the bed in the corner. The feeling of her tight wet pussy clamped around me already had me right at the edge of my control, and I wanted more. When I got to the bed, I dropped her down onto her back so I landed over her. I plunged into her a few hard times, and then her hands pressed against my chest.

She rolled me over, lost the robe, and sank her nails into my shoulders. "There's something intriguing about you. I want to know what it is."

I didn't have any idea what that was supposed to mean, but she could say whatever she wanted as long as she kept bouncing just like she was.

"Find it, baby," I slurred, wondering what the hell I'd gotten myself into.

It wasn't like I'd been fighting off the hot women wanting to jump on my cock recently. Usually, it took a bit more effort. Who the hell was this woman? For all I fucking knew, she was a secret agent trying to manipulate national secrets out of me. Or a monster getting ready to fuck me up. Either way, I might be up for it.

"Just need to taste you." She dismounted my cock and moved down my body, biting and licking as she went.

"Do anything you want," I groaned.

I totally meant it. I felt like I was losing grip on reality, but I didn't care. She really could be an assassin and take this second to finish me off, and I'd tap dance to Hell with a smile on my face.

2

I couldn't tell if I was waking up or in the middle of a fucked-up dream. I shifted around and knew I was coming out of sleep I didn't even realize I'd fallen into. I didn't remember drifting off. All I really remembered was the woman I was fucking biting me when I thought she was going to suck my cock.

Groaning, I pried my eyes open. The room was only half lit, but even that little bit of illumination was too much for my sore eyes. I squeezed them closed again for a few seconds. When the feeling of needles poking into my skull stopped, I opened them again. The woman was gone. So, she hadn't stuck around after getting primal with me. Not that

I expected to cuddle all morning and then go out for fucking crepes or anything, but damn.

I stood up and immediately felt like a truck had hit me. I was groggy and felt like shit, but the headache and feeling like I'd been drugged weren't unfamiliar sensations. I felt pretty much like I always did after a hard night of drinking and fucking. It would pass. Probably just in time for me to want to do it all again.

I didn't know where I was. Obviously, I wasn't at home. After a few seconds, I realized I was still in the room where I'd found Blondie the night before. I was upstairs at Solomon's, which meant the walk downstairs would be awkward as fuck.

Before I could worry about that, I had to find a bathroom. I stumbled out of the room and down the hallway. I figured if there was a room with a bed up there, there had to be a place to clean up and piss nearby. They just went together. The room two doors down proved me right. I sidled up to the toilet and dropped my pants.

Something immediately caught my eye. My thigh looked strange, and I bent down to look closer. The whole inside of my upper leg was red and swollen. The more I looked at it, the more aware I was of how much it hurt. It burned like shit, and when I looked even closer, I noticed two little holes in the middle of the red area. It looked like a bite and felt like it had been pumped full of something nasty.

The pain got worse, and my skin felt like it was searing. Something had gotten me. I thought for a second it might have been a bug, but that would have had to be one big-ass spider to leave that kind of damage. I thought about the woman from the night before and the way her mouth roved over me. She had nipped at my skin in a way that didn't feel exactly playful. Could she have left that kind of mark?

And how the fuck didn't I notice? Actually, I knew exactly why I didn't notice.

If my thigh looked that bad, though, what did the rest of me look like? I looked around the small, dingy bathroom for a mirror. There wasn't one. That struck me as weird. What bathroom didn't have a mirror? Especially in a bar. Didn't people need to be able to make sure they looked good enough to get some ass? Or at least didn't have puke clinging to their hair when they'd had too much. Maybe some dude in the same intellectual class as the morons from the night before had smashed it when they got pissed off.

I pulled out my phone and snapped a picture of myself. I had to make sure I didn't look too rough before I went back downstairs. Looking at the screen, I was shocked at the image I saw. I was expecting the same paunchy face and dark under-eye circles I'd been dealing with for months. Instead, my face looked thinner. Bags big enough to carry all of Mary Poppins's shit were gone. I actually looked awake and healthy. I pulled the phone back a little farther to take another picture of myself. This one showed more of me, and I noticed more changes. My hair was actually thick again. I'd been waking up to gray hairs, but all of those premature little fuckers were gone. I looked as good as I did when I was twenty-one. I didn't know how the hell it happened, but it felt good looking at a version of myself that didn't look like life had run over me with a tractor.

I was intrigued by what I was seeing. If my face looked that much better, what else might be different? Not really caring I was standing in a grungy bar bathroom, I stripped down and started looking over the rest of my body. The gut I'd developed was gone. I actually had abs. My arms were thick, the muscles obvious again. My entire body looked tighter and younger, like I'd gone back years. I didn't know what was happening, and it was messing with my head a little. I thought back to all the drugs I'd used when I was younger. I'd essentially traipsed through the alphabet sampling a little of everything that was available. Some I did a lot more than sample. I didn't think they had much lasting effect other than the general crumbling of my life, but now I was wondering if the impact on my brain had been a lot more than that. How long does it take for the rest of the brain to find out about the deaths of their cell friends? Maybe I was just now starting to get the effects of some of those drugs and that was what was what was making me believe all this was really happening.

I squeezed my eyes closed, telling myself I was the same greying, softened man I had been when I walked into the bar the night before. The changes couldn't be real. When I felt like I'd had enough of a talk with myself, I snapped another picture and looked at it, expecting to see the same me staring back. Nope. I still looked young, smooth, and fit.

I decided to go with it.

What the hell. I might as well enjoy it while my brain was still on its vacation from reality.

3

I HAD to admit I felt a bit of swagger in my step as I made my way out of the bathroom and back toward the steps down into the bar. It was hard not to when you looked as good as I did. I felt better than I had since I was at my peak. Maybe even better than that.

As I got to the top of the steps, I ran my hands down over my abs. I couldn't even remember how long it had been since I had actually been able to feel my muscles through the layer of fat on my gut, but now the fat was gone. There were actual abs there again. Maybe my brain hadn't been cooked by the drugs. There could be another explanation. Maybe it was possible to fuck hard enough to lose seven years' worth of pizza, cigarettes, and whiskey in just a few minutes. If so, I had found my way to make a shit-ton of money. Maybe I'd whip up an infomercial and start marketing my revolutionary new health and fitness plan.

Pound Your Way to Glory.

It worked on so many levels.

I looked around as I made my way down the steps, not really knowing what to expect. I wasn't going to pretend I hadn't been in plenty of bars well before it was five o' clock anywhere, but actually waking up in one brought the concept of day drinking to a whole new level. The bar looked surprisingly similar to what I remembered it looking like the night before. Despite it being sometime in the morning, the inside of the bar still looked dark and smoky. It had the solid doors and heavily curtained windows to thank for that. I was halfway down the steps when I noticed the same bartender from the night before was standing behind the bar.

She looked even hotter than she had when I first saw her. Not having the crowd of drinkers surrounding her might have been a part of it. I could see her better, and there was plenty to look at. The daringly low scoop of her neckline gave me an eyeful as she leaned over the counter to continue wiping it. The clingy fabric barely held back her ample cleavage, and I could tell she hadn't bothered to put on a bra when she got dressed. If she leaned forward a bit more, her nipples would probably pop out to say good morning.

Not that I would have complained.

My feet hit the landing at the bottom of the steps, and she looked toward me. Straightening, she gestured for me to come over to her. I complied, sidling up to the bar and dropping down onto the same stool I'd sat in the night before. I wondered if she noticed the change that had come over me. Now that I was closer, I got an even better view of her. My eyes roved over her, and I took in the abundance of smooth, milky skin exposed by her clothes. Her thick red hair tumbled around her shoulders and down to the tight nip of her waist. A sprinkle of freckles across the bridge of her little nose and her cheekbones only made her sexier.

My hungry stare couldn't get enough of her. I didn't even bother to try to look away from the lush swells of her tits or pretend I wasn't full-on staring at her. Usually, I wasn't that brazen with women. I'd never pretend to be chivalrous or say I didn't like to get my fill of staring at hot women, especially when they were as sexy as this fiery bartender. But usually, I was a bit subtler about it. Not today. Even I was surprised by how completely nonchalant I was about staring at her.

She seemed to notice I was transfixed by her and made a decidedly not subtle sound of clearing her throat.

"Hey," she said. "I'm up here."

I looked back at her face and saw her looking at me with an understandably exasperated expression, bordering on disgusted. She probably got stared at like that most of her life and didn't need more of it first thing in the morning.

"Hey," I said.

Just the fact that I was paying attention to her seemed to assuage her annoyance some. She held out one hand toward me.

"I'm Ashe," she said.

"Hayden," I said, shaking her hand.

Ashe tilted her head at me. My eyes flickered to Ashe's cleavage again, and she gave a half-grin.

"Welcome to the Underworld," she said.

It was my turn to give her a quizzical look.

"The Underworld?" I asked. "I thought this place was called Solomon's."

Ashe nodded. "To the average guy who walks in here without knowing where he is, it's Solomon's. To members of the kin, to your kin, it's called Solomon's Fang. It's a favorite among us."

"Us?" I asked, feeling confused. "My kin?"

"You're a part of the Underworld now, Hayden. You have a whole new existence ahead of you. Well, hopefully."

"I don't understand," I said.

The half-grin returned. "You're confused," she said. "I guess that's understandable. It's not like you walked in here last night thinking you were going to meet a vampire, much less plunge your cock into one."

I felt like I had just gotten smacked in the face with a brick. I tried to process what Ashe said, but it didn't sink in.

"A vampire?" I asked. "I don't remember seeing a vampire."

"It's funny that you think you'd know if you did," Ashe said.

"What do you mean?"

"I'm not talking about fucking Dracula," she said. "Vampires don't go walking around in giant collars, black capes, and powdered wigs. Well, usually. I mean, I guess some of them might get their kicks out of that. But the one whose eye you caught isn't going to be inspiring any Halloween costumes anytime soon."

Realization hit me. "Blondie?" I asked.

Ashe gave a short, mirthless laugh. "I wouldn't let her hear you call her that," she said.

"So, let me get this straight. You're telling me I hooked up with a vampire last night? And that's why I changed like this?"

She nodded. "You catch on quick."

"I thought I had just gotten back in shape," I said, feeling a hint of disappointment.

"Overnight?" Ashe asked sourly. "Even you should know it was going to take more than a few minutes of burning calories to work off that gut. And when was the last time you heard of cardio taking the gray out of hair?"

"So what *did* cause it?" I asked.

"Like I said, you met a vampire. She was interested when she saw you, she got you into that room, and she hopped on. Did you notice anything… odd when you were fucking her?"

"Other than that it was happening in some upstairs room of a bar, and I hadn't even said a word to her?" I thought about it for a second, and then something came to mind. "She bit me. I just remembered that. She went down on me, and she bit me."

Ashe nodded again. "Are things becoming a little clearer to you?" When I didn't answer, she leaned against the counter again. "Let me spell it out for you. She bit you, and she took your blood. That means she started the change."

"She turned me into a vampire?" I asked.

"Not quite. Like I said, she started it. You have to finish it. You've got four days to complete the change."

"What happens if I don't complete it?" I asked.

"You die," she said matter-of-factly.

"Fantastic." I drew in a breath. "Four days?"

Ashe pushed back from the counter. "Well, that part is kind of misleading. It's quite common to sleep through the first twenty-four hours because the body undergoes so many changes so fast. Best to plan on a solid three days, just to be safe."

She bent down to pull a crate of bottles out from under the bar, and I let out an audible moan at the sight of her ass in her tight little pants. Ashe stood up and shot me a glare.

"That's all a part of the transformation, too," she said. "You're going to have a much stronger affinity for sex now. It's just the nature of the beast. You'll get used to it."

I still felt like I wasn't totally grasping what she was saying to me. I couldn't make myself believe it. This had to be one big-ass elaborate prank they liked to pull on the drunk chumps who fell asleep in the upstairs rooms. I leaned forward with my arms on the bar and stared at Ashe for a few seconds.

"Prove it," I said.

"What?" she asked.

"I don't believe you. Vampires don't exist. Especially not sexy vampires who turn you during sex and crank back the years with their enchanted pussy."

Ashe shot me another glare. "I can tell you for a fact it wasn't her pussy that turned you. Enchanted or otherwise. You said it yourself. She bit you."

I shook my head. "I don't know what kind of joke is being pulled here. I'm pretty sure any second now, some dude is going to jump out from under one of the tables with a camera and tell me he's going to post all the footage on YouTube. It's going to be boring as hell, though, because I'm not fooled."

"What do you mean?"

I leaned toward her, lowering my voice to a mock conspiratorial whisper. "There's no such thing as vampires," I said again.

"There's not?" Ashe asked. "Thank you so much for telling me. I really appreciate you breaking through the delusion."

I rolled my eyes. "You're going to keep it up?" I asked. "Look, you are unbelievably sexy. I'm not going to lie. You're so hot, I forgot how to function for a few seconds there. But it's not enough to make me start believing in urban legends and spooky campfire stories. You didn't even offer me a s'more."

"But you're so quick to believe you can just wake up and all of a sudden and your gut is gone? And you've somehow managed to shake seven years of disappointment and failure funk off just because you spent a few minutes with a woman?"

I shrugged. "I personally find that easier to believe than a horde of the undead just roaming around New York."

"You're not in New York," she said.

I looked at her incredulously. "I might not have known what end was up when I woke up this morning, but I know what city I'm in. I came for my high school reunion, and since I went to high school in New York, I think it's a safe bet to say that's where I am."

"Then I suggest you keep your ass out of Las Vegas, or even Atlantic City for that matter. You would lose that bet."

"Where do you think I am?" I asked sarcastically.

Ashe held out her hands as if to encompass the bar around us. "Solan City," she said. "It's a perfect mirror of New York but designed for our kind." She grabbed a menu from the end of the bar and slid it toward me, turning it so I could look at the logo on the front. "See that?"

I looked down at the burgundy faux leather of the menu cover. I wouldn't have thought a place like this would have a menu at all, much less one that fancy. If I'd seen it when I first went into the bar, I might not even have noticed the symbol on the front. Now that Ashe had it right in front of me, her fingertip tracing the gold embossing, I couldn't miss it. *Solomon.* A complex tribal pattern surrounded the name of the bar, and she touched it almost adoringly.

"Do you know what this is?" she asked.

Her voice had that tone that meant she knew I didn't. She asked the question in the way people do when they know you don't know the answer but want you to admit it.

"No," I said.

"It's a character in ancient vampire language. It means 'fang'."

"I still don't believe you."

Ashe let out a sigh and took a step back from the bar. Locking eyes with me, she opened her mouth. I watched as her teeth started to shift, and my heart pounded as I watched sharp, glistening fangs slide into view. She let them stay that way for a few seconds, just long enough for me to know they were definitely real. They slid back up into place, and she closed her mouth.

"Convinced?" she asked.

"Holy shit," I muttered. My mind cleared suddenly with a jolt of realization. "Wait. How did I manage to wander into a vampire bar? I was walking around New York. I didn't say an incantation or go through a fireplace or some shit."

Ashe rolled her eyes. "Did I say you've been transformed into a wizard?"

"I'm just trying to figure out how I went from being in New York to getting into here, and now I'm supposedly in some other city."

"It's both," Ashe said.

"Both?"

"Solomon's Fang isn't just one place. It's a nexus between the two worlds. It exists in both New York and Solan City simultaneously. When you come here, you can step through the gateway between the two worlds and fully enter the Underworld."

"I'm not in New York anymore." It came out resigned, like I was convincing myself.

"So now that you're caught up to speed, where did she bite you?"

"What?" I asked.

I felt like I was most certainly *not* caught up to speed.

"Where did she bite you?" Ashe asked again, speaking slowly and pronouncing each word carefully like she didn't think I understood her.

"On my leg," I answered.

"Let me see it," she said. "I'll show you how the fangs fit."

I got down off the stool and walked around behind the bar. Ashe reached for my belt and loosened it. The feeling immediately tightened my stomach and made my cock twitch. She unceremoniously dropped my pants around my ankles and crouched down to get a better look at the bite. Her soft hand ran along my skin as she pressed her fingertips into the still swollen and tender area around the punctures. It was starting to feel better but being turned on by having the sexy bartender on her knees in front of me was probably doing its part to dull the pain. Her fangs sank down out of her mouth again, and she tilted her head so I could see the pointed tips perfectly aligned with the holes in my leg.

"See?" she asked. "Looks like a good, clean bite. She really knows what she's doing."

The affinity for sex Ashe had mentioned reared its head. I reached down and ran my fingers through her silky hair.

"Why don't you show me what *you* know how to do?" I asked.

Ashe nipped at me with her fangs, just catching the skin of my thigh. She climbed to her feet and flipped her hair back over her shoulder.

"Soon," she said. "There'll be plenty of time

for that. But right now, you need to get your ass in gear. I told you, you only have four days after the bite to finish the turning. If you don't, you'll die. Time's ticking. You've got to get going." She gave me a regretful look. "But, honestly, I wouldn't hold out too much hope."

4

I didn't like the sound of Ashe's last statement. She stepped away from me, and I pulled up my pants.

"What do you mean you don't hold out too much hope?" I asked.

Ashe tilted her head thoughtfully, looking like she was trying to figure out the right words to say. She seemed to almost be debating with herself about what she thought she should tell me. Finally, her shoulders dropped resolutely, and she looked me directly in the eyes.

"Alright, let me put it this way. The woman you called Blondie? Which, just to reiterate, I recommend you never, *ever* do again. That's Aurora. She is the daughter of one of the highest-ranking vampires in our world. Do you know what that means?"

I thought about it for a second. "She's royalty?" I asked, just throwing it out there.

Ashe gave a hint of a nod. "Essentially," she said. "You need to think of Aurora as a princess, and you are a peasant. That is how untouchable she is to you. She is completely beyond you, and you can't pursue her, just like a peasant would never try to go after a princess. Do you understand?"

I stared at Ashe, still trying to get her words to sink in. When did I stop being able to understand what a woman was saying to me? Not that I'd call myself a sparkling conversationalist or anything, but usually, I could at least follow along with a basic talking to. Even when I was distracted by fantastic tits and creamy skin. Right now, I felt like Ashe's words were coming at me through a block of Jell-O.

I frowned. "Okay, so let me get this straight. The vampire who found me so irresistible she just had to make me her bar snack is apparently some big deal in the vampire world, so I'm not even supposed to try to talk to her again?"

"Yes," Ashe said.

"Bullshit," I said.

Ashe sighed and grabbed two mugs from the rack above the bar. She filled them with sudsy beer and stalked around the side of the bar toward one of the tables. She didn't say anything, but her body language told me to follow her. Actually, language didn't have anything to do with it. I'd follow the swish of those hips anywhere they went, whether they were telling me to or not. She walked up to a table and set the mugs down firmly. I vaguely remembered that particular table getting kicked out of the way the night before during the brawl.

Had it been the night before? Ashe mentioned that people going through the *turning* sometimes slept for the first twenty-four hours because of all the changes happening to their bodies. Had I done that, too?

"Look," Ashe said, dropping down into a chair. "It's not my problem Aurora zeroed in on you. I don't know why she did it."

I sat across from her. "Well, that's hurtful."

She shrugged. "Also, not my problem. I'm trying to tell you that she isn't just some bar skank you can track down after a one-night stand and bring out for greasy Chinese food in some hole in the wall you think is romantic."

"Have you been following me?" I asked with a grin.

Not impressed. Damn. This girl just wasn't giving me an inch.

"Aurora does what she wants, and who she wants, when she wants," Ashe said.

"So, the city is crawling with her little collection of vampires?" I asked.

Ashe shook her head. "No, that's the thing. She doesn't usually bite the men she picks up for fun."

I took a swig of the beer and set the mug back down. What the hell time was it? Not that it mattered. I wasn't above drinking no matter what time it was. "Well, that makes me special, then. Doesn't it? And I'm not giving up. I'm not just going to sit around with my memories and long for her like I'm in some pathetic women's network movie."

"Are you particularly familiar with those?" Ashe asked flatly.

I ignored her teasing. "I don't know how this whole vampire thing works, but I really don't care. If I want to go after a woman, I'll go after her. Even if she thinks she's above me."

"She doesn't *think* she's above you," Ashe said, leaning slightly toward me. "She *is* above you.

Therein lies your problem. Remember, you are a peasant. You can't just stroll up to the princess and expect her attention. Unfortunately, if you don't, you are fucked, and not in the way that got you here in the first place."

"What are you talking about?" I asked.

Ashe took a deep sip of her beer. "I told you that you have to complete your turning within four days after you get bitten."

I nodded. "Or I die. Yes, that stuck with me."

"Yes, you die," she said. "A very slow, very prolonged, *very* painful death. It takes a at least a week. Sometimes more. The venom from the bite starts to break down at the point of the bite, and your body goes along with it. It's not a kind or gentle death. All these benefits you're enjoying from the bite? All the youth and sexiness? Gone."

I was unnerved by the matter-of-fact tone of her voice and the unaffected expression on her face. I would have preferred if she put some drama into it. Some flailing. A few meaningful gestures. Even just an increase in the volume of her voice would have made it less chilling.

"Gone?" I asked.

"It came to you as a gift of the turn," she said. "If you don't complete the change within the set time, it's taken from you, along with everything else. Your skin that has become so smooth and youthful will go gray and slack. It will start rotting away, sliding off your bones. The blood going through your veins will become like acid and will eat away at you from the inside."

I felt my stomach turn at the thought and nodded. "That's really lovely, but I think I have the basic idea now."

She kept going. "You'll lose the feeling in your fingers and toes."

"Oh, there's more? Lovely." I hung my head for a few seconds, drawing in a breath to try to keep myself from throwing up.

She nodded. "They'll turn black, then start to fall off one by one."

"At least I'll know when that's going to be over. I'll just do the most depressing New Year's Eve-style countdown from ten ever done. I'd just have to go through it twice." I folded my arms on the table and dropped my head down onto them. I felt dizzy thinking about everything Ashe was saying.

"Well, it would be a countdown from eleven for one of them, technically," she said in her same flat tone.

"What?" I asked without lifting up my head.

"Eleven," she said again. "It's already a fairly shaky metaphor you've got going there, but if you want to go with it, you might as well be accurate about it. You'd have to do a countdown from eleven if you really wanted to make sure you knew when appendages were going to stop falling off during the death process. Ten fingers, then ten toes, and one…"

My head snapped up from my arms to look at Ashe. "No," I said.

She nodded. "Yep," she said. "Just like everything else. It would turn gray and—"

"No," I said, shaking my head.

"It would lose all feeling."

"No," I groaned.

"And it would fall off."

"My dick?" I managed to ask, my voice squeaking. "No, not my dick."

"It's not a pretty picture," she said. A smile turned up her plush lips, and I noticed her eyes travel up and down me briefly. "Well, the falling off part isn't. Before that is yet to be seen."

The hunger rose up inside me again, and it took everything to keep sitting in the chair, rather than diving over the table and taking Ashe for a spin right there. The image of my dick falling off helped dampen my urges a bit. That was one scare tactic the public-school system should grab hold of and run with. They could show all the oozy, gross pictures they wanted, but teenagers were still going to fuck. Throw them one mental image of coming across the wrong one-night stand and their dick going grey and falling off, and the teen pregnancy rate would drop to nothing.

"So, what am I supposed to do?" I asked. "I'd definitely like to avoid the dick falling off scenario."

"And the death?" Ashe asked.

I shrugged. "Well, yeah. It's a package deal."

"You have to drink Aurora's blood," she said.

"I have to what?" I asked.

"Aurora is the one who bit you and started the turn," she said. "You have to bite her and drink her blood in return. That will complete your transformation, and all the changes will be permanent."

"You *just* got finished telling me I'm not even supposed to consider getting near this chick because she's some eternal princess," I said, shaking my head. "Now you're telling me the only way to keep myself from decomposing to death is to not only get near her, but to drink her blood. That's just perfect."

Ashe shrugged. "Now you see why I said not to hold out too much hope."

I shook my head. "No, I'm not going to accept that. You can't just tell me I can't approach this woman after she did this to me when she's the only chance I have. That's not happening. I'm not just going to give up and sit around waiting for the next four days."

"Three days," Ashe corrected.

"What the fuck ever. Three days, then. I'm not going to sit around waiting to die for three days so I don't offend the princess. I'm going to find her. And you're going to help me."

Ashe's eyes widened slightly. "Me?"

"Yes," I said. "You're the one who told me Aurora was interested last night—or the night before—whenever it was I met her. You told me to go after her, and now you're telling me about all this. Whether you like it or not, you've taken me under your wing, and you're going to tell me where she is, how to find her, and then what to do."

Ashe's eyes narrowed. Her glare told me she wasn't used to people standing up to her. I expected her to lash out at me and tell me I was on my own. Instead, she took a long swig of her beer and squared her shoulders.

"Fine," she said. Her eyes traveled up and down me again. "I don't know why, but I'm going to help you. Usually, I don't care about people in your situation. It's not in my nature to care what happens to those who are in the process. Too disposable. I don't like to get attached, just in case things don't turn out. That's not something you want to watch happen to a person you have any connection to. But there's something about you."

It was the same thing Aurora had said to me when I first walked in the upstairs room with her. The fact that Ashe said it now struck me, but I didn't mention it.

"Where do we start?" I asked.

5

"I don't know where Aurora is," Ashe said. "She moves around as she pleases and isn't the easiest to follow. If we're going to find her, the best thing we can do is figure out where she isn't."

"Are we communicating in riddles now?" I asked. "If so, I'm going to need a few minutes to come up with mine."

"It's not a riddle," Ashe said. "Come with me."

She stood, and I followed her toward the back of the bar.

"Where are we going?" I asked.

"Downstairs," she said. "There's somebody I want you to meet."

I'd watched enough horror flicks to know it was rarely a good thing when somebody asked you to go downstairs in a building you didn't know. Especially when they also told you they had somebody they'd like you do meet. Usually, that meant there was going to be a monster or a torture chamber with rusty implements involved. But since I was already staring down the barrel at a pretty nasty death if this whole find-Aurora mission didn't work out, I decided to go along with her.

We made our way through the bar and to a black door in a dark corner. If I'd seen it after just wandering in, I'd probably have thought it was a storage closet. The small etching of the emblem from the front of the menu into the doorknob was the only thing giving me any indication it was something different.

Ashe took hold of the knob and pushed the door open. It was anticlimactic in a way. I thought there was going to be a special secret knock, or a password, or something. At least a key. She opened the door like we were just going on a casual stroll to get some extra paper towels.

The door opened onto a set of steps, and she started down them. I followed her, pushing the door closed behind me as I went. We were immediately engulfed in complete darkness, and I heard Ashe muttering to herself as she hurried the rest of the way down. A few seconds later, I heard a click, and a light turned on over my head. I was still making my way down the rest of the steps toward Ashe on the landing when a man came around a corner toward us.

Big and muscular, the man looked angry as he stalked toward Ashe. I felt a protective urge to defend her, but when she glanced over her shoulder, she didn't seem bothered by his advance.

"What's going on?" the man demanded.

"Hey," Ashe said. "I was coming to look for you." She gestured toward me. "This is Hayden."

I stepped toward him with my hand extended. "Hey," I greeted.

The man said nothing, and Ashe gestured toward him. "This is Tybalt," she said.

I grinned. "Hey, Tybalt. Sorry to hear about your cousin Juliet." I laughed. "That Shakespeare dude really knows how to do a downer, doesn't he?"

Tybalt's expression didn't change as he reached out to shake my hand. It was a firm, almost painful grip. "Will was a good man," he said. "I miss him."

I wanted him to laugh. He didn't.

My hand fell away from his, and I looked back to Ashe. She didn't look at all fazed by his comment, and something told me she'd heard stories about this man's time chumming it up with good ol' Will.

"Ty is my bouncer," she explained. I noticed him stiffen, as if the word made him angry, but she didn't elaborate. "Hayden is a new member of the clan. At least, he's on his way to becoming a new member of the clan. He's in process."

"I thought he had an unfinished look about him," Ty said.

I wanted to say something back, but Ashe pushed ahead to drown me out.

"We need to go to the portal," she said.

Ty scrutinized me for a beat, then gave an almost imperceptible nod. He turned, and Ashe started following him deeper into the basement. I fell into step behind them and tried to pay attention as we weaved through a honeycomb of rooms. In case they were planning on just abandoning me somewhere down here, I wanted to have at least some chance of making my way back out. Finally, we reached another door. Ashe hung back slightly as Tybalt approached it.

I leaned toward her so I could whisper in her ear. "What's up with him?" I asked.

She shook her head sharply. "Ty doesn't talk about his past," she said.

It was vague, but the tone in the words shut me down instantly. I straightened again and watched as Ty reached into the neck of his shirt and withdrew a chain. Hanging from it was a large, complicated-looking key. He took the chain from his neck and inserted the key into the hole just beneath the handle on the door. When the lock clicked, even before opening the door, he put the chain back over his head and tucked the key into his shirt again. He opened the door and stepped inside. Ashe waited a few seconds and then followed him, with me right behind her.

We walked into a room that was almost completely dark. A faint light shone from somewhere across the space, but I couldn't see what it was. I had the distinct feeling there was something there I couldn't perceive.

"Where are we?" I asked.

"Ty is also the keeper to the portal to the Underworld," Ashe explained.

"So he's a bouncer for both worlds," I said.

"You can say that," Ty said flatly. He looked to Ashe. "You can pass through, but you have to pay the blood price."

That didn't sound promising. "Blood price?" I asked.

"Before we do that," Ashe said, ignoring me. "Have you seen Aurora?"

Ty looked at her strangely. "Aurora?" he asked. "I saw her upstairs last night."

So it *was* just last night. The drugged feeling I'd had since I woke up was still dragging on me, but at least having some grasp of how long I'd been out made me slightly less disoriented.

"Have you seen her since?" Ashe asked.

"No," Ty admitted. He sounded almost confused. Then a sinister smile curved up one side of his lips. "Wait, Aurora?" He looked at me. "Aurora bit him?"

"Yes," Ashe said. "Apparently, he caught her eye, and she bit him in the thigh. She didn't drain him, so his time is ticking. We need to find her so he can take some of her blood and finish the turn."

"Before my dick falls off," I offered, leaning slightly toward the massive man in the hope of creating some sort of camaraderie.

He glared at me. "Good luck with that," he said. "Aurora hasn't passed back through the portal. Not since she came through a few days ago."

"Shit," Ashe said.

"What does that mean?" I asked.

She shook her head. "If she didn't pass back through the portal, she hasn't gone back to the Underworld. It still wouldn't be easy to find her if she was there, but at least I know most of her usual spots. As it is, she's still somewhere in New York. That's going to make it even harder to track her down."

"Then we better start looking for her," I said.

"I'll text your phone if I see her, or if she tries to pass through the portal," Ty offered.

"Thanks," Ashe said. She looked at me. "Come on."

"Happy searching," Ty said to me with a dark glint in his eye.

Ashe and I started back through the basement toward the stairs up into Solomon's.

"You know," I said. "I don't think that dude likes me."

"Tybalt doesn't like anyone new," she said. "Let's just hope we find Aurora in enough time that you'll get a chance to change his mind."

6

Ashe didn't hesitate as we made our way into the bar. She made a beeline for the front door, but I hesitated slightly. I still didn't know exactly what time it was, but I was vaguely aware it was daytime. Every piece of vampire lore I'd ever heard told me that sunlight was lethal.

I assumed Ashe was aware of the time, but I didn't relish the idea of following her out on to the sidewalk and watching her burst into flames in front of me. I was also shaky on just how much of a vampire I was at the moment. I knew a large part of me was still human, but how much? How would the part of me that had already changed react to the sun?

Ashe was almost at the door when she noticed I

wasn't following her anymore. She stopped and turned to look at me. "What's wrong?"

"It's still daytime, right?" I asked.

"Yeah," she said. "Like I said, you slept most of the day, but it's still afternoon. Why?"

"Is it sunny?"

"I guess," she said. "Why? Do you have a thing for sunscreen? Need to protect yourself from the UV rays?"

"I mean… shouldn't I?" I asked.

"Oh," she said, seeming to realize what I was getting at. "You think we're going to go crispy if we go out in the sunlight, don't you?"

I shrugged. "At least you, anyway. I don't know if still having some human in me provides a guard against that or not."

Ashe laughed. It wasn't a taunting laugh but something genuine. The sound made me want her even more. She definitely hadn't been kidding when she said my desire for sex was going to get stronger.

"That's all fiction, Hayden," she said. "Just stories. The sunlight isn't going to bother you, I promise. I'm even known to do a little sunbathing every now and then." Her long lashes lowered as she gave me another smoldering look. "I'm particularly fond of the nude beaches."

That was enough to get me following her again. She slipped out of the building, and I went right after her. The sunlight was a stark contrast to the dim environment of the bar, but I was relieved when it just felt warm and comforting, rather than violent and burning. Ashe smiled at me from a few feet away. The sun made her red hair even brighter and brought out the creaminess of her skin even more. She had decidedly not burst into flames. I took that as a victory.

"Nice day," I said.

Ashe nodded. "You don't have to be afraid of wooden stakes, either, by the way."

"Really?" I asked.

"Getting stabbed in the heart by one is enough to piss you off, but it's not going to kill you."

"Has that happened to you?" I asked.

She shuddered. "A few more times than I find amusing," she said. "People will try all kinds of ridiculous things when they think they're going to kill a vampire."

"Let me guess. Those encounters didn't end well for them?" She just flashed me a look, and I knew the answer. "So, what do we do now? Where do we start looking for Aurora?"

"The first thing we need to do is *not* look for Aurora," Ashe said.

"Isn't that kind of counterproductive to finding her?" I asked.

"Yes, we need to find her, but what I'm saying is you aren't in any condition right now to be looking for her. You need to get freshened up. And aren't you hungry?"

My stomach grumbled, answering for me. "Maybe. Wait. What am I going to eat?"

I was thinking about the row of various vaguely ethnic fast food restaurants a few blocks over in a much different way than I usually did, and I was feeling a bit queasy.

"Whatever you want, I guess," Ashe said. "The part of you that's still human needs food, and it will for a while. Didn't you wonder why there's a menu at a vampire bar?"

"You said it yourself. That bar exists in both the real world and the Underworld. I figured it was probably for the patrons who don't end the night with puncture holes in their thigh as a souvenir of being picked up buy a ravenous woman."

"Well, yes. Them. But also for those in the

process. Makes it easier on them. But it's really only convenient if the person knows where to find the one who bit them. Where do you live?"

"Not too far from here," I said.

"Good," Ashe said. "Let's go to your place. You can order some delivery, take a shower, and get into a change of clothes. I promise you'll feel better after."

I nodded, and I led her in the direction of my apartment. We could probably have grabbed a cab or waited for a bus, but I didn't want to deal with it. I looked better than I had in years, and even with the brain fog still lingering, I felt good. I told myself I just wanted to be able to talk to Ashe without a nosey cab driver or fellow passenger listening in. In the back of my mind, though, I knew I really just wanted to strut.

We'd only gone a few blocks when that idea kicked me right in the ass. I started feeling weaker, and the drugged feeling got worse until I felt like I could barely process what was going on around me. Needing a break, I stepped into an alley and leaned back against the cool brick of the wall.

"You okay?" Ashe asked.

I shook my head. "I feel awful. This sucks."

"I know," she said, leaning against the wall beside me.

"You do?" I asked.

Ashe looked at me sideways. "Do you think I was born a vampire?" she asked, then laughed. "No. Not even close. I was changed just like you were." She paused. "Well, maybe not *just* like you were."

"What happened to you?" I asked.

She shook her head. "The details don't matter. But I *do* remember what you're going through. The process isn't easy. But it gets better when it's over."

"Is that the only option?" I asked.

Her eyes narrowed slightly. "What do you mean?"

"It getting better when it's over," I said. "Is the only option going through the whole change? There's no way I can just stay like I am and not go all the way through the turn?"

Ashe looked around, then glanced at her phone before shoving it into the pocket of her tight jeans. "Come on," she said. "We need to keep moving. We can get a ride if you don't think you can keep walking."

I nodded, and we walked out onto the sidewalk

again. It could be difficult to get a cab in the middle of the day, but all Ashe had to do was throw a hand up, and a cab skidded to a stop beside us. To be honest, she probably didn't have to wave at all. Her ass in those jeans and the cleavage spilling out of her shirt could have hailed the ride all by themselves. I gave the driver my address, and we started across town.

"Yes," she said after a few blocks.

"Yes?" I asked, barely remembering the question.

"Going through the process is the only option," she said. "Other than dying, of course. If you don't want to go that route, the only thing you can do is finish the turn."

I looked at the back of the driver's head in front of us. He had barely paid any attention to us since we got into the back of the car, not even glancing into the rearview mirror at us. I'd lived in New York long enough to know that didn't mean he wasn't listening. In fact, him putting so much effort into keeping his eyes in front of him gave it away that he was probably taking note of every word we said.

As a test, I stayed quiet for a few seconds while watching him. There it was. He leaned back slightly, his ear almost twitching as he strained to hear the rest of the conversation.

Ashe and I made eye contact. She didn't seem bothered by the idea of this man listening to us. She probably just assumed he'd think we were crazy if he did hear us. It was a safe assumption. I would have been the same way less than two days before. Even so, I didn't want to keep talking. I wasn't ready to let my vamp flag fly just yet.

I stayed silent for the rest of the ride. As we rode the elevator up to my apartment, I looked at Ashe again. "What's it like?"

"What's *what* like?" she asked.

"Being a vampire," I said.

Ashe seemed to think about my question for a moment. "It's not all that different." She laughed. "Except for not having to worry about dying anymore and never being able to get enough sex."

She laughed again and then grabbed my face with both hands, pulling me in for a kiss. The taste of her was electrifying, and I instantly wanted more. I reached for her, but Ashe flattened her hands on my chest and pushed me back.

"Not yet," she said. "You need to get cleaned up and get something to eat. We've still got a lot of work to do, and I'm not using up the last of your strength."

I unlocked my apartment door and ushered her in. Walking into the kitchen, I grabbed the handful of delivery menus from the drawer under the microwave.

"Want anything?" I asked.

"Not unless you're going to hold down the delivery person for me," Ashe said.

I wanted to laugh, but I knew that she wasn't joking. "I'll just get a pizza," I said.

"Well, that isn't predictable at all," she said.

I knew she was right. Truth was, I didn't really have a craving for pizza. I was just hoping one of the guys I used to work with would show up and see how good I looked. Maybe catch a glimpse of Ashe. I didn't know what being a vampire entailed, but something told me I wasn't going to be slinging pies anymore.

I knew I was hungry, but I hadn't realized how completely ravenous I was until the pizza got there. I downed almost the whole thing within minutes after it arrived, barely even tasting it. Eating made me feel stronger, but it also made me aware of how grimy I felt.

"I'm going to grab a shower," I said. Ashe

nodded. "Make yourself at home." I took a few steps toward the bedroom, then looked back at her. "Unless you want to join me."

"Persistent, aren't you?" she asked.

I shrugged and shuffled into the bedroom. Tossing my clothes aside, I went into the bathroom and turned on the shower full blast. When the room filled with steam, I stepped into the searing water. It immediately hit the punctures in my thigh, and I hissed with the pain. Turning my bite mark away from the water, I did my best to get clean without getting anything else into the wound.

I'd gotten a good chance to check myself out when I was in the room when I first woke up, but this was a better opportunity. As I washed, I admired the muscles that had reappeared and the tautness of my skin in places I hadn't even noticed had gone slack. Seeing myself virile and youthful again just made the tightness in my belly stronger, and I couldn't stop thinking about Ashe. She'd been teasing me since I had come down the stairs earlier, and I was feeling like I wouldn't be able to control myself around her much longer.

Not that I wanted to.

When I got out of the shower, I grabbed a towel

to dry off with as I made my way back into my bedroom. I hadn't gotten any clothes before I got into the shower, which meant I was completely naked when I walked into the room and found Ashe sprawled out across my bed. She was flipping through a book I'd had on my nightstand, but it didn't take long for her to look up and notice me standing there. Her eyes locked on my body and roamed over me the way they had earlier. Only this time, there wasn't anything to stop her from seeing every inch of me.

"Mmm," she murmured, her lips curving up in a smile. "Aurora definitely did you good."

My cock had been throbbing all day, but now, it sprang all the way to life. Ashe climbed to her knees in the middle of the bed. Her intense eyes were securely on my dick, as unabashed in her staring as I had been earlier. I could see the hunger wasn't just limited to people new to the clan, or to the men. She was looking at me with the same desire as Aurora had, and I was happy to oblige her.

I walked up to the side of the bed, keeping my body on full display for her.

Ashe smiled, licking her lips. "I love men who are just getting started," she said, low in her throat.

"So much delicious, pent-up lust. So much tension."

She took hold of the hem of her shirt and pulled it off over her head. Her heavy tits bounced out, her nipples taut. I reached forward and rested my hands over them, kneading their soft flesh. She moaned a little, and I leaned down to kiss her, wanting more of the taste I'd gotten before we had come into the apartment. Before I could get my lips to hers though, Ashe moved her face out of the way and brought her mouth to my neck.

Her breath was hot as it trailed down my skin. The tip of her tongue ran along my neck as she moved down, then brushed over my collarbones. I could feel my heart pounding at the base of my throat, and she flicked her tongue there. I wondered how long it had been since she'd been with a man who still had a heartbeat.

Ashe crawled forward slightly so she could continue her progress down my chest and onto the muscles of my belly. They twitched at the touch of her lips, and my cock jumped in anticipation of more attention. The tip bounced against one of her breasts, and she wrapped her hand around it. Her skin felt soft and smooth as she tightened her grip around the base of my engorged dick and gave a slight squeeze.

She licked along my stomach and nipped at the trail of hair leading down from my navel as her hand started stroking my shaft. I wasn't looking forward to the idea of her fangs, but she kept them up, and by the time her sweet little mouth closed around the head, I didn't care anymore.

Ashe drew her mouth off the tip before going down all the way. Then she ran her tongue along the slit at the tip of my cock. I watched her tongue gather up some of the clear fluid she pulled out of me, and she made another of her sexy moans. I leaned my head back for a few seconds, my mouth opening and my eyes closing. But then I lifted it again to look back down at her.

Ash had been so much in control from the first second I saw her. I was enjoying that I had managed to take away some of that control. A renewed flicker of excitement moved through me, and I pushed my hips forward to urge her on. Her mouth opened, and she welcomed all of my length in and cradled it against her tongue. The feeling was completely dizzying. The delectable sensation of my engorged cock filling her mouth was almost too much for me to handle. The hot, wet feeling brought to mind the image of sinking inside her, and I felt my erection grow even harder.

Ashe's hand tightened around the base of my cock, and she held it still as she increased the speed of her mouth. Each of the fast, intense glides sent a shiver of sensation through me, and the occasional deep suck was enough to drag groans out of my chest. She was bringing the tip far into her mouth, and I felt it dip just into her throat.

I reached forward to dig my fingers into her hair, and I pulled her head forward slightly. I didn't have to say a word. That suggestion was enough. Ashe moved back slightly to get into a better position, and she twisted her hand around as she dipped her head deeper. Finally, she pulled me all the way in so my cock sank into her throat. Letting out a grunt, I grabbed onto her shoulders to give myself leverage.

Ashe murmured, sending a slight vibration through me, and I pushed my hips forward in response. I started thrusting into her mouth, and Ashe accepted it eagerly. I was about to come. I could feel it rushing toward me, and I didn't want to fight it.

I let out a deep groan and felt Ashe's hands come to my hips. Her fingertips dug into my skin to hold me in place as she took back complete control. Her mouth met each of my thrusts, sucking and drawing on me until I felt myself on the very brink of control. With one final hard draw, she pushed me over the edge.

I cried out as my orgasm crashed over me, and I felt my cock tighten even more in her mouth. Ashe didn't move. Instead, she continued to milk me, licking me clean as I shook and trembled with the waves of pleasure.

"Feel better?" she asked as I crawled up onto the bed beside her and dropped down face first onto the pillows.

"Yes," I groaned.

At least, I think I did. It was possible I just made a primal sound.

"Good," she answered. I felt her lean down and suck my earlobe into her mouth briefly. "You tasted delicious, too."

With that, I let myself fall asleep again.

7

I woke up to Ashe shaking me. I'd been having a dream about going over a rope bridge in the middle of a jungle, and I briefly couldn't tell the difference between hanging on for dear life over the open mouths of the swarm of alligators beneath me and the sexy bartender pushing on my shoulder. It took a few seconds of her shaking me before I groaned and opened my eyes. I felt groggy again, and when I lifted my head off the pillows, I felt the world spin.

"Am I ever going to get used to that?" I asked, squeezing my eyes closed again.

"I don't care," she said. "You need to get up."

I opened my eyes again and looked at her questioningly. "Did you just say you don't care?"

"Yeah, right now, I really don't. How you feel when you wake up isn't really my issue right now. It shouldn't be yours, either. You need to get up and get dressed."

I finally felt like I was coming into consciousness, and I realized she was dressed again. Her hair was pulled up into a ponytail behind her head, and all hints of the slumbering, lusty expression that had been on her face were gone. It was replaced by seriousness that got me to my feet.

"What's going on?" I asked.

"I got a text from Tybalt," she said. "A traveler at the bar told him he'd heard Aurora had some business to attend to at Nakatomi Tower. That wasn't too long ago, so there's still a good chance she's there. We might be able to track her down and get you through your turn."

Nakatomi Tower. I knew that name. It was a massive fifty-story building in the business district. I'd never had a reason to go inside, but it was hard to miss for anyone who frequented that part of the city. It occurred to me that if Aurora had business to attend to there, it meant that building likely had something to do with the Underworld. I grabbed clothes out of my dresser and closet and carried them into the bathroom with me.

"Do we have to go barefoot when we go to Nakatomi?" I asked.

There was a pause.

"What?" Ashe finally asked.

"Barefoot," I said. "I mean, I know it's not quite Christmas and I'm trying to save my own ass and not my daughter, but is there a rule that if you're on a quest when you enter the building, you have to go without shoes?"

Another pause.

"What?"

"*Die Hard*?" I asked. Silence. "Never mind."

I stared into the bathroom mirror after brushing my teeth, looking at myself for the first time, other than the picture I'd taken when I first woke up. It was a shock to feel like I was looking backward almost a decade. Maybe more. I didn't even know if I looked that good when I was younger. As I looked at myself, I thought of Ashe's fangs sliding down out of her mouth and wondered what it would feel like to have them. Even more than that, I wondered what it would feel like to sink them down into somebody.

The bite in my thigh burned, and I looked down at it. "Oh, shit."

Ashe came to the doorway. Her gaze hit my

thigh, and she reached forward to touch her fingertips to the skin beside the punctures. It was redder, more swollen, and as she touched it, a new wave of agony rushed through me.

"That looks painful," she said.

"It is," I said. "What's wrong with it? Am I getting sick or something?"

"You're not going to get rabies from a vampire bite," Ashe said.

"That's not what I asked." It had definitely been what I was thinking. "Why is it getting worse? I still have time before I start turning grey and falling apart, right?"

"That's not it," Ashe said. "This happens sometimes. It means Aurora is close. She's still in the area. That's a good thing."

I started dressing. "Yeah, it feels delightful."

When I was ready, I followed Ashe out of the apartment and locked the door. As we were getting into the elevator, I heard her phone buzz. She fished it out of her pocket, and I saw her face drop when she looked at the screen.

"It's Ty again," she said.

"What did he say?" I asked.

"He said a couple of Shades were seen in the

area of the Nakatomi Tower. They didn't look happy."

We stepped out of the elevator and rushed out of the building.

"What are Shades?" I asked.

"Not what. Who. The Shades are bodyguards. They protect an extremely important family within our world."

"Why are they called Shades?" I asked. "Because they sink into the darkness?"

She gestured for a cab, and we dove inside as soon as it slowed beside us.

"Because they always wear sunglasses with crimson lenses," she responded.

"Oh," I said. "What family do they protect?"

"The Prime and his family," she answered. "He likely heard someone is after his daughter and sent them to protect her. Aurora would already have one Shade with her. She always does, but the Prime likely sent two more just to make sure she's safe."

I looked at Ashe. "Who the fuck is the Prime? Do you have a manual I could read? A handbook or anything to get me up to speed?"

8

The Nakatomi Tower looked even larger when we got up close to it. I had no idea what kind of business was done inside the enormous, mirrored building. As I looked at the revolving doors, it occurred to me that even if I had thought I knew what happened there, I probably would have been wrong.

Ashe didn't hesitate to walk straight through the door and into the cavernous lobby of the building. I followed her, impressed by the interior as soon as we got inside. As enormous and impressive as the mirrored exterior of the tower was, the interior was just as daunting.

The floors were covered in pale gray marble, and huge columns rose up high toward a dizzying ceiling. Expensive-looking pieces of furniture created small clusters in various places throughout the lobby. They were all empty, and I wondered if anyone ever actually used the seating areas to sit and relax. This didn't exactly strike me as the type of place where people went to kickback and share a couple of laughs with their colleagues. I suddenly got the urge to shout just so I could hear the reverberation through the eerily still space.

"I don't see anybody," she said. She looked across the lobby. "Stay here. I'll be right back."

She walked away, and I saw her headed toward a curved green marble desk at the far end of the lobby. I hadn't even noticed the woman sitting there. She had been completely silent when we had come inside and still hadn't said anything. From a distance, all I could see was her inky black hair cut in a severe bob to just beneath her chin, and pale skin that made her eyes look just as black in the expanse of her face.

Ashe rushed up to the desk and leaned against it as they spoke. The acoustics of the lobby made it so I could hear the muttering and murmuring of their voices, but I couldn't make out any of the words they were saying. I looked around, and a bank of shimmering elevators caught my eye. They were partially obstructed behind two columns and several planters. I didn't know if that was on purpose to keep the flow of the lobby intact or just an accident of design. One elevator stood out among the others.

Surrounded by delicate scrollwork, this particular elevator had its own dedicated button set apart from the one used to control the rest of them. But it wasn't the decorative scrolling or high shine of the doors that held my attention. Instead, it was the two massive men who flanked those doors.

The men stood so still, they almost looked like they weren't alive. It occurred to me then that they probably weren't. But that didn't mean they weren't living. Both stood with their hands clasped in front of them. The position put their broad chests and powerful shoulders on display. These weren't men anybody would want to meet in a dark alley. They weren't men anyone would want to meet in a fully lit business tower lobby in the middle of the day. The only word I could think of to describe them was sinister.

Neither of them was moving, and they were both staring ahead of them, completely expressionless. It was hard to tell if they were waiting for someone to come out of the elevator or were preventing others from getting in. Neither option was very uplifting.

Something else about them stuck out to me, but I couldn't put my finger on it. The drugged, groggy feeling that was keeping me from being able to think straight was seriously starting to piss me off. I looked over at Ashe again and saw her still engaged in deep conversation with the woman behind the desk. They leaned closer to each other, and I saw the woman's eyes flicker over in the direction of the elevators. She gestured toward them, and Ashe looked across the lobby. Her eyes locked on the center elevator and the men standing on either side. The feature that was standing out to me clicked in my head just as I saw her push away from the desk and come running toward me.

They were both wearing sunglasses with crimson lenses.

The Shades noticed us before Ashe got to me. They started toward us as she reached out and grabbed onto me, yanking me with her.

"Run!" she commanded.

We burst out of the lobby, back out onto the sidewalk. There weren't as many people bustling through the business district that afternoon as there would have been on a weekday, but there were still enough to provide both an obstacle and a help as we ran. Ashe had continued to hold on to me for the first few strides we took down the sidewalk, but soon, she let go to give both of us the opportunity to move more easily. She maneuvered her way around a small group of women in pantsuits, and I dipped the other way to meet her.

"Those are Shades, aren't they?" I asked.

It didn't matter to me anymore if anyone was listening. All of this was going on right around them every day, and none of them noticed. It made me wonder how many times I had walked by a vampire or gone into a business that was actually a front for the Underworld and never even knew.

"Yes," Ashe said. "Particularly nasty ones. You don't want to be on their bad side."

"I don't want to be on any of their sides," I said.

Without giving me a warning, Ashe darted out into the middle of the road. Horns blared as cars skidded to a stop to try to avoid hitting her. I wondered what would happen if they did. I knew it wouldn't kill her. If a wooden stake through the heart was only enough to piss her off, getting pegged by an angry New York City cabbie was probably just an annoyance.

Fortunately, I didn't have to see if she would fling herself to the ground and try to sell an injury. The cars managed to miss her, and she didn't even give them a glance as drivers leaned out of their windows to scream creative strings of obscenities at her. If I didn't have two villainous-looking vampire bodyguards on my ass, I probably would have paused to commend them on their linguistic gymnastics.

I hazarded a look over my shoulder and saw that the Shades were close behind. Their faces hadn't changed. Their expressions were still emotionless, but the way their bodies moved was enough to know they weren't happy about chasing us through the city. When I looked back ahead of me, I realized I had lost track of Ashe.

She had disappeared somewhere on a busier stretch of sidewalk, and I felt my stomach sink. I realized as I scoured the crowd for her that I wasn't as worried about myself as I would have thought I'd be. Instead, I was thinking about Ashe and wanting to make sure she was safe. Ignoring the protests of the people I pushed past, I forced my way down the sidewalk, checking every face I saw for her.

This better not be some sort of messed-up

vampire hazing ritual, or I was going to be uber pissed.

I heard a shout behind me and knew the Shades had found their way across the street as well. I felt a hand grab me and yank me so hard, I was nearly off my feet. My back slammed into a wall, and I was about to start swinging when I realized it was Ashe in front of me.

"Stick to the alleyways," she said in a harsh, ragged voice. "Don't go back out on the sidewalk."

"Why?"

"There are too many people. We're not going to be able to get away fast enough."

"Won't having people around help?" I asked. "With people watching, they're not just going to snatch us up."

"You have a lot to learn about being a vampire," she said. "Shit like this happens every day. Humans? They never notice what's actually happening. If you don't want to end up on the news as the next case of police brutality or a gang mugging, you'll stick with me and stick to the alleyways."

She pushed away from me and started down the narrow, shadowy alley. The farther I went, the more I felt like I was leaving the real world behind.

I stayed as close to her as I could as we slipped between buildings to access another alley. She ran up toward the sidewalk and then scrambled up onto a dumpster. I followed, watching her as she leapt without hesitation. Her fingers grasped the edge of a window grate, and she dragged herself up. There was no way in hell I was going to be able to do that. Ashe got onto the window grate and swung up to the one above her. When she was standing at the edge, she looked down at me.

"What are you doing?" she demanded.

"What do you mean, what am I doing? What are *you* doing?"

"We have to get to the other side of the building," she said. "Then we can drop down into the alley and keep going from there."

"I thought I was a vampire, not fucking Spiderman."

"You can do it," she encouraged.

"No," I said, shaking my head. "You seriously think I can launch myself up there like that?"

"You wouldn't have hesitated when you actually *were* twenty-one, would you?" she asked.

"No," I admitted. "That doesn't mean I would have succeeded. I very well might have busted my ass slipping and falling."

"But you would have tried," she said.

I heard angry shouting from the sidewalk, and I knew the Shades had gotten in someone's way.

"Yes," I said.

"You can do a lot more now than you ever could then," she said. "The change is happening inside you. It might not be complete yet, but that doesn't mean you don't have access to some of the abilities. You need to trust me. Actually, I don't care if you trust me. You just need to fucking do it because they're going to be here any second, and you don't want to be dangling from the window when they arrive."

At that, I decided I'd rather at least have a chance than to be standing on the dumpster like I was on display when the Shades got to the alley. Bracing myself for what I figured was the inevitable splatter of my body to the cement below, I jumped toward the window grate.

I was stunned when I felt my hands grab onto the cold metal. Only giving myself a second to feel successful, I pulled myself up and mimicked Ashe to swing over to the next window. When I climbed up, I was relieved to see a narrow ledge that made it easier to scramble up a few more feet until we were on a section of the building that was higher than the one behind it. This gave us room to maneuver our way toward the alley ahead of us. We jumped down onto a stack of crates and then onto another dumpster before touching ground again.

"Where now?" I asked.

Ashe looked up and down the alley and then back to the sidewalk. "We're going to cross the street again," she said.

"Are you kidding me? After that, you want to go back out onto the sidewalk again?"

"If we have any luck, the Shades figured out we came back into these alleys. They'll be trying to follow us. We'll cross the street into those alleys and make our way back toward Solomon's. If we can get there, we're safe."

I knew I didn't really have a choice. The number of people out on the streets was already dwindling. Soon, it would be nightfall, and even though Ashe hadn't said anything about it, I had a feeling the last thing I wanted was to still be trying to get away from the bodyguards in the dark. She took a steeling breath and shot down the alley. I watched her leap toward a car, planting her foot on the hood to launch herself the rest of the way across the street.

I ran after her, darting behind the shocked driver and into the alley where Ashe had disappeared. We ran through dirty puddles and over piles of cardboard to get to the small passage that led into the next alley. We'd only taken a few steps when the Shades stepped into view at the end.

Ashe gasped and scrambled to a stop. Grabbing onto me again, she turned and started toward the next alley. We got into it but had to stop almost immediately. It was wide , and the size made it possible for a truck to park diagonally across it, blocking the way. Massive metal shipping containers sitting on the ground on the other side obliterated any chance for us to slip under the truck. We turned around to start back, but the Shades came into view once more.

We were trapped. *Shit.*

There was nothing we could do. We couldn't run. We couldn't escape. There was no choice but to face them and fight. As soon as I squared up against one of the Shades, he launched toward me. His body hit mine, his shoulder digging into my torso. I grunted as I crashed to the ground.

The man on top of me drew up to his knees and planted a punch directly into my face. I felt the pain, but I also felt something else. It was like a sharp crack cut through the fog and sent a rush through me. I managed to push the Shade off me, but before I could get to my feet, the other kicked me in the ribs. I felt another powerful surge of adrenaline and energy, and a smile started to come to my face.

"Again," I said.

The Shade paused for a second, seemingly confused, but then kicked me again. The other swung, punching me in the side of the head. Lights burst in front of my eyes, but I felt my blood pumping through me like it was carrying new power to the tips of my fingers and down to my toes.

One of the Shades walked away from me, and I heard Ashe yelp. That brought me to my feet, and I lunged at the man in front of me. He caught me halfway, and we latched to each other. Though we were barely moving, we were both grunting and growling with the exertion of the clash. The longer I fought him, the stronger and more powerful I felt. I gathered it up inside me and pushed it forward in one massive blast that sent him flying. He crashed to the ground, and I threw myself toward the other. I could see the second man getting back up as I fought, and I looked to Ashe. It was obvious she was thinking about getting in on the fight, but I shook my head at her.

"Go!" I shouted. "Go *now*."

I didn't say where I wanted her to go. I didn't know the details of how this all worked, and I didn't want to give away Solomon's if they didn't already know about it. Ashe hesitated. One of the Shades grabbed me by both arms, and the other punched me in the back of the head, but I didn't buckle.

"Ashe, go," I commanded.

She ran past us and back down the passage that led to the other alley.

"Get her," one of the Shades growled to the other, and he broke away from us and started after Ashe.

Now that there was only one of the men holding me, he had no chance. I surged against him, battling him to the ground and holding him down as I stared into his face. He was nothing against me, dominated fully, and I suddenly felt more alive than I had in a long time.

9

Leaving the Shade unconscious on the pavement, I ran out of the alley and back onto the sidewalk. I could feel blood running down my face, but I didn't care. I looked around for Ashe or the other Shade, but I didn't see either. Not wanting to go back in the direction of the Tower, I ran in the opposite direction and hailed a cab.

I didn't know if the driver would know where to find Solomon's, so I directed him to the neighborhood and bailed out of the car a block from the bar. Darkness had settled by the time I got to the door, and the light from inside felt welcoming when it poured out as I entered.

"Hayden!"

I heard Ashe before I saw her. I scanned the

bar for her, noticing the eyes of a dozen patrons who had wandered in looking at me. Finally, I saw her standing against the side of the bar. She rushed toward me, and I opened my arms to her. She hugged me tightly and then grabbed my hands as she stepped back to look at me.

"Are you all right?" I asked.

She nodded. "I'm fine." She reached up and wiped some of the blood from my face. "You're hurt."

"It's not a big deal," I said.

"Come on. Let's go upstairs."

She pulled me through the bar and back up the stairs toward the room where I'd met Aurora. She pushed me into the bathroom and shut the door behind us. I had wanted the strength and energy I'd felt when I was fighting the Shade to stay, but within seconds of me entering the bathroom, I felt it start to drain out of me. I leaned back against the wall and drew in a breath.

"What happened back there?" I asked.

Ashe grabbed a paper towel and ran it under cold water from the faucet. She dabbed it to my face, and I drew in a sharp breath at the sting. Frustration filled me.

"Another gift of the change," Ashe said.

"What do you mean?"

"That strength you had? The extra speed? That is part of you now. It's part of your power as a vampire. That was only a fraction of what you'll actually be able to do when your transformation is complete. You'll gain more control over it as time passes. For now, your abilities are still unstable. You'll experience bursts of energy, strength, and speed, but they aren't going to last. But each time it happens, it will be stronger and last a little longer. They'll happen more frequently, but that can be dangerous because they can be harder to control. I have to admit, I'm impressed."

"You are?" I asked.

Ashe nodded. "I've never seen someone have bursts like that so early in their transformation. It was incredible. And it tells me we can't lose momentum. We need to find Aurora. She either needs to give you her blood, or you need to take it in order to complete the turn."

"Take it?" I asked.

Ashe tossed the paper towel into the trash can and nodded. "This isn't an Easter egg hunt, Hayden. Aurora isn't going to pop out at the end of it and congratulate you before giving you a little vial of her blood to sip like a holiday drink. She also hasn't forgotten about you."

"What do you mean?" I straightened up from where I was leaning and grunted through gritted teeth as a sharp pain coursed through my side.

Ashe pushed my hand away from it and pressed her fingertips into the tender area. I growled in protest, but she didn't stop until she'd made her way around the entire bruise.

"You have a broken rib," she said. "Maybe two. Don't worry about it. It will heal in a few hours. My kind heals from injuries like that very quickly, but it will take a little longer for you. You're still in the middle of the transformation, so the human part of you is going to try to keep you from mending as fast as the vampire part."

"I guess that's why a wooden stake through the heart just pisses you off," I said.

Ashe nodded. "Exactly." She looked me in the eye briefly. "Alright, let's just lay it all out."

My brow furrowed. "Lay what out?"

"We've already gone over sunlight. Warm and pleasant. Not going to make you crispy. Wooden stake in the heart—"

"Just pisses you off," I said.

"Right," she said. "We also don't turn into bats or anything else. We don't fly."

"That's kind of a bummer," I said.

"And we can't communicate telepathically with each other. Sometimes, the strongest of our kind are able to influence humans, but it's not a hypnotism situation like in the movies. And very few of us eat human food after our transformations are complete, but those who do can have as much garlic as they want. I know a woman who loves shrimp scampi with so much of it, you can smell her before she's even in the room with you."

"So, bulb necklaces aren't going to do anybody any good?" I asked.

She nodded. "Exactly. So, there you go. All the big old vampire lies the world tells you, debunked by one who has faced it all."

"Silver bullets?" I asked.

She gave me a disgusted look. "That's werewolves, idiot. And, no."

I smiled, but then the grin melted away as I remembered what she said before she noticed my ribs. "What did you mean about Aurora?"

"What about her?" she asked.

"You said I might have to *take* her blood and

that she didn't forget about me. What did you mean by that?"

Ashe opened the bathroom door and started down the hall. I followed her, waiting for her response.

"Aurora doesn't do anything accidentally," she said. "Like I said when I looked at the bite, she knows what she's doing. She doesn't do things carelessly. The position you are in is not pleasant."

"I'm aware," I said.

"My point," Ashe said, "is that the human world might like to see our kind as monsters, but vampires really aren't brutal just to be brutal."

"Inhuman but not inhumane?" I asked.

She paused in front of a closed door nearly at the end of the hallway and turned to smile at me. "Yes. We don't make people, human or otherwise, suffer just for the sake of doing it. I mean, obviously some do. That's just reality. There are humans who are horrible and cruel, and there are vampires who are as well. It's not the norm, but it happens."

"I don't know where you're going with this," I said.

Ashe opened the door and stepped through. She gestured for me to come inside, and I walked into what looked like the front room of a small apartment.

"In our world, it's considered a major taboo to just leave somebody in your condition. When we bite someone, we either do it with the intention of going through with the complete transformation, or we completely drain them and let them die quickly and easily. We don't just let them linger in this limbo to suffer such a horrible death."

"It feels like you're about to tell me Aurora doesn't know about that specific cultural norm," I said.

"Oh, she knows about it." Ashe headed farther into the apartment and dropped down onto a dark blue couch. I sat down beside her, and she looked over at me. "She just doesn't care a lot of the time. As royalty, she doesn't bother herself too much with doing things the way others do it. She has a nasty habit of simply discarding her victims when she feels like it. Especially if she gets distracted when something or someone better comes along. She has her fun and then just walks away without giving a second thought to the person, or what's going to happen to them."

"Does she always do that?" I asked.

"Not always," Ashe said. "There are some she

changed on purpose. And there are some she killed on purpose. And there are some she abandoned and allowed to suffer on purpose. She won't pretend otherwise. She does what she wants. But most of the time, it's not that she wants to do it. She just doesn't care enough not to do it."

"Which is why I might have to take the blood from her?" I asked.

Ashe nodded. I was still letting it all sink in when she stood up.

"Come on," she said. "I want to change."

I got up and followed her through the apartment into a bedroom in the back corner, sitting down hard on her bed.

"How did it get to this point?" I asked. "How did all of this get so complicated?"

Ashe kicked off her shoes. "What do you mean?" she asked.

"I didn't even know what was happening to me when I woke up. But somehow, the Shades knew about me and what happened with Aurora. How is that possible?"

Ashe drew in a breath. "I don't know. I have no idea how they would know who you are or that you would try to find Aurora."

I wanted more of a response from her. She was

my source for everything I knew about what was happening, and I needed her to give me an answer. Instead, Ashe looked like she was at a loss. It didn't exactly make me feel better about the unique situation in which I found myself.

She reached down and grabbed the bottom of her shirt. In one movement, she pulled it off over her head and tossed it aside. Her full breasts on display, she reached for the button on the front of her tight jeans and released it. She slid her zipper down and hooked her thumbs in her waistband.

My mouth watered as I watched her wriggle her jeans down her curvy hips and let them drop to her feet. I could feel my blood pumping through my body, swelling my cock until it ached. My mind raced with thoughts of grabbing Ashe and bending her over the bed so I could plunge into her.

I climbed off the bed and wrapped my arm around her waist, yanking her up against me. My mouth crashed down over hers. Her lips parted so I could thrust my tongue between them, and I felt her arms wrap around my neck.

Keeping one arm holding her tight, I used the other hand to start working at my fly. I had just gotten my pants open and was starting to work my way out of them when I heard a heavy knock on the apartment door. I kept kissing Ashe, but another loud knock made her step back away from me.

"Later," she said, patting me on the chest.

She walked toward her closet, and I left the bedroom to go to the front door. There was no peephole, so I just pulled it open. Ty stood on the other side.

10

"Oh, hey, Tybalt," I said. "Ashe is getting dressed, but I'll go get her for you." I started to turn away.

"No," he said. "Actually, I didn't come here to talk to her. I came to talk to you."

That struck me as odd. "Why did you come to Ashe's apartment, then?" I asked.

"I didn't know where else to look for you. You two seemed pretty friendly when you were down in the basement. I knew she came back here after your run-in with the Shades, and I figured if you survived, you would be here with her."

"*If* I survived? Thanks for the vote of confidence," I said. Ty didn't look moved, and I stepped back to let him the rest of the way into the apartment. "Come on."

We walked over the couch and sat down. I looked expectantly at him.

"Who are you?" he asked. "Why are you here?"

That wasn't the question I was expecting him to ask. I didn't know what I was expecting, but somehow that wasn't it.

I shrugged. "My name is Hayden. I came here last night because I was supposed to go to my high school reunion and I didn't want to go in. I decided having a drink by myself had to be better than mingling with a crowd of people who would only want to talk about all the shit I *haven't* done in the last ten years."

"How old are you?" he asked.

I grinned. "It's a little late to be carding me, don't you think?"

He didn't laugh. Ty was a tough crowd. "How old are you?" he asked again.

"Twenty-eight," I told him.

Ty drew in a breath and let it out slowly. "Who are your parents?"

I shook my head. "I don't know."

"Stop bullshitting me," he said, a hint of anger spiking in his voice. "Tell me about your parents."

"I'm not bullshitting you," I insisted. "I don't know anything about my parents. I was orphaned when I was a baby. I never even knew their names."

Ty looked at me like he was trying to decide if he believed what I was telling him. "Where did you grow up?"

I leaned back on the couch and let out a long breath. "As far as I can remember, I was with a foster family. I don't have too many memories from before I was about four or five, but my foster family had pictures of me from when I was younger than that. As far as I know, I was always with them."

"And when you got older?" Ty asked.

I wanted to make a joke about his probing questions, but the effort would be wasted on Tybalt. So, I just answered. "When I was in middle school, I started playing football. I stuck with it in high school and was really good at it. I was the star of the team. I got a full scholarship into college and was on the fast track to a professional career. Then I got hurt, and my entire life went to hell."

We had gone from casual conversation to midafternoon talk show real quick. Ty didn't say anything, but his expression changed as he stared at me. Now, he looked at me like he recognized me, but he couldn't figure out who I was or *how* he knew me.

I tilted my head at him. "Do you know me?"

I didn't know why I asked it. The question just came out of my mouth, and I wasn't aware of it until I actually heard myself ask it.

Tybalt's eyes didn't move away from me. It looked like he was trying to burrow into me to find out something hidden beneath my surface. He didn't answer my question, and before he was able to say anything else, the bedroom door opened and Ashe came into the room.

She was wearing fresh clothing, and it looked like she had brushed out her hair and applied a new coat of makeup. My stomach tightened as the underlying hunger I always felt for her reared up again. I wanted her naked body back in my arms.

"Hi, Ty," she said brightly. "It's a surprise to see you here tonight."

Ty didn't say anything. He stood up from the couch and walked out of the apartment without another word. The whole interaction struck me as very odd, and I turned to look at Ashe, expecting some sort of explanation. She rolled her eyes and shook her head as if she wasn't surprised by Ty's weird behavior at all.

"What was that all about?" I asked.

She narrowed her eyes at me slightly. "I think I should be the one asking that question. You were who he came to talk to apparently. What did he say?"

"He asked me who I was and why I'm here," I told her.

"That doesn't seem all that strange," Ashe said. "I told you, he doesn't take too well to new people. He probably just wants to know more about you."

I shook my head. "It wasn't like, 'hey, what's your favorite team, and do you like peanut butter and jelly'."

"Are those questions you frequently ask people when you're trying to get to know them?" Ashe asked teasingly.

"It's important information," I said.

"You never asked me," she said.

I took a step closer to her. "What's your favorite team?"

"I don't have one," she said. "I find sports insufferable."

I grinned. "Do you like peanut butter and jelly sandwiches?"

"I never had one," she said. "Way after my time."

"Interesting," I said.

"So, what did he ask you?"

"He asked how old I am and about my parents."

A quizzical look passed across her face. "About your parents?" she asked.

I nodded. "Yeah, and he didn't seem terribly pleased when I told him I actually don't know anything about my parents because I was orphaned."

"You were?" Ashe asked.

I nodded. "Before I was even old enough to be aware of anything. It's not some sad, dramatic story. It's just like anybody else, only the first memories I have are with my foster family."

"I wonder why any of that would matter to Tybalt," Ashe said.

I shrugged, then took another slight step toward her. "Is something going on between the two of you?" I asked.

"Between Ty and me?" she asked.

"Yeah," I said. "He didn't seem very happy when you brought me down into the basement, and he was really digging into me, trying to find out more about me."

Ashe scoffed. "You've got to be kidding," she said, then shook her head. "No, there isn't anything going on between Ty and me. He's the portal keeper, and he's been a bouncer for me for years. That's it." She gave me a teasing look. "Why? Are you jealous?"

I took the two strides to get to her and pulled her up against me, holding her the same way I had before Ty interrupted us.

"Why don't you show me why I shouldn't be?" I said.

Ashe looped her arms around my neck and brought her mouth up to mine. I bit her bottom lip, and she ignited. Our mouths played hungrily across each other as she walked backward toward her bedroom, pulling me along with her. I kicked the door closed behind us to create another barrier. I didn't care if Ty came back to the door with another round of Hayden, This Is Your Life. I wasn't going to answer. I felt like I'd been waiting far too long for Ashe as it was, and I was going to explode if I had to wait for her any longer.

Her hands pulled at my clothes, casting my shirt

aside so she could rake her fingernails down my chest. I repeated the favor and was surprised to find she had put on a bra beneath the clingy white T-shirt she changed into. The last two times I'd seen her take off her shirt, it had been the only thing keeping me back from her luscious tits. This time, there was something else, and somehow, that added layer was even sexier.

I cupped my hands over the flimsy white fabric, running my thumbs across the lace edging on the cups. I could feel her breasts becoming heavier in my hands as her desire built up. Ducking my head down, I sucked one taut nipple into my mouth through the fabric. I flicked my tongue over it and then gave a brief bite before moving on to the other one.

Moans of appreciation slipped through Ashe's lips as she fought to get her pants over her hips. I let go of her long enough to step back and wrestle out of my own clothes. Then I yanked her against me again. I could feel the heat of her body through her bra, and I finally reached around behind her to flick the hooks open. It loosened, and she let it slip down her arms and drop to the floor. I could finally feel the pressure of her tight nipples pressing into my chest, and as we kissed, her breasts rose and fell against me.

I scooped Ashe into my arms and walked over to the bed. Sitting on the edge, I settled her across me so her legs were on either side of my hips, and she hovered above my lap. I licked the pad of one thumb and brought it between her legs to massage into her clit. Ashe's head fell back as she gasped.

Her hips pressed forward to seek out more of the attention, and I obliged her for a few more seconds. My cock strained toward her, and I finally wrapped one hand around the base to hold it steady as I lowered her down over it. I sank into her in one movement, and the hot, silky feeling of her walls wrapping around me wrenched a growl of pleasure from my lips.

Ashe and I kissed passionately as I led her hips to rock against mine. We moved at a fevered pace, and it was only seconds before I could already feel myself rushing headlong toward another mind-blowing orgasm. I didn't want to leave her behind, so I began to stroke her with my thumb again. Rubbing her pearl in tight circles, I ducked my head to suck on one of her nipples. Ashe whimpered and moaned, her hands clutching at my shoulders.

Finally, I felt her body start to shake, and I pounded into her harder and harder as I gave myself over to the sensations. Her fingernails dug into my skin, but I was relentless. She screamed out, and I felt her pussy clamp down on me. It was enough to send me into oblivion, and I slammed up into her as hard as I could, holding myself deep inside her as I poured out.

When it was over, I dropped back onto the bed, wanting to sleep, only to sit right back up. I hissed and grabbed onto my thigh.

"What is it?" Ashe asked.

"My leg," I said, gesturing toward the angry-looking punctures. "It's getting worse."

"She can't be far," Ashe said. "We have to find her."

11

I HAD NEVER BEEN a big fan of waiting around for things. It just wasn't one of my strengths. I could be lazy as fuck, and not do anything but sit around on my ass and shove pizza in my face for long stretches of time, but that wasn't waiting. That was *doing* something. Now, I was figuring out that even more impatience was another thing that came along with the constant need for sex, and strength that made me want to experiment with an Iron Man competition. Waiting was something I could barely even think about doing, and now that I was down in the bar with Ashe while she worked, I was not having a good time.

She had told me she needed to take care of some business at the bar, so I'd gone downstairs with her and perched on one of the bar stools to wait. I'd specifically chosen the one in the furthest corner so I could see everything that was happening in the room. Now that I knew what the bar really was, I wanted to watch and see if I could sift out the vampires from the hapless humans who followed in my footsteps and wandered in completely unknowing. It was fun at first. The guy over there in the tight black jeans…vampire. The girl, sitting in his lap…hopefully a vampire or tonight was going to be a major eye-opener for her. The burly man in the red flannel…not a vampire. This kept me amused for a little while, but after twenty minutes of playing Spot the Blood Sucker, I was bored.

I turned my attention to watching Ashe work next. I enjoyed watching her round little ass in her tight pants sashaying side to side as she moved along the bar. It took some of the edge off the boredom, and made sitting there on the uncomfortable stool with only a watered-down beer in front of me more tolerable. I took a swig from the glass out of force of habit. The taste was way off, and Ashe told me that was the way it was going to be now. It wasn't that I couldn't consume human food anymore, or that it would somehow hurt me now that I was no longer strictly human. There were some vampires who continued to eat human food for decades after their change. Some never stopped. Nothing was ever going to taste the same, though. She'd heard there were some things that actually tasted better after the change was complete, but since she hadn't eaten any human food since she was bitten, she couldn't attest to it.

Three men walked into the bar and approached the stools directly opposite me. They didn't sit down, but stood staring at Ashe until she noticed and made her way over to them. Ducking her head down, she started talking to them. I couldn't hear what any of them were saying, but by the way Ashe kept nodding and leaning closer so she could speak without raising her voice, it looked like it was something intense. After a few minutes of this, I decided I needed a change of scenery. I didn't want to just sit around anymore. As after-school-special as it sounded in my head, I was changing, and the world around me was changing too. I wanted to go out to explore and clear my head, and find out exactly what these changes meant. The fight with the Shades had been a revelation. Ashe had been telling me about the changes I was going to experience as I moved through the transition, and the new abilities I would develop. Seeing them in action was a different thing entirely. Suddenly I could take out two men far larger than myself, and I barely broke a sweat. I wanted to see what else might have changed.

I slid off my stool and walked around to where the three men were standing and talking to Ashe. They looked over at me, and it was obvious they weren't happy about the interruption. I didn't care. They were in my way, and I had no desire to be polite or wait any longer.

"Ashe, I need to talk to you," I said.

She looked over at me. I half-expected to see aggravation and frustration in her expression. Instead, her eyes got that look in them again, that look I'd seen in her apartment that made my stomach tighten and my dick harden. Stepping to the side, she leaned across the bar toward me.

"What do you need?" she asked.

"You know exactly what I need," I said. "But since you're working, I don't think I'm going to get it right now."

Ashe grinned.

"Not yet," she said.

I resisted the urge to reach out and touch her, because I knew if I did, I wouldn't be able to stop myself from tossing her over my shoulder and bringing her back upstairs to her bedroom.

"I'm going to go for a walk," I said.

"A walk?" she asked, looking unsure. "Are you all right?"

I nodded.

"I'm fine," I said. "I just don't feel like sitting around here anymore. I'm going to go walk around outside for a while."

"Sure," she said. "I shouldn't have to be here for too much longer. I'll meet up with you at the park in a while."

I agreed and headed for the door. When I glanced over my shoulder just before leaving, I saw her walk back over to the three men and start up the conversation again. I slipped out the door and walked slowly toward the park, taking in everything around me. I felt like my senses were heightened. My eyes seemed sharper, smells seemed stronger, and the sounds of the city seemed clearer and louder. I didn't know if that was actually the case, or if it was my mind playing tricks on me.

When I got to the park, the quiet contrasted with the noise of the street I had just walked down. This calm let me focus and try to find the strength I'd had during the fight. I tried to summon it, wanting to feel it rushing through me again. I felt like I could take on the world, and I started looking around for something impressive I could do. Maybe there was a tree about to fall and crush some little old woman and I could catch it, or a mugging going down and I could toss the bad guys in the bushes. I was feeling the need to live out some superhero fantasies when I noticed a woman leaned against a nearby light post. She was looking at me through lowered eyelashes, and when I met her eyes, she licked her lips.

The woman pushed away from the light post and came swaggering toward me. She swept her long black hair back over her shoulder and lifted her face to examine me as she approached. Big, vibrant green eyes stood out against her dark skin, and they didn't move away from me as she came closer.

"Hey, baby," she purred as she approached. "You shouldn't be walking out here all by yourself."

"Oh, really?" I asked.

She shook her head.

"No. Why don't you let me keep you company for a little while?"

"What did you have in mind?" I asked.

She took another step toward me and reached out to run her hand down my chest.

"I'm sure we could come up with something," she said. "My place isn't far from here. Let's go there so we don't waste any more time. I don't want to wait any longer to feel you inside me."

Before I could think of a way to respond, I felt a hand touch my back, and I turned around. Another woman was standing behind me, her almond-shaped hazel eyes flitting back and forth between me and the other woman.

"Don't give this park leech any more attention," she said.

"Park leech?" I asked.

"She'll latch onto anything that walks past," she said.

"Not anything," the first woman said, walking up to me again. "But she might be right about calling me a leech." She leaned closer to whisper in my ear. "I do suck."

What in the living hell was going on?

The second woman tugged on me again, and I turned back to her. She took my hands and guided me away from the first woman, who stumbled slightly when she no longer had my body to lean against. The second woman had a more innocent, nurturing look on her face, but she wasn't fooling me. That was a look I was familiar with. Admittedly, I had gotten it much more before the injury that blew my chances at stardom all to hell, when women would try every trick in the book to get my attention. This situation was the equivalent of having an angel and a devil standing on each of my shoulders. On one side I had the woman ready to strip me down and fuck me right here on the walking path. On the other was the woman batting her eyelashes and pretending she was the sweet girl next door who I might have the chance to deflower.

I had to say, they were both fairly effective techniques.

"Let me take you away from this tramp," the good girl said. "I'll save you from her and take you home with me."

"He doesn't want to have a tea party," the bad girl said. "You don't have anything you can offer him."

"You don't know that," the second woman snapped, some of the sugary sweetness leaving her voice as she faced off against green eyed woman. "You don't know anything about me."

"I know there's no chance he'd choose

someone like you when he has an offer from me." She grabbed me by the wrist and turned me around to face her. "The things I could do to you," she said. "You have no idea. I'd change your life."

I doubted that. Nothing could come close to changing my life as much as the past twenty-four hours had. Not that I would object to letting her try. The two women glared at each other for a few more seconds, then moved around me to lunge toward each other. Before they clashed, I heard a voice make a sound similar to the one my mother used to make when our dogs fought when I was a child. I looked up and saw Ashe striding toward us.

"The two of you need to back off," she said, eyeing the other two women.

I thought I was about to be in the middle of a three-woman smackdown, then realized she was looking at them like she knew them.

"Why?" the first woman asked.

"Hayden is not to be messed with," Ashe replied. "Aurora has already taken a liking to him."

That was enough to make both women back away from me.

"That's not fair," the second woman protested. "Why does she get to claim all the good ones?"

"I want him," the first woman said. "Just a little taste of him."

"No," Ashe said forcefully, stepping up so she stood between me and the other two women.

I had no idea what was going on, but I couldn't deny that I liked it.

"And who decided you were his bodyguard?" the first woman seethed at Ashe.

"I did," Ashe replied, undeterred. "He's not yours to play with."

"When is Aurora going to finish her turn?" the second woman asked.

"When she does," Ashe replied.

The first woman's lips curled up in a vicious smile that told me she knew of Aurora's reputation for not being the most attentive when it came to finishing the conversion for those she started. She stepped to the side and moved closer to me.

"Visit me if she doesn't," she said. "I'll make sure you go out with a bang."

Before my dick shrivels and falls off. She didn't say that, but I knew she was thinking it. It would be kind of hard not to.

Ashe took hold of my arm and guided me away from the two women. We headed out of the park, and I looked over at her. She was shaking her head, and there was an almost angry look in her eyes.

"What was that all about?" I asked. "It's like those women couldn't resist me."

"They couldn't," she said. "There's something different about you, Hayden. I don't know what it is, but something about you is intoxicating. Even I feel it. Whether I'm near you or not, there's this intense arousal. It just gets stronger when you're close."

I stopped and turned toward her. Taking her hand, I yanked her up against me.

"It does, does it?" I asked. She nodded, and I leaned down to crush my mouth against hers. "Show me."

12

The door to the VIP room at Solomon's Fang was barely closed before I pushed Ashe up against the wall and yanked her shirt off over her head. I dropped it to her feet and dipped my fingers into her bra to pull the cups down. Her breasts spilled out, and I ducked my head down to catch one in my mouth. My tongue swirled around her nipple as my fingers worked at the button of her pants. She grabbed her waistband to wriggle out of them while I shucked my shirt and fought my way out of my own pants. When I was finally naked, I lifted Ashe up and plunged into her without any hesitation. She pressed her hands against the wall on either side for leverage as I pounded into her hard and fast.

Our mouths tangled roughly with each other, and she wrapped her legs around my waist. I grabbed onto her hips and carried her over to the other side of the room where I set her down on one of the large, plush chairs. Getting on my knees in front of her, I pushed her thighs wide and leaned down to swipe my tongue up through her glistening wet pussy. Ashe whimpered and wriggled against the cushion of the chair. I moved my tongue up to her clit and flicked it, swirling it around until I saw her hands clench on either side of her. She was groaning, her back arching as I lapped up her juices. All it did was feed my frenzy. Holding one thigh down with one hand, I used the other to sink two fingers into her. She let out a strangled cry, and I felt her walls spasm around my fingers. I pushed them as far up into her as I could, and held them there as I watched her face. When she relaxed, I withdrew my fingers and pulled her up, turning us around so our places were switched.

Without prompting, she dropped to her knees in front of me and wrapped her hand around the base of my engorged cock. A few strokes of her soft little palm had me rock hard. Ashe opened her mouth and sucked just the plush head between her lips. The tip of her tongue dipped into the slit at the tip, and she squeezed slightly with her hand. Stroking up and down my length, she moved her mouth slightly lower. The teasing was pushing me close to the edge, and I let out a little growl.

"I want to taste his blood."

It was Ashe's voice, but how could she be talking to me when her mouth was full of my dick?

"I want to know how he tastes. But what would that do? Would it change the ritual?"

There it was again. I was positive I had heard her that time. She must have felt me tense up, because she lifted her head and looked up at me.

"Is something wrong?" she asked.

"I thought I heard you say something," I said.

She looked at me strangely, her hand still moving in slow, distracting glides up and down my shaft.

"What do you mean?" she asked.

"Just a few seconds ago," I said. "I thought I heard you say something."

She got a little smile on her face like she thought I was playing with her.

"Oh? And what did I say?"

"You said something about wanting to taste my blood, but you don't know if you should because you don't know how it would affect the ritual."

As soon as I said it, Ashe's face dropped. Her hand fell away from my dick, and she looked shocked. I had the feeling I had said something wrong, or at least something she wasn't expecting to hear.

"You heard me say that?" she asked.

"I thought I did," I said, trying to laugh a little. "I mean, obviously you couldn't have said anything. Your mouth was otherwise occupied at the time."

I wanted to break the tension, to bring back the fun, playful mood we'd been in. Instead, she continued to stare at me.

"I was thinking it," she said.

"Thinking it?" I asked. "Like in your head?"

Ashe rolled her eyes.

"That's usually what people think with."

She pushed back and stood up.

"I don't know," I said. "You still haven't gotten back to me on that manual."

She gave me an incredulous look. She was not amused.

"So, I heard your thoughts?" I asked.

Ashe nodded.

"It seems that way," she said. "That was exactly what I was thinking just then. I could see where Aurora bit you, and was thinking about how much

I'd like to take a little taste myself, but I didn't because I don't know what that would do. Two vampires biting the same human isn't something that happens unless it's already been established that human is a sacrifice."

"A sacrifice?"

"Meant to be fully drained and killed anyway," she clarified.

"That's lovely," I said, my stomach turning at the thought of the blood.

"Sometimes that means several vampires will bite the same victim at the same time, but then it doesn't matter what's going to happen. That person's dead by the time the group's done with them. But you...you're in the middle of your turn. I have no idea what would happen to you if I bit you as well. It might mean I would need to give you some of my blood as well as you needing some of Aurora's, but it might also just kill you. I don't know."

"Thanks for not deciding today was the day to take risks," I said.

Ashe shrugged.

"Aurora would be pissed if I managed to kill you before she even got the opportunity to decide whether she's going to turn you or not."

I stared at her blankly for a few seconds.

"I'm glad that's your priority," I said.

"Actually, my priority right now is figuring out how you could hear what I was thinking," she said.

"I don't know why you're so worked up," I said. I reached out and took her wrist, trying to pull her toward me. "Maybe it's just one of the abilities I'm developing during my turn. I'm sure there are plenty of other vampires who are able to read thoughts."

She shook her head.

"Do you really think I'd be reacting like this if it was a completely normal thing for vampires to be able to do? Regardless of the fact that you are still in the middle of your turn, you shouldn't be able to do that. Even fully developed, high-powered vampires don't just go around listening to other people's thoughts. Is this something you've always been able to do?"

"Seriously?" I asked. "If I could just hear what everybody around me was thinking, I wouldn't have been wasting my time out on the football field. I would have been able to find a way to manipulate the shit out of it, and I'd have all the money I ever wanted. Yours are definitely the first thoughts I've heard."

"I don't know what this means," she said. Then she looked at me with a mischievous glint in her eyes. "But I don't really want to think about it anymore right now. Where were we?"

She dropped back to her knees, and I felt her tongue glide along me again. I let her suck for a few seconds, then pulled her to her feet and into my lap. Slamming up into her, I kissed her deeply and fucked her hard until she came. Ashe pulled her mouth away from mine to let out a scream, then dropped her head to my shoulder. She didn't lift it again, and for the first time since waking up I wondered what time it was. It had been the longest day of my life, and I was ready to go to bed. I jostled Ashe until she lifted her head, and looked at me with equally sleepy eyes.

"Let's go to your apartment and go to bed," I said.

I didn't want to drag myself all the way back to my apartment. Part of me also just wanted to stay near Ashe. At the back of my mind, I could feel the time ticking away, and something told me to stick close to her if I wanted to live. She was the one telling me how to get through this, and I didn't want to do anything that might decrease my chances of surviving. She nodded her agreement and we got dressed.

The next thing I knew, I was being woken up by the sound of someone pounding on a door. I didn't even remember getting into bed. I remembered walking out of the VIP room with Ashe, but everything else was fuzzy. The pounding continued, and I opened my eyes. Looking to my side, I saw her stretched out in the bed beside me. She was sleeping completely naked. The sight of her body against the cool white sheets was enough to get my blood pumping again, and I wanted to flip her onto her back and go for another round. The knocking was getting louder, though, and I knew I wasn't going to get away with it. She shifted in her sleep, moaning slightly.

"What the hell is that?" she asked.

"Someone's at the door," I said.

Ashe rolled over and lifted her head to look at me questioningly.

"Who is it?" she asked groggily.

"I don't know," I said. "I'll get it."

She nodded and I got out of bed, pulling on my pants as I crossed the apartment to the door. I pulled it open and saw one of the Shade guards from the night before standing just outside. His expression was stony, but his stance told me he wasn't happy to see me. I tensed, ready to fight him again. I noticed his friend wasn't there with him.

"What do you want?" I asked.

"What are you doing here?"

I looked over my shoulder and saw Ashe coming into the room.

"I'm here with a message," he said. He looked back at me. "You are to come back to Nakatomi Tower. Aurora requested a meeting with you."

He didn't say anything else, just turned around and stalked away. I closed the door and faced Ashe.

"Is this a trap?" I asked. "If this was a movie, I'd be screaming at the characters not to go."

"Do you see someone filming?" she asked. When I didn't answer, she shook her head. "I don't think there's anything to worry about," she said. "You don't have to be afraid of them."

"I'm not fucking afraid of them," I said. "I just want to be prepared for what I'm walking into."

"What are you going to do? Go buy some wooden stakes first?" she asked.

"Hilarious," I said, following her back into the bedroom so I could finish getting dressed.

"The Shade have plenty of ways to, let's say, *convince* people to do what they want them to do.

They don't need to resort to thinly veiled traps. Complex and intricately planned traps, perhaps, but they aren't going to walk up to the door and tell you someone wants to talk to you and then toss you in a dungeon when you show up. If that Shade was sent as a messenger and not as a guard, it means Aurora really did send him. She wants to talk to you."

"Beats the hell out of searching around for her," I said.

Ashe shrugged.

"We'll see. Get ready. We don't want to keep her waiting."

13

WE WALKED out of the apartment a short time later and found a note stuck to the door with a push pin. Ashe pulled the note off the door and handed it to me.

"Looks like our Shade friend wanted to make sure we didn't forget he came by for a visit," she said.

"Who travels with their own push pins?" I asked.

I unfolded the piece of paper and looked down at the note. Any thoughts that it might have been the Shade who wrote it were gone as soon as I saw the handwriting. Any man that big and rough would have handwriting that matched. Either his big hands and strength would make his script messy and illegible, or his intense control would make it chunky and square. The handwriting on this note was neither. Instead, it was smooth and flowing. The script felt formal and old-fashioned, like it came from a different time. I remembered what Ashe had told me about Aurora, and knew the note had to be from her. I didn't know why, but I got a thrill out of holding the piece of paper and knowing she had written the words on it. It was like I felt like I was getting closer to something I didn't yet understand.

"You are hereby summoned to Nakatomi Tower. Thirty-seventh floor," I read.

"That's it?" Ashe asked.

I nodded, flipping the paper over to make sure I hadn't missed anything.

"That's it," I confirmed. "She sure doesn't waste time on niceties, does she?"

"I told you, Aurora isn't the warm and fuzzy type. She's not going to go out of her way to make you feel...well, much of anything, to be honest. Not unless she gets something out of it. She wants you at the Tower, so she's going to tell you that. Plain and simple. She doesn't need to invite you, or hope you want to come. She wants you there, so you'll be there."

We got to Nakatomi Tower twenty minutes later and walked in through the revolving doors. Despite what Ashe had said about the Shade, part of me expected the guards to jump us as soon as we got into the lobby. I was on edge until we'd gotten all the way inside and hadn't been smashed into the marble floor. We looked around, but didn't see anyone who seemed to be waiting for us. Ashe started across the lobby toward the desk where she had gone the day before, and I fell into step behind her. As we approached, the same woman looked up at us. She gave what looked like a corporate smile, one of those half-grins that only seemed to tug up part of her lips and didn't reach her eyes.

"Good morning," she said in a bland, not quite cheerful voice that matched the smile.

"Hi," Ashe said. "I was here yesterday."

The woman nodded once.

"I remember."

"We're meeting someone here. She's expecting us."

I didn't know why Ashe was being evasive. She didn't seem frightened, or like she was trying to protect Aurora or the Shade. Instead, it sounded almost like a test, like she was trying to determine if this woman knew all the inner workings of what was happening in the building. When the woman stared back at Ashe without a response, I stepped up to the desk. I held the note out to her.

"We got this," I said. "It was left this morning."

I didn't feel the need to tell her about our visit from the Shade. I'm sure she remembered the run-in from the day before. She took the paper from my hand and looked at it, then lifted her eyes to me before handing it back.

"Just a moment," she said.

She picked up a phone on the desk beside her, and pressed a button.

"He's here," she said without greeting.

She hung up the phone just as promptly, and gestured further into the lobby.

"You can wait there," she said. "Someone will be with you in a moment."

Ashe and I walked past the columns in the center of the lobby and stood amongst the plants that had shielded the Shade guards from my view yesterday. I noticed they weren't standing by the elevator this time, and wondered what had come of the guard I had left lying on the ground in the alley. Only seconds passed before the elevator doors slid open, and the guard who had been at the apartment stepped out.

"Come with me," he said.

Ashe and I followed his instructions, crossing the rest of the lobby and walking into the elevator. When the doors shut, the guard pulled a keycard out of his pocket and inserted it into a slot on the control panel. Only a few of the numbers had been illuminated, but once his card was in place, the others lit up as well. He pressed the button for the 37th floor, and the elevator started to slide upward, moving rapidly. Soon the car stopped, and the doors slid open again. The Shade stepped out and waited for us to follow him. He escorted us down a long hallway with grey carpeting and lights in elaborate sconces every few feet.

"What's with the card?" I asked.

"Nakatomi Tower has several purposes," the Shade responded. "It's best only some enter certain areas."

"There are forty floors in the tower," Ashe explained. "But the top 10 are only accessible by special authorization. That was technically a private elevator and no one is supposed to use it but those on the top floors. The keycards are just another layer of security. The elevator would be unable to access those floors without it."

We reached a door at the end of the hallway

and the guard used his key again to open it. As soon as we stepped inside, I felt like I had walked into an invisible wall. Aurora was sitting at an ornate desk in the center of the room, and the force of seeing her and being in the room with her, was tangible. It hit me so hard I could barely breathe. It was as if the attraction I felt for her was physically pulling me toward her. As I looked at her, I could see her breaths become deeper. An even larger guard stood to one side of her. She gestured toward him with one graceful hand. All I could think about was how it had felt for that hand to run along my body.

"This is Jaxxim," she said. "My personal guard."

I nodded an acknowledgement toward him, but I couldn't tear my attention away from Aurora for long.

"Touch me."

Just like when I had heard Ashe's thoughts, I heard Aurora speak, but her mouth didn't move. I didn't say anything. The way Ashe had reacted was strong enough. I didn't want to do anything that might push Aurora away before I got what I wanted from her. Her hands were folded on the top of the desk in front of her, and I could see them tense, like she was trying to control herself. The way the women in the park had acted came to mind, and I wondered if she was feeling the same attraction Ashe had described. I decided to take my chances. I took a step toward the desk.

"I know what you did to me," I said.

"Of course you do," she said. "You wouldn't be here if you didn't."

"*Stop, Aurora. Not yet.*"

She was holding back, fighting with herself to resist me, but I didn't know why. All that mattered was getting her blood and finishing this turn. It wasn't something I relished the thought of doing, but it was better than the alternative.

"You need to complete the ritual," I said. "Ashe told me you sometimes just don't finish turning people. Not me."

The draw I felt to her was unlike anything I'd ever experienced. It was more powerful than any attraction I could have imagined. It was challenging just to keep my thoughts straight enough to talk to her.

"You think I should complete your turn, do you?" she asked. "And you know what the ritual involves?"

"You took my blood when you bit me – which

still hurts, by the way – so you have to give me some of yours. That will complete my change."

Aurora looked amused and made a quiet, affirmative sound.

"That's a lot to ask, you know," she said. "To have some of my blood. I'm not just any old vampire you might find on the street." Her eyes slid over to Ashe. "Or in a bar."

It was a nasty, snide comment, but I didn't get the impression she expressly disliked Ashe. Instead, it felt like a subtle barb, a comment made to remind the people around her of her station, and of theirs.

"I know," I said. "But it's also a lot to ask for me to just sit around and wait to fucking shrivel up like a raisin and die. You didn't ask me if I was up for *that.*"

"Unfortunately for you, it's not up to you," she said. "I can do as I please. And I haven't come a decision yet as to whether I'm going to allow you to have some of my blood."

"Then why did you bring me here?" I asked.

Her smile got only slightly larger.

"You're a clever one, aren't you? Why *would* I bring you here if I didn't have the intention of completing the ritual? Or…perhaps…of just finishing up and killing you?" She lifted her hands so they folded in front of her and rested her chin on them briefly as she looked at me. "There's something about you, Hayden. Something I can't quite put my finger on."

"So I've heard," I said.

She gave a nod.

"I'm sure you have. I want to know what it is. I want to know what makes you different."

I had the feeling she was going to deny me, and the image of my poor dick rotting away flashed through my mind again. I couldn't let that happen. Remembering what Ashe had said about Aurora either giving me her blood, or me taking it, I made a split-second decision and rushed the desk. I had taken only a few steps when Jaxxim shot away from his position and grabbed me around the neck. He lifted me off my feet and glared up into my face as he held me off the ground. It was instantly obvious that as fast and strong as I thought I was, Jaxxim was greatly more so. I clawed at his hands, and he finally put me back on my feet.

"What the fuck?" I asked, struggling to drag in a breath.

"Now you see why I have him as my personal guard," Aurora said. "He is very strong. Very fast.

Very powerful. Things you could be, if you were to complete your change and come into your full powers. The operative word here being 'if'. That's still a decision I have to make. You see, finishing the ritual to turn you isn't just about you. Changing you would make a major impact on my life as well. If I was to give you my blood and finish the ritual, it would tie you to me forever, make you my lord, and eventually my king. I don't take that lightly. I haven't lived this long and stayed free just to be locked down to a human with a glow. I want to know what it is that makes you so different, and then, and only then, will I consider finishing the ritual."

"So, that's it?" I asked. "You're dangling my life over me because you can't decide if you want to be linked with me for life?"

"Not life, Hayden," Aurora said. "Eternity. Or until one of us is decapitated."

"Beautiful sentiment," I said. "You should really add that to your online dating profile. Look. Why don't we just decide that's not how it would have to work? We don't have to be bound to each other just because you change me. I'll just say thanks for the offer, but no, and we'll move on."

"That's not how it works."

I turned toward Ashe, who was still standing just inside the room.

"What do you mean that's not how it works?" I asked.

"Just that," she said. "You don't get to decide how the change affects either of you. Aurora is a princess. Her station sets her apart. The depth of her bite and the amount of the toxin she puts into you when she bites you determines the intensity of your bond to each other if she chooses to complete your turn."

"You've always been such a good little student, Ashe," Aurora said. "She's right, Hayden. My bite is special. It can mean little, or it can mean a lot. Most of the people I change I can't even remember. They go on having whatever existence they're going to have, and it literally has no impact on me. For some reason, you strike me as different. The night I saw you at the bar, I was drawn to you, and I wanted you right then. Giving you the amount of venom that I did was a spur of the moment decision. But if I choose to finish the transformation, it can't be changed."

"What does that mean?" I asked. "Do you want me to give you the run-down of myself? Tell you all the names of my childhood pets, my favorite sushi spot, and that I love long walks on the beach while discussing fine literature?"

"I don't need you to romance me," Aurora said flatly. "I've had enough people try during my existence. I need answers. Find out what makes you special, and I will trade you my blood for the answer. Seek out Malakan in Solon City. I will hear the answer from him."

My eyes locked on Aurora, and I didn't want to look away. I felt Ashe's hand wrap around my wrist and start pulling me backward. I wanted to stay there in the room with her. I didn't want to be away from her.

"Come on, Hayden," Ashe said. "We have to go. We don't have much time."

Finally, I tore my eyes away from the gorgeous woman gazing back at me and followed Ashe out of the room. Just as the door was closing behind me, I heard her voice again.

"I will only believe the answer from a friend I trust."

I immediately wondered if she had actually spoken the words, or if I had heard another thought.

We walked back down the hallway and into the elevator. As the doors shut, she smashed the button for the lobby.

"I thought you needed a key card to use the floors this high up in the building," I said.

"Just to get up to them," Ashe said. "You need special authorization to access these parts of the building, not to leave them."

"I guess it's reassuring to know they can't keep anybody hostage here," I said.

She looked at me seriously.

"Why not?" she asked.

I opened my mouth to respond, but decided it was best to just let that train of thought end.

14

I was still trying to wrap my head around everything that had happened in the tower when we walked through the front door of Solomon's Fang. It all seemed completely outlandish, like I was a part of some sort of incredibly complex prank. Of course, I didn't know anybody who was smart enough, or creative enough, to go about orchestrating a plan like this. To be completely honest, I probably didn't know anybody who gave enough of a damn about me to try. It was all real, and that meant I really did have one hell of a challenge ahead of me.

"Are you feeling better?" Ashe asked as we walked through the door and immediately crossed through the bar.

"Feeling better?" I asked.

"You've been really quiet the entire way back," she said. "Are you dealing with everything all right?"

"I'm fine," I told her. "I promise I'm not going to start moping around and bemoaning my fate. Unless I notice any sign at all of dick rot. If that happens, I can make absolutely no promises about how well I'll handle it."

She laughed, and suddenly turned to face me.

"You seem tense," she said.

I nodded and shrugged, trying to look casual even though I knew she could sense the tension in me. More than a day had passed, and time was going by quickly. It seemed challenging enough to find Aurora and convince her to change me when it didn't also involve having to bend to the whim of the princess and go on a quest to bring her back the answer to some riddle. At least she hadn't requested my heart on a silver platter, though there was still no guarantee of me coming back alive.

"Maybe a little," I said.

"Well, going through the portal isn't going to be easy," she said. "Maybe you'd like a quick tumble in bed to take the edge off."

That intoxicating glint was in her eyes again.

"Well," I said, walking toward her she had to back up against the steps. "We do have a few minutes to spare…"

She laughed as I chased her up the stairs toward her apartment. When I gathered her up in my arms and tossed her onto the bed, I was already hard and ready to sink into her. Feeling her hot, wet pussy close around my cock was exactly what I needed to distract me from our visit to Nakatomi. I rolled Ashe over onto her stomach and used my knee to shove her thighs apart so I could get on my knees between them. I plunged into her again and used my leverage to slam into her fast and hard. Her ass bounced against my thighs with each thrust, the sound of our skin slapping against each other only arousing me further. She let out a moan, and I gave her ass a sharp smack, causing her to cry out. Her hips lifted slightly, and I did it again. I growled at her sounds of pleasure and took hold of her hips so I could ride her until I came in a blinding rush.

I was sitting on the edge of her bed half an hour later when she came back into the bedroom. I had showered before her, but was still only wearing my pants.

"Something wrong?" she asked.

"The first time you and I went down into the basement and you introduced me to Tybalt," I said. "He mentioned that there's a blood price to go through the portal to Solon City."

Ashe tossed the towel she had been using to dry her hair into a hamper in the corner.

"Yeah," she said. "It's not that bad. All the portals require it. It's how we're able to pass from this world into the Underworld." I shuddered, and she looked at me strangely. "What is it?"

I drew in a breath.

"I don't like blood," I admitted. "I know, it sounds ridiculous. But I really fucking hate it. I always have, ever since I was a kid. I'm sure a few hours stretched out on the psychiatrist's couch could give me some sort of deep insight into whatever trauma that happened to make me so squeamish around it."

"Or you could be like a lot of people," she said. "You see, most people don't go wandering around talking about how much they love blood."

"I guess," I said. "It just really bothers me. I don't like admitting it, but I'm anxious about this whole blood price thing."

"You better get over that shit," she said. "There's a whole lot more after the piddly little blood price. Remember, you have to actually drink Aurora's blood to complete the change."

"I know," I said, swallowing hard to try to keep my stomach under control. "I'm not really looking forward to that."

"Like I said, it's best you find a way to get over that real fast. Not being able to stand the sight of blood is an odd affliction for a vampire to have. It's like a human being afraid of a cheeseburger." She brushed her hair up into a ponytail at the back of her head, tied on a pair of black boots, and let out a breath. "You ready?"

I looked down at myself.

"I'm half-naked," I said.

"I know," Ashe said with a grin. "I hoped you were planning on staying that way."

"Probably not the best idea," I said.

I finished getting dressed, and we walked out of the apartment. Walking down the stairs felt familiar now, and I realized just how much I was leaving my old life behind. I had barely even thought about it, which was comforting in its own way. We made our way through the main floor of the bar toward the door to the basement. As Ashe opened it, my anxiety about the blood price came back. I tried to think about what it could be as we walked down the next set of stairs and through the chambers of the basement. I was surprised when Ty didn't step out of the shadows like he had the first time.

"Looks like your bouncer is asleep on the job," I commented.

"Not today."

The sound of Ty's voice came from the room behind me.

"Ty," I said. "Always lovely to see you."

Part of me expected him to launch back into the stream of questions from when he had come up to the apartment the day before. Instead, he didn't even acknowledge me and walked toward Ashe.

"Do you need something?" he asked. "I still haven't heard anything else about Aurora."

"We did," Ashe said. "One of the Shade from the scuffle yesterday showed up at my place with a note requesting Hayden meet her at Nakatomi."

"I take it that visit didn't involve her stretching her neck out to him, or handing him a little vial of blood so he could tip it into his coffee," Ty said.

"Not exactly," Ashe said.

"I got sent on a mission," I said.

"A mission?" he asked.

"Aurora doesn't want to change him yet," Ashe said.

I was getting seriously tired of them talking about me like I wasn't even there.

"Yeah," I said. "Turns out she's having second thoughts."

"I wouldn't exactly put it like that," Ashe said. "I don't think Aurora has had a second thought in her entire existence, alive or otherwise. That's just not her. What Hayden means is she gave him a bonding bite, but she hasn't decided whether she wants to go through with it yet."

"Really?" Ty asked. "I never thought I'd see the day."

"She played it off like it was no big deal, but you know as well as I do it's not something she does all the time. In fact, I think she has only done it one other time, ever."

They looked at each other like they were sharing some kind of secret, but I couldn't hear any thoughts coming from Ashe. A realization suddenly popped into my mind, and I grabbed her arm to pull her away from Ty.

"I need to talk to you," I said. "There's something I need to tell you."

"Now?" Ashe asked. "We really need to get through the portal."

I glanced at Ty. I didn't want him to hear me, so I nodded.

"I'll tell you later," I said.

She gave a single nod, then turned back to the bouncer.

"She said there's something different about Hayden, and she won't consider finishing the change until she finds out what it is."

Ty's eyes slid over to me and he scrutinized me for a few seconds before looking at Ashe again.

"So why are you here?" he asked.

"I'm supposed to talk to somebody called Malakan," I said.

"Aurora said she wants the answer from him, and she'll trade her blood for it," Ashe said. "So, we need to get through the portal and find Malakan."

"How would he even know anything about me?" I asked. "I don't even know who he is. How could some vampire in a world I've only known existed for twenty-four hours tell me what it is about me that's so different."

Ty and Ashe exchanged glances again.

"Don't tell him."

Ashe was thinking it in repeat, and it occurred to me Ty couldn't hear her, she was just hoping to send the vibe to him.

"I need to get you through the portal if you're going to go," Ty suddenly said. "I have things I need to be doing."

It was a bullshit answer to get past my question, but I wasn't going to push it. I'd had enough of Ty, and was ready to move on to whatever was waiting for us on the other side of the portal he guarded. I followed Ashe into the room where they had told me about the portal, and watched Ty walk up to a cabinet I hadn't even noticed the first time we were there. He reached in and pulled out several objects. He laid them on a table, and I looked at them. The only thought that went through my mind when I saw them was that they looked like antique surgical implements. I watched him cross the room and reach up to light a candle in a large sconce in the wall. It produced just enough glow to illuminate him as he lit several others, until there was enough light in the room for me to look around. Directly in front of me was a wall covered by a tapestry that looked old and worn. Ty moved the tapestry to the side, using a loop woven into the pattern to attach it to a hook in the wall.

The movement exposed an area of bare stone, but he didn't do anything else. He came back to us, and looked back and forth between us.

"Which one of you is going to make the payment?" he asked.

Before I could even open my mouth to answer, Ashe stepped forward.

"I am," she said. "Hayden has been going through a lot the last couple of days."

"All right," Ty said. "Come here."

Ashe walked up to him without any hesitation. She didn't seem afraid or worried, even when he reached over to the table and picked up one of the knives. I reminded myself she had gone through this process countless times before, and it probably didn't bother her anymore. As the only person in the room who had no idea what was going on, I was bothered. She extended her arm to him, and Ty took her wrist. He flipped her arm over, exposing the pale, soft underside of her forearm. Without a word of warning, he drew the blade along her skin. I tried to watch without reacting, but as soon as I saw blood rising up to the surface, I felt my stomach flip. Despite the feeling, I forced myself to keep watching. I wanted to know what was going to happen. She was paying this price for me, and I felt the compulsion to know every step of it. I needed to understand what was happening.

Ty placed the knife back on the table and picked up a long, narrow piece of black material. It looked like dark wood, but I couldn't fully tell. He brought it over to Ashe and stroked it over the wound he had just made. She didn't react as he scooped her blood up onto the object and carried it over to the wall. She kept her arm in the same position, and I watched as the blood stopped beading up and dried. By the time she gestured at me to follow her toward the far wall where Ty was headed, it was visibly healing.

We stopped a few feet from the wall, and Ty reached up to run the black object along it, spreading Ashe's blood onto the stone. There was a faint hissing sound and the stone seemed to absorb the blood, then the stones melted away.

"Come on," Ashe said, patting my arm.

She walked forward, and I followed her through the wall.

15

I didn't know what to expect when I got through the portal. Part of me thought we would go through the wall and end up in another basement. Instead, it seemed like we were suddenly standing in an alley. It looked very much like the one where we had fought the Shade guards, and I looked around. Everything seemed so familiar. It didn't feel like we had done anything but step outside the building.

"Did we just pass through a wall into the alley behind Solomon's?" I asked.

"Do you really think we would go through all that just to do a parlor trick into an alley?"

"No," I answered. "I'm just trying wrap my head around it."

"That," she said, gesturing at the building beside us, "is the Solan City part of Solomon's Fang. Around here, people just call it the Fang. The portal to get into the city comes out here rather than inside because it would be annoying as hell for people to be traipsing up and down from the basement all the time."

"Is it the only way?" I asked.

"No, there are other gateways throughout the city."

I noticed her glance at her arm. "Thanks for doing that," I said.

"No problem," Ashe said. "It's not a big deal for me. I've paid the blood price more times than I can count. After what you told me, I knew you probably wouldn't be too enthusiastic about being the one he had to cut. I'm already almost healed, anyway. But I'm letting you know right now, it's not always going to be like that."

I gave a short laugh.

"I got it," I said.

"Good," she said. "Now, let's go find Malakan."

We walked out of the alley, and I was struck again by just how much this place looked like New York City. All of what surrounded us felt exactly like home. I couldn't pinpoint anything that set it apart, or anything that made me feel like I was in some other world. On a whim, I grabbed my phone out of my pocket, and glanced down at it.

"I have cell service!" I exclaimed, holding my phone out to Ashe as though she had asked for proof.

"Yep," she said.

"Look, I don't get this. You and Ty made this big deal about moving through a portal, and going into another world. Supposedly we are in a different city, and yet I can't tell the difference at all. I mean, I know we're not on the same block, but it still looks exactly like New York."

"It's supposed to," Ashe said. "That's how it was designed."

"What do you mean?" I asked.

"Ages ago, the mages designed Solon City. They are an extremely powerful magic species. They wanted to create a world that was a mirror to the one of the humans. They used their magic to exactly replicate New York City. The trees, the skyscrapers, every blade of grass. It's just the same as the human version."

"The human version?" I asked. "So there are other vampire cities?"

"Not vampire cities," she corrected. "Underworld. There are many more species here than just the vampires. Like I said, it was designed by the mages. But, no, it's not the only city. There are other Underworld cities throughout the world, all of them designed to exactly mirror their human counterparts."

As we walked along the sidewalk, I noticed several of the people we passed turn to look over their shoulders at me. A few sniffed the air, leaning toward me as if trying to figure out something about me. I looked at Ashe, who wasn't paying any attention to anyone around us.

"Tell me about this Malakan guy," I said. "You didn't explain why Aurora would want me to go to him. Is he some sort of vampire guru?"

"He's not a vampire," Ashe said.

"He's not?"

I was shocked by the revelation. I had just assumed the princess of the vampires would send me to another vampire to prove myself.

"No," Ashe said. "And it's not something that's necessarily well-received among our kind. Malakan is a mage, a warlock. A very old warlock. He was exiled by his people, and now he lives in the slums of Solon City. The vampires and the magi don't have the friendliest of histories with each other. The war claimed many lives on both sides, and even though it's mostly a stalemate now, there is still a tremendous amount of tension. There is a lot of distrust on both sides, and Malakan is at the center of a lot of it. Many vampires don't believe he's actually separated from the rest of the warlocks. There are rumors he's here in Solon City as a mole, feeding information back to his people. But not everybody feels that way. There are just as many people who think his presence here has done a lot to offset the danger from the warlocks, and is continuing to ease the tensions and turmoil between the two races."

"Why would Aurora send me to him?" I asked.

"Malakan has been a close confidant of Aurora's for a very long time. It's not something that's well-known, and not something she likes to advertise. But she thinks very highly of him and his opinions. It seems to me, though, that it must be more than that."

"Why do you say that?"

"She's not sending you to him so he can give you the once-over, and then tell her whether he thinks you two are a match. This isn't like when a girl sends her best friend over to infiltrate the group of guys so she can get the intel on whether a certain one likes her. If that was the case, she wouldn't have a problem bringing you out and putting you on display at a banquet. There would be plenty of people to tell her what they thought. There has to be a specific reason she wants you to talk to Malakan. She said he would be able to give you the answer."

We walked by another group, and their conversation stopped as they watched us pass. I glanced over my shoulder and saw them staring at me, their eyes trained on me intently. Shaking my head, I forced myself to focus.

"I told you I needed to tell you something," I said.

"Go ahead," Ashe said.

"I heard Aurora, too."

She narrowed her eyes at me.

"You heard her, too?" she asked. "As in, you were standing there in the room with me, and you heard the same things I did? Because I already knew that."

I shook my head.

"No. I *heard* her. Like I told you I heard you."

"You heard her thoughts?"

Ashe sounded stunned, and I nodded.

"Yes," I told her. "When we first went in, she wanted me to touch her. Then she was convincing herself to stop thinking about me. When we left, though, I heard her, but I wasn't looking at her. I don't know if she was actually saying it, or just thinking it. She said she would only accept the answer from her trusted friend."

Ashe stopped, and turned to search my eyes.

"She said that?" she asked.

"Yeah," I said. "What do you think it means?"

"Remember how I said Aurora has never second-guessed anything in her existence?"

"Yes."

"She knows something. She might not want to say it, but there's something on her mind. She just wants to hear someone else say it."

16

NEITHER OF US knew what else to say. Even though I could see the seriousness in Ashe's eyes, and I knew that the revelation carried weight, I didn't know enough about what it all meant to respond. Instead, we just started walking again. All around us, I could see people staring at me. Women walking out of buildings would stop in their tracks to watch me pass, and a few even fell into step behind me for a few paces before peeling off. The hunger was building inside me again, and I was enjoying the attention they were giving me. We walked toward another group, and I saw them all turn to face us. They let Ashe go by, but before I was able to pass them, three women stepped out to stand in a line across the sidewalk. I paused in front of the wall they had created with their bodies and smiled at them.

"Hello," I said, letting my eyes trail up and down each of them.

One of the other women from the group suddenly reached out for me. She grabbed the belt loop on my pants and pulled. The movement was so unexpected that I stumbled slightly, giving her and another woman the opportunity to take hold of me and push me up against the wall of the building behind them. As soon as I was standing with my back against the cold brick, all of the women swarmed in around me. Their hands roved my body, and I couldn't even tell which of them was touching me. The woman who had been in the middle of the line across the sidewalk stepped up in front of me and crushed her mouth against mine. Her tongue plunged into my mouth and tangled with mine as if she was trying to taste as much of me as she possibly could. On either side of me, two other women kissed along my neck. I could feel their tongues slip out of their mouths and glide across my skin. Two more women pressed up close to them and reached around them to slip their hands up into my shirt to feel along my stomach and chest.

Not to be outdone, the woman kissing me loosened my belt just enough that she could shove her hand down into my pants. At this point, my cock was already hard, and her hand stroked along it eagerly. She moved her head out of the way, and another of the women took the opportunity to kiss me. I noticed she had a distinctly different taste than the first woman. Neither of them tasted like Ashe, or what I remembered of Aurora. It was like a new sense I was developing. I could discern the flavor of each of these women, and it only made me hungrier for more. I pulled my mouth away from the woman kissing me, and turned my head just enough so another could catch my lips. The combination of the different tastes, the tongues on my neck, and the confident, willing hand around my shaft was intoxicating. I had been shocked at first when they pushed me against the wall, but now I was losing myself in the attention. This was like sex in surround sound, and I couldn't get enough of it. My body and my mind were welcoming it, drinking it in, and feeling as though this was the way life should be. For the first time in as long as I could remember, I felt like I was in my own skin.

As suddenly as I had been swarmed by the women, I felt them step back from me.

"Get off of him," Ashe commanded.

She pushed the woman in front of me away, and reached to pull me away from the wall.

"Why?" one of the women asked.

"He's not here for you," Ashe replied.

"What's that supposed to mean?" another of the women asked.

Their hands grabbed at me, as if they were desperate to keep me close. One stepped up behind me and I felt her arms go around my waist and run along my chest and stomach. They slipped down further to stroke over my hips and between my thighs.

"It means get off of him."

"But he's just so delicious," another woman said, stepping up closer so she could run her tongue up my neck.

"We're just looking for a little snack," the woman who had been in front of me told Ashe.

"Find somebody else," Ashe commanded.

She pulled me away from the women, and we started at a fast pace down the sidewalk.

"That was even more ridiculous than in the park," I said.

"And it's just going to get worse," Ashe said. "Aurora completing the change will take some of the edge off, but you're going to keep getting this type of attention. Until we figure out what in the living hell it is about you that is drawing all of this attention, we're just going to have to deal with it."

"One of them said something that brought up a question," I said.

"What was that?" she asked.

"That woman told you they just wanted a little snack," I said. "How exactly do you deal with that when you're here?"

"I don't think I know what you're asking," Ashe said. "They want to snack on you the same way I do."

"That's not what I meant," I said. "What do you do about food here when you're away from humans? It's not like you're going to call for delivery. Somehow, I sincerely doubt Ty is going to swing through Solomon's and collect a few humans for take-out to bring here for everybody to drink blood from. So, what do you eat?"

"Drinking blood isn't exactly the same thing for vampires as eating food is for humans," she explained. "Humans need to eat every day, but that's not how it is with us. We need it, obviously, just not as often. We can go for weeks between feedings. Some of us are even so disciplined that they can go for a few months at a time and not have to drink blood. Even if the time for a feeding is getting close, we don't necessarily have to go hurt anyone. There are ways now to comfortably and reliably acquire blood without having to go on any violent forays into the human world."

"How convenient," I said.

Ashe nodded.

"Yeah, the wonders of the modern world. Who would have thought technological advances came to the supernatural folk as well? What we really need is sex. Sex works for us the way people assume blood does. We need it intensely, and regularly. Our appetites can be insatiable, and the longer a vampire goes without, the more unpredictable and unhinged they can become. They can get physically weak and the abilities they have can start fading. They become ravenous. Frequent sex to satisfy our lust is the only way to keep us fulfilled and alive. Fortunately, we have worked out ways to simply be able to take care of those needs amongst ourselves, to an extent."

"But you still like to sample the goods elsewhere," I said.

She looked at me, and I saw a flicker of concern in her eyes.

"You haven't been taking care of yourself. You're going to need your strength to get you through this. I think I know somebody who can help."

"Who?" I asked.

"Her name is Stephana. She lives nearby. She's one of the vampires I told you about who still eats human food. She always has. She says she believes continuing to eat human food even after the transformation is beneficial to a vampire. She's also older. She's been around a long time, and she was older when she was changed. She is very wise, and knowledgeable about the city and its inhabitants. I'll bring you to her. She'll be able to help you, and she might be able to lead us in the direction we need to be going."

We continued down the sidewalk, and she gestured toward the crosswalk. We both looked both ways and then started across. The sound of muttering followed us, and we both looked over our shoulders to see the women who had cornered me following several paces behind us. Two other women saw their pursuit and joined them, and I saw several men glare angrily at me.

"What are we going to do about them?" I asked.

"We need to get off the streets," Ashe said. "Give everybody a little time to cool off."

We rushed the rest of the way across the street and down the first block. Cars filled the space behind us just in time to keep the women from following closely behind. Ashe noticed this, and took the opportunity to grab onto me and pull me into a small clothing store.

"Going to do a little shopping?" I asked.

"We're going to hunker down in here to get away from some of the attention you're drawing. We'll keep going when things have died down."

17

As soon as we ducked into the shop, Ashe began flipping through the racks of clothing as if browsing the store's selection. It was a good cover for the confused looking woman standing at the cash register, but I wasn't sure how long we were going to be able to keep up with the ruse. The shop wasn't very big, and the selection of clothing was limited. Particularly for me. Unless, of course, I decided to begin wearing floral prints. In that case, this would be the perfect place to broaden my wardrobe.

I followed along behind her, flipping through the same racks she was, and occasionally holding out an article or two toward her. We hadn't been in the shop for long when the door opened. The cluster of bells hanging above the door rattled almost violently, signaling the entrance of three men. I looked over at Ashe and saw her nodding in the direction of the changing rooms. They were on the other side of the small shop, and we needed to pass through an almost completely empty section of floor. We moved as quickly and subtly as we could and dipped into one of the changing rooms. She eased the door most of the way closed, and we moved our faces close to the gap to watch the men. It didn't seem like they had noticed our run for the dressing room, or if they had, they didn't care.

The men moved slowly through the racks. It was obvious they were searching for something, but they weren't looking at any of the individual articles of clothing. Instead, it seemed like they were looking into the displays themselves. It took me a few seconds before I realized I only saw two of what had been a trio.

"Where's the third one?" I asked in a low whisper.

Ashe leaned closer, her eyes darting through the store to try to find him. Out of the corner of my eye, I noticed a flicker of movement through the slats in the dressing room door. Instinct tightened my muscles, and I touched Ashe in warning.

A second later, I planted my foot in the middle of the door. The kick sent the door flying open and into the man who had been standing on the other side. He stumbled backwards as the door slammed into him, falling into a rack of clothes. Ashe and I burst out of the stall and into the shop. The sound caught the attention of one of the other men. He turned toward us and came at me as Ashe and I tried to rush out the front door. His eyes were wide and bloodshot as he ran toward me. I drew back my fist and sent it exploding forward. I made contact with his jaw, feeling the crunch of his teeth breaking and his jaw dislocating, the spittle flying through the air. Suddenly, he was on the ground, several feet back from where he had been when I had hit him.

I sensed the second man only an instant before his arms wrapped around me. He was trying to wrestle me to the ground, and I didn't want to know what would happen if he got me there. The strength I had been trying to summon in the park was rushing through me, making me feel even more powerful than I had during my fight with the Shade. The man grappling with me was far larger than I was, and if I was still human, I would have folded instantly under his strength. But he was no match for the power coursing through me now. I crouched down and exploded back upward, my arms breaking free of his grasp before I spun to face him. His black eyes were fixed on me, and they were wide with surprise. He hadn't expected me to break free from his grip. He recovered quickly, swinging his fist at the same time as me, and we each landed blows on the other's face.

Beside me I heard Ashe grunt, and I looked up to see her direct a kick into another man's stomach. He rocked back, but continued to pursue her. I grabbed the rack of clothes closest to me and shoved it toward him. He didn't fall under the pressure of the rack hitting him, but it was enough to distract him and allow Ashe time to get several feet away from him. By this point, the man I'd knocked over with the door to the dressing room had dragged himself out of the tangle of sweaters he'd fallen into and was coming toward us. The woman who had been standing behind the cash register when we came in wasn't standing there anymore, but I could hear her whimpering. She must have crouched under the counter to avoid the fray. Massive fights breaking out in the middle of her shop was probably not something she experienced on a daily basis, even if she lived in the Underworld. Part of me felt bad for luring this type of attention into her store, but I didn't have much attention to spare for that line of thought. I had to focus on the three men who were coming at me from different angles.

The harder I fought, the more I was able to tap into the strength inside me. I could feel it radiating to the tips of my fingers, and I let it explode as I lashed out at each of the men in turn. Ashe held her own as we made our way through the shop. Clothes flew in all directions, and I heard the shattering of glass as a rack I slung out of my way smashed into the mirror hanging on the wall. The sound inspired me, and I grabbed the man in front of me with both hands. Growling as I called forward all of my strength, I lifted him into the air and threw him ahead of me. His body crashed through the huge window at the front of the store. Bits of glass rained down, and I watched him crash onto the sidewalk outside.

This was enough to shock the other two men into backing off. One of them made eye contact with me, glaring at me as he backed away, then he turned and ran out with the other man. They grabbed their fallen companion by the back of his shirt and dragged him several feet down the sidewalk before he was able to regain control of his feet enough that he could get them under him. I watched them until they were out of sight. People were rushing toward the shop from outside, and I turned to see the woman behind the register slowly stand up from where she had been hiding. I looked over at Ashe, who was standing with her hands on her hips.

"So much for keeping a low profile," she said.

Concerned onlookers had started spilling off of the sidewalk and into the shop. They were so dumbstruck by the mayhem and damage that they weren't even paying attention to us. I didn't know how Underworld worked, such as if there might be a police force, but I did know I didn't want to be there if they came. My time was already so limited. I couldn't waste any of it sitting around in some supernatural jail cell. I backed up a few steps, and Ashe came along with me. When we had disentangled ourselves from the worst of the damage, we turned and ran. We burst through the door that led to the back storeroom and ran directly for the exit. We kept to the alleys, and neither of us said anything until we were several blocks away. That's when the exhaustion hit me.

I slowed and stopped. My back hit a brick wall,

and I leaned my head against it. Dragging in breaths, I tried to clear my mind. The same drugged, groggy feeling I'd had yesterday came back, and I felt like all of my muscles were totally empty of fuel.

"Just give me a second," I said.

"The fight weakened you," Ashe said. "You still don't have full control over your powers, and exerting yourself that much drains you. You can't keep going like this. You need to rest. Let's get to Stephana's place."

I peeled myself away from the wall and followed her, forcing myself forward through the weakness and the pain in my thigh, which kept growing stronger.

18

The pain in the punctures in my thigh had gotten so intense by the time we got to the brownstone that I was limping. I dug my fingertips into the skin around the bite to try to lessen the pain, and forced myself to keep going in. Each step felt like I was fighting my way through water, and it was getting harder to move the further we went. I gripped the handrail beside the steps and used it to pull myself up the stairs. When we got to the door, Ashe pressed the buzzer.

"Yes?" a voice said through the intercom.

"It's me," Ashe said. "I need help."

The door clicked, and Ashe opened it. I knew it was just a little further, and I pushed through the pain. When we finally walked into a precisely decorated apartment, I tipped over into an overstuffed chair.

"What's going on?"

I looked up and saw what appeared to be an older version of Ashe come into the room. It was strange to see, and I wondered if the exhaustion had somehow gone to my brain and I was starting to imagine things.

"This is Hayden," Ashe said. "Aurora bit him."

"As she does," the woman, who I could only assume was Stephana, said wryly.

Ashe shook her head.

"This is different," she said.

She gave the brief version of everything that happened in the last day, and I felt myself slipping in and out of consciousness. I struggled to stay awake. I didn't want to miss anything. When Ashe finished, Stephana looked down at me.

"You need something to eat," she said. "Very few people in Solan City would have anything to offer you. Fortunately, I'm not like other vampires. I believe there's still plenty of benefit to eating a normal human diet, at least part of the time. I find comfort in it, and I enjoy eating it, but I also think it has advantages over the normal vampire diet. Not the least of which is the ability to help someone still going through their process. Wait here. I'll make you something."

I nodded, and she walked out of the room. Ashe settled onto the couch and leaned toward me.

"How are you doing?" she asked.

I shook my head.

"It's even worse than yesterday," I said.

"You'll feel better after you eat," she said. "Then you can get some rest."

"I can't," I groaned. "We don't have time for that."

"What we don't have time for is you falling on your ass while we're looking for Malakan and not being able to get up, or us getting into another fight and you not being able to fight back. You need to give your body a chance to heal and rejuvenate. Stephana knows more about Malakan than I do. She'll be able to help us."

"How do you know her?" I asked.

"She's my Sire," she said. "She's the one who turned me."

I don't know why it surprised me as much as it did.

"Is that why the two of you look alike?"

"We hear that a lot," she said. "I don't think it

has anything to do with her siring me. If it did, you would end up looking like Aurora."

"I don't know," I said dryly. "Maybe it could work for me."

Ashe laughed, and I managed a smile. A few moments later, the older woman came back into the room. Now that I had more of a chance to look at her, I saw just how beautiful she was. She was definitely older than Ashe, but the effect of the years was a richer, more established type of beauty. She walked toward me and settled a large plate on my lap. It was covered with a variety of foods, and she placed a huge glass of milk onto the table beside me. I eyed it questioningly.

"It will make you feel stronger," she said. "Eat. Get as much in you as you can."

I picked up a sandwich first and sank my teeth into it. The emptiness of my stomach was suddenly obvious. I'd been ignoring it, but now it was the only thing I could think about. I ate ravenously, feeling like I hadn't had a single bite to eat in weeks. I finished the sandwich and moved on to a pile of potato salad. One bite Illustrated what Ashe had meant when she said some foods would taste even better. The mustard was bright and sharp, more delicious than I ever would have expected. It felt ridiculous to be so excited by mouthfuls of potato salad, but it was yet another discovery, another revelation about this new existence.

"Thank you," I finally said, realizing I hadn't acknowledged her since she had handed the food to me.

Stephana nodded, then turned to Ashe.

"Would you like anything?" she asked.

Ashe shook her head.

"No," she said. "I still don't have any interest in human food, Stephana."

"I don't know why you're so closed minded," the older woman said. "It might do you some good, you know. You would have gotten through your first few days so much better if you had just been willing to eat something."

I tilted my head at them.

"You didn't complete her turn immediately?" I asked.

By the disgusted way Ashe had talked about people not finishing the turns of the humans they bit, I had just assumed her change had been smooth and easy. Then I remembered her lamenting the difficulty of the change, and commiserating with me in my first moments as I had tried to process the information. The two women glanced at each other, then back at me.

"Not exactly," Ashe said.

"She was extremely stubborn," Stephana said. "She tried to resist as long as she could. She didn't believe me when I told her what could happen to her if she didn't let me finish. Time was almost up by the time she relented to letting me do it."

"Really?" I asked.

I reached beside me and picked up the milk, taking a long swig. I couldn't remember the last time I had chosen to drink milk on purpose when it didn't come from the bottom of a bowl of cereal. The milk did just what Stephana had said, though. As soon as I swallowed it, I felt more of the exhaustion slip away, and some of my strength return.

"We're not here to talk about me," Ashe said, shutting down that line of questioning.

"Are you feeling better?" Stephana asked, looking at me.

Her eyes were trained on me so hard it was obvious she was making a point to Ashe. In only the brief time I'd seen them together, I had noticed an interesting dynamic between these two women. I wasn't sure what it meant, but I had a feeling I'd find out more over time.

"Much," I said. "Thanks again."

"Of course," Stephana said. Her eyes roved over me. "I have to say, you look a little worse for wear."

I looked down at myself and realized I was dirty and that my clothes were torn from the fight.

"Yeah," I said. "I think I need to find better friends."

She gave a small smile and stood.

"Why don't you get cleaned up?" she said. "I always keep some extra clothes around for situations like this. I'm sure you'd feel even more like yourself if you were clean. Then you can relax a little while we figure this out."

She looked over at Ashe, who nodded.

"Go for it," she said. "I'll get all this cleaned up, then I'll get some rest myself. These last couple of days haven't exactly been leisurely for me either."

I snatched the last of the pile of fruit as Stephana took the now-empty plate from my lap. She handed it to Ashe, then reached for my hand. I gave it to her, and let her guide me through the home and into a bathroom that felt like it had come from another time. The floor was a classic black and white check tile, and a massive clawfoot tub sat in the middle of the room. The wrap-around curtain was pulled back, revealing a showerhead built into one side. Without hesitation, the woman reached for my clothes and started peeling them away from my body. She examined me, running her hands over my body appreciatively. Once I was naked, she walked over to the tub and reached in to turn on the water. Almost immediately, the bathroom began to fill with steam. I breathed it in deeply, and felt it rejuvenate me even more. She turned on the showerhead, then glanced back at me.

"Would you like some company?"

My stomach tightened and my cock twitched.

"Absolutely," I said.

I watched as she disrobed in front of me, never taking her eyes away from mine. She stepped backward into the tub and reached out a hand to me. Taking it, I stepped up over the high edge of the bathtub and into the warm water. I had taken a shower earlier that day, but there was something different about this. Maybe it was because of how exhausted I had become, and everything that made a little bit of the tiredness slipped away felt extraordinary. I stepped under the stream of water and let it rinse over me. Stephana picked up a bar of soap and began to run it along my body, washing me with a sweet-smelling lather. She focused on my chest and stomach first, then turned me around and started on my back. Her hands moved over my muscles and massaged the soap into my skin. She washed down my arms, and then I felt her touch run along the sides of my ribs and waist. She wrapped her arms around my waist, her hands traveling down from my navel into the tangle of coarse hair at the apex of my thighs. I heard her moan slightly and felt her lips touch my back. They brushed across my skin, and her fingers combed through my hair as they moved closer to my cock.

I leaned back against her and looped my arms around behind me to grip her ass. She took this as an invitation and one hand wrapped around my cock. There was absolutely nothing slow or gradual about the way she touched me. This was a woman who knew exactly what she wanted, and had absolutely no qualms about going after it.

"Fuck me, Hayden," she said into my back.

I turned around sharply, and pulled Stephana up against me to kiss her. My tongue shot forward into her mouth, and she sucked on it eagerly. Dipping my hand between her thighs, I found her clit and massaged it in tight circles, coaxing it out from under its little hood. Replacing my fingertips with the pad of my thumb, I turned my hand and plunged my fingers into her hot pussy. She was surprisingly tight, and I pumped my fingers into her appreciatively. Stephana lifted one foot and rested it on the side of the tub to open herself up more to me. It was too much to resist. Grabbing her by both ass cheeks, I tucked my hips down, then thrust into her. Stephana's head fell back and she let out a loud groan. Not hesitating even for a second, I slammed her hips against me as I rocked into her.

"Harder," she growled, and I complied, digging my fingers into her skin to give me leverage for even more intensity.

I came hard, the rush of my orgasm hitting me so fast I hadn't even felt it building up. Stephana rolled her hips in energetic circles as I poured out into her, and I felt her clamp down onto me as her own orgasm crashed over her.

"Much better," I said.

She smiled at me and lowered her leg, then stepped forward into the water to wash herself.

"Good. I'm always glad to help."

19

I was exhausted again by the time we stepped out of the shower. Stephana led me into a side room and gave me fresh clothes to put on. My hands shook as I pulled on the pants, and I could barely button up my shirt.

"I think I need something else to eat," I said.

Stephana dropped a shirt down over her head.

"No," she said. "You ate plenty. You need some sleep."

"I can't sleep. I don't have enough time as it is. I can't waste any."

"You aren't wasting it. You have to sleep. That's just part of existing, and going through the change is exhausting. If you don't get the rest you need, you're going to end up crashing, and then you're going to be less than useless."

"Thanks for the vote of confidence."

"It's true, Hayden. You're dealing with a lot more than most people do when they are going through this process. Most people aren't pursued and forced to fight, and most people don't have to try to jump through hoops to convince their Sire to finish their process. You need as much energy and strength as you can get. That means resting when you need to. Ashe said she was going to lay down for a rest. You should, too. Take advantage of this chance. You're safe. No one will come looking for you here. And even if they did, they would have to get past me before they got to you. You don't have to sleep for the rest of the day. Just lay down for a little while, and let your body recuperate. You heal a lot faster than you did when you were fully human even though you haven't completed the transition yet. But to heal, you need rest."

I had to admit the big bed looked incredibly welcoming. The piles of pillows were calling to me. I crawled onto the dark blue bedding thinking I would just rest my eyes for a second. I didn't need the sleep, whatever Stephana said. Then my head hit the pillow, and the world faded away.

Coming out of sleep when you didn't realize you had even fallen into it is always disorienting, but this time it was particularly jarring. I snapped awake feeling breathless, my heart pounding like I was in the middle of a fight. I wasn't afraid of anything, and didn't feel like I had been having a nightmare, but I was on edge, just like I had been in the seconds before fighting the men in the shop. Images from the fight flashed through my mind, and I realized something that hadn't occurred to me before. Tossing off blankets I didn't even remember getting under, I rushed out of the bedroom and toward the living room. I heard muffled voices coming down the hall and knew Ashe and Stephana were both awake.

"How long have I been asleep?" I asked frantically.

Stephana looked up at me from where she was curled in a chair.

"Only a couple of hours. Calm down."

"You needed the sleep, Hayden," Ashe said. "It's going to be fine."

I noticed she was holding a mug in front of her, and steam was rising up out of it. I pointed to it questioningly.

"I thought you didn't eat or drink anything

because it was disrespectful to your culture or some shit like that."

"Well, I don't think I said all that, specifically," Ashe said. "But, you're right. I don't eat anything humans do, and with the exception of alcohol, I don't usually drink anything they do, either. But before my transformation, I loved drinking coffee. I still like wrapping my hands around a warm mug. It's comforting for some reason. There's nothing in here but hot water."

I wasn't expecting that from her. I'm not sure what it was about the comment that struck me so much. Maybe it was because it made her seem almost vulnerable, which wasn't something I was accustomed to thinking when it came to Ashe.

"Can I get you something?" Stephana asked.

"Coffee actually sounds amazing," I said. "Lots of cream and sugar."

I felt like I needed the boost from the sugar to break through the fog. Stephana went into the kitchen and came back a few moments later with a mug. She settled it into my hands, and I took a deep sip.

"Good?" she asked.

I nodded.

"Good," Ashe said. "We were just talking about

everything that's going on. I was asking Stephana about Malakan."

The mention of his name perked up my interest.

"What do you know about him?"

"Honestly?" she said. "Not a lot. They call it exile for a reason. He's extremely reclusive and mysterious. From what I do know about him, I believe he is a warlock defector. The only reason he's able to live anywhere near the city is because he is under the protection of Darien."

I waited for an explanation, but didn't get it. I rolled my eyes and looked at Ashe, who recognized the blank expression.

"The vampire Prime," she said. "Also, Aurora's father."

"Again, a manual. It would be so helpful and would save us a lot of time."

Ashe laughed and shook her head at me.

"So, you've never met him?" I asked Stephana.

She took a sip of her own coffee, then set the mug down on the table in front of her.

"No," she said. "I've never been anywhere near the man. I also don't know where to find him. All I know is rumor has it Aurora often seeks his counsel, as does Darien."

"So, I've been sent to find a man no one knows, no one has seen, and no one knows how to find," I say. "Awesome. I'm just going to get right on that."

"It's not that no one has seen him," Stephana said. "It's just not easy to find him. But there is someone who would know where he is."

"Yeah, Aurora. But she's the one who sent me to find him. She's not going to tell me where to look. Somehow I think she's getting a kick out of this whole scavenger hunt thing."

"Not Aurora," Ashe said. "A member of the Shades. She'd have her guards with her any time she went to visit him. They would know where he lives, or at least where he meets with her."

"I don't have the best track record with those guys," I pointed out. "I don't have the best track record with the Underworld in general, come to think of it."

Stephana looked at Ashe questioningly.

"What's he talking about?"

"I told you we got into a bit of a scuffle," Ashe said. "Three men attacked us on our way here."

"Not members of the Shades?"

"No," I said. "They weren't wearing their snazzy matching getups. The red shirts and sunglasses and all. They also didn't seem quite as powerful as the guards."

"Part of that may also be the fact that you are getting stronger as you move further through your transition," Stephana pointed out. "Every passing minute, you are getting closer to being complete."

"Do you know who it could have been?" Ashe asked.

Stephana shook her head.

"I don't know," she said. "But I've heard the Prime's men have been having some problems with warlocks in the city recently."

"They've been in the city?" Ashe asked.

"Is that a problem?" I asked.

Ashe nodded.

"Remember when I told you people don't like that Aurora hangs out with Malakan, and she keeps it quiet because of that?"

"Vampires rarely think too kindly about warlocks roaming around our city," Stephana explained. "They don't want them anywhere around, much less patronizing businesses or interacting with people. It's always a dangerous situation when they start showing up."

"But if those guys did have anything to do with the warlocks, why would they be going after

Hayden? Malakan was exiled a long time ago. Why would they care if he was looking for him, or if Aurora sent him?"

Stephana shook her head.

"I don't know," she said. "But it's important that you find him as soon as possible. If someone is coming after you, there's a reason, and they might not stop with you. They could be after Malakan as well."

"What do we do?" I asked.

"We talk to Ty," Ashe said.

"Why Ty?"

"He was a Shade," Ashe said. "It was a long time ago, and he hasn't associated with them since he left the group. But he might still have the information we need, or at least know how to find it."

"Why did he leave?" I asked.

"It doesn't matter right now," Ashe said. "Let me call him and see if he'll come meet us. I don't want to have this conversation with him over the phone."

Setting her mug of hot water on the table, she stood up and walked away as she dialed. I heard her muttering down the hallway, but I couldn't make out anything she was saying. A few moments later, she came back into the room.

"He says he'll meet us at The Foundry tonight," she said.

"What's that?"

"It's a club downtown," she said.

"Tell him the truth," Stephana said. "He should know everything he needs to."

Ashe didn't look happy about it, but she turned to me.

"The Foundry is a club, but that's not all it is. It also acts as a front for an underground organization known as Lunaris."

"An underground organization in the Underworld?" I asked. "That's a whole lot of secretiveness."

Both women nodded.

"The group is made up of some of the outcasts of society. They're the ones who don't really fit in, and aren't always accepted."

"Who could possibly be an outcast in a vampire city? I mean, other than warlocks, apparently?" I asked.

"I told you, the Underworld is much more complex than just the vampires and the warlocks. Most of the time they stick to their own cities, or their own neighborhoods, but in the case of Lunaris, they come together. There are vampires with alternative beliefs, lycan, hybrids, demons, even a few humans who have wandered over from their slice of reality. The group has existed for as long as anyone can remember, but it's been essentially quiet and self-contained until the last couple of years. It's been gaining strength recently. Nobody really understands why."

"Is that why we're going there?" I asked. "To meet with them?"

"No," Ashe said. "It's a warning. Just something for you to know, in case things don't go as planned."

20

The sun was just starting to set when Ashe and I approached The Foundry. I looked around for Tybalt, but didn't see him. Instead, my attention locked onto the man standing beside the door to the club. I'd call him a bouncer, but it didn't seem like he was actually controlling the crowds. Instead, people who walked up to him tended to look into his face, then turn away. Something about him struck me as familiar, and it took a few seconds for me to realize he was one of the men who attacked us in the clothing store. I patted Ashe's leg beside me, and nodded in the direction of the man. We walked up to him, and the man smirked at me as he opened the door beside him. I paused long enough to look into his face. Empty black eyes stared back at me. His irises were dark, with nothing to differentiate between them and his pupil. The effect was chilling, and I instantly knew this man wasn't human. I doubted he ever had been.

Ashe and I walked into the club, and the door slammed behind us. It felt final.

"I think they knew we were coming," I said.

The club looked exactly like any number of clubs I'd visited when I was younger. It could have been on virtually any street of New York City. Loud music throbbed from speakers positioned in the corners, and bright, flashing lights pulsed around us. Despite having watched the guard intimidate nearly everyone into leaving, the dance floor was full of people. I wondered if there was another entrance we hadn't seen, or if these people had come earlier in the day.

"How would they know?" Ashe asked.

I looked across the club and noticed a solid black door. The vibrant lights didn't break through the shadows shrouding the door, or the man standing guard beside it.

"I don't know," I said. "But I'm going to find out."

I strode directly to the door and stared down the guard.

"Let me in," I demanded.

"You will have to wait to be summoned," the guard said.

"What?" I asked. "What are you talking about?"

"The Dragon will not see you until it's ready."

Ashe looked at me curiously as I stalked back toward her.

"What happened?" she asked.

"You know that manual I keep asking you for? I need to put it in an order for a glossary as well."

"What did he say to you?"

"He refused to let me inside, and said I was going to have to wait until the Dragon summoned me."

"The Dragon?" Ashe asked.

"I take it you aren't familiar?"

She shook her head.

"If that ends up in your glossary, let me borrow it."

"No problem." I sighed and looked around. "I still don't see Ty. What are we supposed to do now?"

"We wait."

I gestured toward the bar.

"After you," I said.

Ashe and I climbed up onto bar stools, which were much more comfortable than the ones at Solomon's Fang. The bartender glanced our way, but didn't approach us. I looked at the menu, curious to see what an Underworld club served. Even if the vampires weren't going to be partaking in mixed drinks and snack platters, Ashe had made it clear there were plenty of other species gathering here. What did a demon like to snack on before picking up a girl for the night?

Were jalapeno poppers too on the nose?

The environment was almost dizzying. The number of people inside seemed to have multiplied, even though I hadn't noticed anyone else coming through the door. The dance floor, which took up much of the center of the room, was overflowing. Bodies writhed against one another while hands reached out to explore whoever was in reach. The lust was palpable, and I remembered what Ashe said about the vampires being able to take care of their need for sex amongst themselves. That became very clear as clothing started falling away or getting pulled aside. A hand looped around to the front of a woman who was dancing with three others and tugged the neckline of her stretchy top down. It was cut so low it was barely managing to cover her nipples as it was, and the yank allowed one of her ample breasts to spill out. The hand cupped it, and one of the men in front of her dipped his head down to catch the swell in his mouth.

My eyes slid over to Ashe. She seemed utterly unfazed.

"I take it things like this happen a lot?" I asked.

She watched the people dancing for a few beats, then looked back at me and shrugged.

"Meh," she said.

She smiled at me, and the way her hand ran up the inside of my thigh and brushed against my cock told me she wasn't actually feeling *meh*. In fact, she was looking more than a little hot and bothered.

"I should have taken a shower with you and Stephana earlier," she said.

I leaned forward and kissed her.

"Yes," I said. "Yes, you should have."

I kissed her again and felt her tongue slip between my lips. I reached for her, but she pulled back.

"We can't get distracted," she said. "We have to remember why we're here."

"So I can fuck you in public?" I teased.

"Where is that bartender?" she asked, craning her neck to look for the man who had ignored us earlier.

In the back of my mind, I was cursing Ty. What the hell was taking him so long? He was supposed to meet us here at sundown. Of course, he was also supposed to meet us in front of the club and not inside it, so it was entirely possible it was actually us who had screwed up the meeting. I turned around, planning on taking a peek outside to see if he was waiting, and noticed something strange. I couldn't exactly describe it, but it seemed like the shadows around the black door were becoming solid. I watched as the darkness deepened and a man materialized in front of me. He reached out and put a hand on my shoulder.

"The Dragon will see you now," he said.

I stood as I started to tell him Ashe would be right back, but before I could even open my mouth, we both melted into the shadows. An instant later, we were standing in an octagonal room. I had seen and been through some messed up stuff in the last couple of days, but that freaked me the fuck out. I looked around frantically, trying to figure out what twisted parlor trick the man had used to get us into the room, but I slowly realized that no parlor trick could be that convincing.

I looked at the man who had somehow escorted me in here. He was standing beside me, but now he was wearing dark robes and a mask over his face. Each of the eight edges of the room had a separate seating area, and in each was another masked man. It was so silent that I thought I could hear the blood moving through my veins and the breath going in and out of my lungs.

"We are the Dragon," one of the men said. I couldn't identify which one. The sound of his voice was like ice water going down my spine. "Why have you come here?" he demanded. "And why should we not kill you where you stand?"

21

"I thought you were known as Lunaris," I said, remembering the warning Ashe had given me.

The man who had spoken scoffed. I assumed the speaker was the man directly in front of me, because he was the one who stood. The large chair he had been sitting on was positioned on a platform, and him standing caused him to tower over me. He glared down at me, and it was obvious he thought he was intimidating me.

"Lunaris is the name of the larger group. It belongs to anyone who has been cast off. They are welcome to gather with us and find strength in our shared power. The Dragon is the core, the strongest, the most powerful."

I had no idea what to say to him. Only one thought came to mind.

"I am the intended mate of Aurora, daughter of the Prime vampire."

The man in front of me gave a bitter laugh. That wasn't the reaction I was hoping for.

"The vampires mean nothing to us," he said. "We don't exist because they allow us to. We exist in spite of the vampires who rule this city. We are the outcasts and the hybrid throwaways who have been forsaken because of our mixed blood. Each of us in Lunaris is unique. Some of us were created in passion, others through violence. Those of us called the Dragon are the most varied of blends. Among the eight of us there are mixes of fae, demon, lycan, and, yes, vampire. The blood that runs through the eight of us brings with it some of the greatest power in all of existence. There is nothing that compares to us."

"Then why are you lurking in the shadows?" I asked.

He disappeared, and seconds later was standing beside me. He had moved through the darkness at the edges of the room just as my escort had when he brought me here.

"We're biding our time," he said in a seething

whisper. "It's coming soon, and when it does, the city will fall, bodies will burn, and only we will walk among the ashes."

"Why did you bring me here?" I demanded.

Dark eyes stared back at me from the mask. Suddenly the man's posture softened.

"We were curious," he said. "We heard you were here in Solan City, and we wanted to have the opportunity to be in your presence. Being what you are; a most powerful hybrid of two ancient bloods."

I felt like I was being given an opportunity. The atmosphere been aggressive and threatening when I first showed up in the room, but that had lessened. If there was a time for me to seek out what I needed to know, now was it.

"I'm looking for someone," I said. "A friend of mine. Maybe you know him. He's a warlock. His name is Malakan."

I waited for a response. This man, who I'd come to think of as the leader of the Dragon, had talked so much about them being the outcasts of society. From what I heard, the warlocks would fit perfectly with that. I'd hoped finding Malakan would be as easy as asking them where to find him. Unfortunately, the leader stared back at me without answering, and I got the sense he didn't want to even acknowledge my question.

"Beware of the people you consider friends," a voice said from behind me.

I was surprised when I heard it. Seeing the figures in their cloaks and robes, I had automatically assumed they were all men. This voice, however, was distinctly female. It sounded mature and strong, but there was a note to it, something that reminded me of flowers and perfume. It was a bizarre response to have to the sound of someone's voice, but the impression almost overwhelmed me when I heard her speak. It was like she was surrounding me with herself, even though she hadn't moved from her position behind me. I was drawn to her, and I took a step closer.

"What do you mean?" I asked.

"Beware of those you consider friends," she said again. "For one seeks to deceive you."

"Who?" I asked. "Who are you talking about?"

"Why do you want to find Malakan?" another asked.

"I need to talk to him," I said. "Do you know where he is? Or where I should look for him?"

I didn't care about the woman's warning. I needed to find the old warlock if I was going to have any chance of survival. Two days had already passed. I couldn't afford to wait any longer.

"We can guide you to him," the woman said.

"That's fantastic," I said. "Where is he?"

"The man of whom you speak is forsaken by his people and cast aside much like us. But he is not one of us. He has turned within himself and lives in seclusion where two rivers meet."

I'd lost patience with the games.

"I want an answer," I demanded. "A real answer. Tell me where to find him. I'm tired of the cryptic responses, and I hate riddles."

I felt my guide's hand clamp down onto my shoulder again. Before I could say anything else, or even fully process what was happening, I was standing in the alley behind The Foundry. He was standing closer to the building, and I pushed him aside to go back in, but there was no door.

"What's going on?" I shouted. "I need to get back in. There are people waiting for me."

He was completely unimpressed.

"The one you came with will not be returned," he said.

"I told you," I growled through gritted teeth. "I'm tired of the fucking riddles. Where is Ashe?"

"She is now considered payment for our council."

I lunged at him, but he was gone before I could get to him. I let out an infuriated, frustrated roar as I examined the wall. Finding nothing, I ran up the alley and toward the side of the building.

"Where are they?" I shouted at anyone who would listen. "Where are the Dragon?"

I felt strong hands grab me by the shoulders, and I thought for a moment I was going to be transported through the shadows and back into the room again. I didn't resist it. If that was the case, I welcomed it. I needed to get back into the building, and to find Ashe. Instead, the hands spun me around, and I found myself facing Ty.

"Hayden," he said.

"Where are they?" I demanded again. "Where the fuck are they?"

"Hayden, calm down," Ty said. I continued to seethe, and he gave me a hard shake. "What's going on? Tell me what happened."

"I need to go back inside the club," I told him. "Right now."

"Back inside?" Ty asked, sounding confused. "I thought you just got in here. Weren't we supposed to meet out front?"

"Yes," I said. "We were supposed to meet out front at sundown. You weren't here when we got here. I need to get back inside. They have to give Ashe back."

"What are you talking about?" Ty asked.

"They said they wouldn't return her," I told him. "They said they were going to consider her payment, but I'm not going to take that shit. I'm going in there, and I'm going to demand they give her back."

I pressed my hands to the wall again and ran them along the brick as I tried to feel for a door. There was no exterior door, no gap in the bricks, not even a window I could slip through. Nothing that led from outside the club to the inside. Pushing past Ty, I rushed around to the front of the club. I forced my way through a small group of people who were braving the black-eyed man at the front door, and into the dizzying lights of the dance floor. I ran for the bar, slamming my hands against it as I leaned toward the bartender.

"Where is she?" I demanded.

The bartender looked at me curiously.

"Is there something I can do for you?" he asked.

"The woman who was sitting with me at the

bar," I said. "She came up to you looking for a drink not too long ago. Where did she go?"

"Oh, yeah," he said. "She was a cute little thing. I was hoping she wouldn't go too far."

"Where is she?" I demanded.

"I don't know," he said. "I went to get her drink, but when I came back, she was gone. I thought maybe she went to freshen up, as they say. But her drink is still sitting there. She never came back."

My head snapped in the direction of the back room. The guard was still standing on the outside of the black door, and I headed straight for him. He saw me coming, and I noticed his hands slip from behind his back to tighten by his side as he prepared for me.

"Stop," he commanded as I approached.

"No," I said. "Get out of my way."

"You haven't been summoned," he said, stepping to the side to block the door.

"Hayden, what are you doing?" Ty asked from behind me.

"I'm going into that room," I said, pointing at the door. "I know Ashe is in there with those creeps, and I'm going to get her back."

"You haven't been summoned," the guard said again.

"I don't care," I said. "They summoned me before. This time, I'm inviting myself."

The guard didn't move, and I planted a punch into the side of his head. He stumbled slightly, then rebounded and came back at me. I avoided the first blow, but he caught me in the back of the head, and I felt myself nearly crumble to the ground. Behind me I heard a grunt, and I turned to see Ty grappling with the guard. I caught the guard around the waist and wrestled him away from Ty, tossing him to the ground. Before he could get up and come at me again, Ty and I slammed our shoulders against the door. It took two hits, then it crashed down. I pushed through, expecting to end up in the octagonal room again. Instead, I was in what looked like another room of the club. The multicolored lights flashed even faster here, disorienting me, and making the people dancing in the middle of the floor look chaotic and spastic.

"Where did they go?" I shouted into the room. "Where did they go?"

"What's wrong?" Ty asked.

"There was a room," I yelled above the sound

of the pulsating music. "Through that door, there was a room where the Dragon met with me."

I saw another door across the room and thought of the guide bringing me through the shadows. Maybe we had passed through more than one door. I rushed across the room, pushing people aside with total disregard. I got to the door and smashed through it. Rather than finding the room on the other side, I ended up in the alley again. Ty followed, and I turned around as he shut the door. The sound of it slamming burst around me. Instantly, the wall looked solid.

"No!" I shouted.

I pounded my hands on the wall. My fury was spiraling, and I was starting to feel out of control.

"They aren't there," Ty boomed behind me.

The intensity of his voice made me stop, and I turned around to face him.

"What do you mean?" I asked.

"You're looking for the Dragon," he said. "They aren't there."

"They were," I said. "I saw them. They were in a back room."

"You might have seen them," Ty said, "but somewhere else. Those who know of the Dragon know they possess a mysterious form of magic that lets them use the shadows as transportation. Wherever there is darkness, they can move to wherever they need to. It only seemed they brought you into a back room here because they wanted it to. They weren't there then, and they aren't there now."

22

"You need to tell me what's going on," Ty said.

I suddenly realized I had no idea where to go. If I was in New York, I'd go back to my apartment, or even to Solomon's. I didn't want to go to the version of the bar that was here, and I didn't have anywhere else to go. Ty seemed to realize what I was thinking and gestured toward the street.

"Come with me," he said.

"Where?" I asked.

"You need to get away from here," he said. "We're going to my apartment."

He started down the sidewalk and I felt into step behind him.

"You have an apartment here?" I asked.

"Where do you think I live?"

"The basement at Solomon's?"

"No," he said. "I don't live in the basement at Solomon's."

"What happens to the portal when you aren't around?" I asked.

I didn't care. It didn't matter to me if he put a lock on it, gave it a pacifier for the night, or folded it up and carried it home with him in his pocket. I was just trying to distract myself on the way to his apartment.

"It stays where it is," Ty said. "I put protections on it to prevent anyone from trying to move through it."

We hadn't gone far when Ty turned down an alley and led me up a set of narrow metal stairs. We walked out onto a fire escape, where he opened a window. Climbing through, he held a heavy golden-colored curtain out of the way so I could follow him in.

After seeing Ashe's apartment in the bar, I expected Ty's to be similar. When I got inside, I saw it was nothing like it. Rather than the large living room and separate bedroom, bathroom, and kitchen in Ashe's apartment, everything seemed to be in one room here. The only thing I didn't see was the bathroom, and a chipped white door to the side probably took care of that.

"It's not much," he said.

"It's a place to go," I said. "Is this your only place?"

I told myself it was just curiosity. If I was being honest with myself, I'd admit it was because thoughts about my own future were constantly churning through my mind. As the finalization of my transformation grew closer, I had to think about what was going to happen to me moving forward. I probably wouldn't be able to pull off trying to go back to my normal life looking like this. Besides, I had no interest in ever flinging a pizza or answering a phone with a stupid company slogan ever again. I didn't know what I was going to do in the Underworld, or even what life might look like once I was completely separated from my human existence, but something about Ty's meager apartment was reassuring.

"I have an apartment in New York, too," he said. "But I prefer it here. You should sit down."

It wasn't until he said it that I realized I was pacing back and forth across the small room. Nervous energy kept me moving, but I forced myself to sit down. Ty came up and sat at the other end of the couch.

"We got to The Foundry right around sundown," I said, launching into the story even before he asked. "We didn't see you, but the man standing at the door let us through. I realized when I saw him he was one of the men who attacked Ashe and me in the clothing shop."

"Wait, what?" Ty asked.

I realized he didn't know anything about what had happened to Ashe and me since we passed through the portal.

"Aurora wanted me to come to see her at Nakatomi Tower," I said. "I went to talk to her, and then afterward Ashe told me I should get some rest. We were walking through the city, and were chased by three men. You didn't hear about a fight in a clothing store?"

"Was there a broken window involved?" Ty asked.

"I might have thrown one of them through the front window of the shop," I admitted.

Ty nodded.

"Is that when you went to Stephana's house?"

"Yeah," I said. "Ashe said she would be the one

to go to because she still eats human food. I needed it because I was completely exhausted."

"When she called me, she told me you were there. She said there was something you needed to talk to me about."

"She didn't want to talk to you about it over the phone," I said. "She said The Foundry would be the best place to go. But when we got there, you weren't there yet. The guy at the door was one of the men who attacked us. I'm sure of it."

"Did he recognize you?"

"I'm pretty sure he did. The way he looked at me," I shook my head as I tried to come up with the right way to describe it. "It was like he had been expecting me to be there. Like he knew I was coming, even though he had no way of knowing it. He opened the door and we went inside. That door, the black one, I saw it and was immediately drawn to it. I don't know why, but I felt like I had to get through it. I walked up to it and told the guard to let me in, but he said I had to wait for the Dragon to summon me."

"You can't see the Dragon unless you're summoned," Ty said.

"You know them," I said.

He gave a slow nod.

"Why did you go to that door? You were supposed to be waiting for me."

"I know. I told you, I don't know what it was, but something about that door just sucked me in. I had to go through it. Like whatever was on the other side was calling to me. Of course, now I know there wasn't anything on the other side."

I was still having trouble wrapping my head around that.

"Did they summon you?"

"Yes," I said. "Ashe and I sat at the bar to wait for either you to get there, or the Dragon to summon us. She decided she wanted a drink, but the bartender couldn't be bothered with us, so she got up to order. Just a second later, a guy appeared in front of me."

"He came out of the shadows."

I nodded.

"He told me they were ready to see me, and grabbed my shoulder. The next thing I knew, I was in some room with them. They told me who they were, and said they just wanted to see me."

"Just wanted to see you?"

"Yes. The leader said I was a hybrid of powerful ancient blood, and they wanted to see me." I was getting frustrated again, and jumped to my feet. "They took Ashe," I said. "The guy who took me to the alley said they weren't going to return her, that she was payment."

Ty looked at me intently.

"Payment for what?" he asked. "What did they do for you? The Dragon never does anything for anyone without payment, but they won't take anything without giving something in return."

"I didn't ask for anything from them, other than if they knew where someone was."

"Who?" Ty asked.

"It's why Ashe and I were coming to see you, she thought maybe you would know."

I knew I was rambling. I wasn't making any sense. But the thoughts in my mind had tangled and I was struggling to unravel them enough to talk to Ty.

"Sit back down," Ty said. "You need to calm down, and tell me what the hell is going on."

I sat down, but couldn't keep one leg from bouncing with the energy and anger still flowing through me.

"When I went to see Aurora, she told me she didn't know if she was going to go through with the transformation. Apparently if she does, she's bonded to me for the rest of existence."

"Shit," Ty said.

"I know. She said if I wanted her to give me the blood I need to finish my process and not rot away into a pile of primordial ooze by next week, then I needed to go talk to a friend of hers and bring back the answer to what makes me different. She promised to trade her blood for the answer, but only if she got it from this man."

"Malakan," Ty said.

"How did you know?"

"He's been her confidante for a long time," he said. His eyes met mine briefly. "Did Ashe tell you I was once a member of the Shades?"

"Yes," I said.

"Did she tell you what happened? Why I'm not anymore?"

"No," I told him. "She just said you might be able to help us find Malakan because you were a Shade once."

"I've never been to his house," Ty said. "The only times I accompanied Aurora and Darien to a meeting with him, it was in one of the buildings at the palace. But I've heard rumors that he lives on the outskirts of the city."

"The Dragon told me he lives where two rivers meet," I said.

"They told you that?" Ty asked.

His voice was tense, and it struck me that there was more significance to that exchange than I knew.

"Yes," I said. "They said they don't know where he is, but how to find him, and that he lives where two rivers meet."

"That's what they did for you," Ty said. "They gave you that information, so they took Ashe in exchange."

I felt my stomach drop.

"They took her because I asked where to find Malakan?"

"They felt they deserved something in return for helping you. But that doesn't seem like enough. Did they tell you anything else?"

I hesitated.

"What do you know about Malakan?" I asked.

"What do you mean?"

"You said you've never been to his house, but you were around sometimes when Aurora and Darien met with him. What do you know about him?"

"I never really met him. I saw him many years ago, but I've never had a conversation with him, and know very little about him. Why?"

"One of them, a woman, told me to be cautious about the people I consider friends, because one of them is out to deceive me."

"That's the council they gave," Ty said. He seemed to think about this, then looked at me again. "We need to find him."

"We need to find Ashe," I insisted.

"Malakan is going to be the way to find Ashe," Ty said. "The Dragon does nothing accidentally. Everything is strategic and purposeful. If they gave you that warning, and then took Ashe as payment, he is going to be the path to finding her. Tell me again what they said about where he lives."

"They said he'd been cut off from his people, and lives at the crossing of two rivers." Ty's face darkened. "What is it?" I asked.

"Only one river runs through Solan City."

23

"The woman specifically said Malakan lives where two rivers meet," I said, as if repeating it would change things.

Ty knew Solan City far better than I did. If he said there was only one river, that meant there was only one river. Besides, if the city really was an exact mirror of New York City as Ashe had told me, then he was right. The Hudson River was the only one that crossed the city. There was no other river to meet it.

"The only thing we can do is go to the river," Ty said. "Maybe we'll be able to find something there. Even if there isn't a second river, Malakan can't be far from the only one there is."

I nodded.

"Let's go," I said.

I had expected to go for another long walk. It was the only way we had been traveling recently, and fortunately my renewed body was better able to handle it than I would have been just a few days before. I was relieved, though, when Ty led me to a car behind the building. We got inside, and he drove us to the river.

"This is the Triking River," Ty said.

We drove along it as slowly as we could, looking for any hint as to what the Dragon might have meant. Of course, there was no second river. I kept going over the words in my mind, trying to find some other meaning behind them.

"Nothing," I said. "It's just one river."

"I know," Ty said.

"What if it's not actually a river," I said. "What if it's just something that's like a river?"

"What do you mean?"

"I don't know. I've never been good at riddles or solving puzzles. I like it when people are straightforward and actually say what they mean."

We fell silent for a few more seconds, then my eyes snapped over to Ty.

"What if it's the name of a place? Is there anything around here with a name that has something to do with rivers? A bar or a restaurant, or even a store called Two Rivers or River Crossing or Meet Me at the Damn River So We Can Find The Warlock?"

"I think that last one is a little wordy," Ty said. "But that's a good idea. I don't know of anywhere around here with a name like that, but it's always possible. Get out your phone and start looking."

I looked at him incredulously.

"Solan City has its own browser?" I asked.

"It's just like the regular world," Ty said. "Right down to the bitter and self-important business reviews."

I shook my head as I pulled out my phone.

"Some of the creatures around here give a whole new meaning to *Yelp,*" I muttered.

I opened the browser on my phone and saw that it had completely changed since we'd gone through the portal. Pulling up a map, I searched around the area, looking for anything that sounded like it might be the place the Dragon had mentioned. I focused my search near the river at first, then gradually widened it to several blocks away.

"Anything?" Ty asked a few minutes later.

"No," I said. "Nothing." I shoved my phone

back in my pocket, then slammed my hands down on the dashboard. "Damn it!"

"Can you think of anything else? Did the Dragon say anything else besides the thing about two rivers meeting?"

"No," I said. "That's all they said. That was their helpful information. That's what they took Ashe for."

We had nearly reached the end of the river and I looked ahead of us. A massive bridge, the mirror of the George Washington Bridge, loomed in the near distance. Something struck me about it. As we got closer, I leaned forward.

"What is it?" Ty asked.

"Pull off," I told him. "Just find somewhere to pull off. I want to go over to the bridge."

Ty checked behind him before making a sharp maneuver and skidding to a stop by the side of the road. As soon as the car stopped moving, I wrestled my way out of the seat belt and got out of the car. I'd been past the George Washington Bridge more times than I could count, but something was different. There was something under the bridge.

"What are you doing?" Ty asked as he jogged to catch up with me.

"What is that? What's under the bridge?"

"Homeless people, I'm guessing," he said. "The Underworld has them, too."

I nodded. That was a reasonable explanation, but something about them drew me in. I was distinctly aware of the pain and burning in my thigh. Aurora's bite was getting worse, and the last time that had happened, it was because she was near. As I got closer, I could see a makeshift town filling the shadowy area under the bridge. Teetering towers of cardboard boxes, torn tents repaired with countless strips of tape, and piles of tangled garbage were illuminated by an occasional trash can fire. People made little groups throughout the space. Some were huddled around the fires, while others sprawled out on flattened cardboard. It was the picture of poverty and desperation.

We started drawing the attention of the people beneath the bridge when we were a few steps away. Two men staggered toward us from where they had been gathered with three others huddled over a pile of sticks that I could only guess was some sort of game. I couldn't tell if they were drunk or had just been crouched for so long their legs had forgotten how to walk.

"Looks like we have some visitors," one of them said.

"What is this place?" I asked.

The other man grinned and made a dramatic gesture with his arm, sweeping down low until he was almost bowing.

"It's our home," he said. "Welcome to Final View."

The other man laughed uproariously like it was the funniest thing he'd heard in a long time. Considering he was wearing one shoe, torn pants, and a sweater so threadbare I could almost see through it, I figured that was probably not saying much. He didn't look like the type of guy who had a lot to laugh about. At the same time, he didn't have the sense of tremendous sadness and hopelessness hanging around him that I would have expected.

"Final View?" I asked.

"Why do you call it that?" Ty asked.

"Well, because every community needs a name, doesn't it?" the other man said seriously, then dissolved into a cascade of giggles.

I looked at him. He didn't look as bad off as the first man. I glanced back at the other man. Maybe it was a fashion choice.

"But why that name?" I asked.

The man glanced up toward the bridge.

"You see that spot? Right up there?"

Several yards away, I noticed a mark on a section of the bridge over a dark stretch of water.

"What is that?" I asked.

"In New York, that is the spot on the bridge where a lot of people decide to," he paused, licking his lips before curling them up into a morbid smile. "Well, let's just say they decide to make a big life decision. Of course, that happens at a lot of spots along the bridge. That particular spot, though, it's special."

"Why?" I asked.

"Because that spot is a portal," the man said.

Ty shook his head.

"There's no portal there," he said. "There's no keeper, no way to protect it. It would be too dangerous."

"A portal doesn't have to have a keeper to exist," the man pointed out. "The danger keeps people away well enough. It's been there for as long as the bridge has, but not everybody knows about it. Rumor has it, one of the warlocks hid it there for his own personal use, and purposely didn't assign a keeper, or a means of locking the portal. That way he could use it whenever he wanted, without needing a keeper or a blood price."

"What does that have to do with anything?" I asked, feeling the frustration building up inside me again.

"The warlock designed the portal to only be safe for those with magic to use. Anyone else who stumbled upon it would not meet a good end. And that's what happens to those people who choose that spot on the bridge. When they jump, the portal is activated, and they travel here. Through the Triking and on to the Styx." He laughed a mirthless laugh. "I like to thank our little home is the last thing they see before they hit the water. We are their Final View."

The explanation of the community's name sent chills along my skin, but it was something else that he had said that stuck with me. I turned and looked at Ty.

"Through the Triking and on to the Styx," I said. "The river Styx."

"Where two rivers meet," he said.

We had figured it out. Take that, Dragon.

Ty and I started toward the community under the bridge.

"I'd be careful," the man said from behind us. "Not everyone who goes through that portal is gone for good. A few have crawled back up and joined our number. They don't always respond well to people who remind them of what they left behind."

Ignoring the warning, I looked around, hoping there would be something obvious that pointed to Malakan. Instead, I saw something I wasn't expecting, and definitely wasn't happy to see. Standing in the middle of the makeshift settlement were several men who didn't fit in. If their tailored suits weren't enough to set them apart, the fact that they wore dark sunglasses even in the deep shadow of the bridge did.

"Shades," I said to Ty. "What are they doing here?"

"Protecting something," he said.

He nodded toward the rocky cliff, beyond the boxes and tents. I hadn't noticed it before, but now I clearly saw a door built into the rock.

"We need to get in there," I said. "That's where he is. I just know it."

The sound of my voice seemed to reach the Shade guards, and they turned to look at me. As soon as they noticed me, they rushed at us. Ty and I braced ourselves for a fight. Around us, people scrambled to get out of the way. Some dove into the tents as if they thought the shabby fabric would somehow provide them protection. Others ducked down behind the trash cans. Some simply backed up and watched. It seemed fights weren't all that unusual around here. That was good, in that it meant the people living under the bridge knew how to respond and were willing to get out of the way quickly. It also meant we weren't going to get any help from any of them.

I ducked down as one of the guards swung at me. He stumbled past, and I ran a few steps forward, but was stopped by an impact on the back of my head. I whirled around and saw him drop a heavy piece of wood.

"Progressing, I see," I said, and lunged at him.

The strength was growing inside me. I could feel it tingling in my fingertips and down through my legs. It was even stronger than last time, and I let it burst out of me as I clashed with the guard. Soon he was crumpled at my feet, and I turned my attention to the next man. Ty was holding his own against two others a few yards away from me, and I focused in on the man squaring off directly between me and the door. My punch made his head snap back, and he returned it fiercely. I brushed away the droplets of blood clinging to my mouth, not looking at them as I wiped them on my pants. My hand shot out and clenched around the guard's neck. Squeezing it tightly, I lifted him up and threw him aside. He landed in one of the trash can fires, and let out a shrill scream. He tumbled to the ground and rolled to extinguish the flames licking along his clothes. I didn't have time to feel any compassion for him. There was another man taking his place, and I focused my energy into a kick to his stomach. He fell, gasping for breath.

I had battled my way through the guards and was nearly at the door. Ty rushed up beside me, and our eyes met briefly before I reached for the door. My hand hadn't even touched the latch when the door shifted and opened. I took several steps back and watched as two figures emerged from the cliff. The pain in my thigh increased intensely as my eyes locked on Aurora. She stared back at me with an emotionless face, then tilted her head slightly to survey the broken bodies of the Shades sprawled on the ground. She looked impressed but said nothing to me. Instead, she glanced up at the man beside her. He was glaring at me and was obviously displeased. He took a step closer to me.

"Who are you?" he demanded. "What are you doing here?"

I noticed his eyes flicker over to Ty, and something dark flashed through them. Ty said nothing but stood his ground. Aurora stepped up closer to the man and rested her hand on his shoulder. Using it as leverage, she rose up on her toes and brought her mouth close to his ear. She whispered something unintelligible to him, occasionally looking over at me. The man's face grew even angrier, and he took two long strides toward me when Aurora stepped away.

"Don't think too much of yourself, young man," he said in a deep, grumbling voice. "You will never get near my daughter. You will be dead in a few days, anyway, so it doesn't really matter. It will be a slow, painful death. Exactly what you deserve for not understanding your station."

He straightened and swept past me. Aurora followed slowly behind him, her eyes on mine until she passed.

24

"So, that was Aurora's father," I said.

Ty nodded.

"That was Darien, the vampire Prime. It didn't look like he was too excited to welcome you as his new son-in-law."

"He also didn't look too happy to see you," I pointed out.

Ty stiffened and glared at me, but he didn't give me any further explanation. He gestured at the door.

"Should we go inside?"

"They came out of there," I said. "They had to have been meeting with Malakan."

"Probably to find out if you'd come to talk to him yet," Ty said.

"Then that means he knows we're coming," I said. "We're as good as invited. Let's go."

I expected something to happen when I opened the door. I didn't know what, exactly, but I figured if I was entering the home of an ancient, exiled warlock, there would be something to mark the occasion. Instead, the door opened easily under my hand, and Ty and I stepped through it into a small, dark entryway. A single flaming torch on the wall provided illumination as he closed the door behind us. Once it was shut, and intense silence closed around us. It seemed the stone filtered out all of the rambunctious noise from Final View.

"Is this it?" I asked. "I would have thought he would have more security. Everybody keeps saying he's exiled and talking about him like he's some mythical being. Somebody like that should at least have an alarm of some kind."

"Did you want a guard dog?" Ty asked.

"Don't you think it's strange?" I asked, ignoring him. "He's exiled, living like the Mayor of Boxtown because people in the city hate him, he's the secret confidante of vampire royalty -- but he just lays out the welcome mat at his home? No lock? No alarm? No booby trap that sends poisoned arrows into us unless we're pure of heart?"

Ty glared at me.

"Did Ashe give you the rundown of all the things that are total fiction bullshit about vampires?" he asked.

"Yes," I told him.

He gave a single nod.

"Remind me to tell you about all of the other species as well."

"Fine," I said. "Forget about the arrows. But you really don't think it's odd there's nothing to keep people out of his house? Anybody can just walk right in?"

Ty took the torch from the wall and held it above his head to spread the light further throughout the space. The area we were in was barely bigger than the space needed for the two of us to stand side by side. It was a rounded room carved into the rock like a foyer. He turned, lighting up a further portion of the space, and revealed the mouth of a long, dark tunnel.

"I don't think he needs security," he said. "At least not here."

"An illusion," I said. "The house isn't actually carved into the rock. It's just the entrance."

"Let's find the rest."

I took the torch from him and held it aloft as I started down the tunnel. It was tight, so close that Ty and I weren't able to walk beside each other. He had to stand behind me as I went ahead first. I realized as we spiraled deeper into the cliff that this was in itself security for the old Warlock. I could imagine plenty of people losing their minds as they plunged further into the darkness without any idea of where they were going, or when they would see light again. The walls were gradually getting closer, and the knowledge that I couldn't just turn around and go back without having to force Ty ahead of me started making my skin crawl.

"This is scary as shit," Ty said, giving voice to my thoughts.

"Scared of the dark?" I asked.

"Scared of something coming out of the dark and you trampling my ass trying to get out of this tunnel," he said.

Fair enough. I lifted the torch a little higher to try to see further down the tunnel. As my hand rose above my head, it hit the ceiling. I hadn't realized that the ceiling was lowering as well. If it continued like this, we wouldn't be able to get much further before we were encased in the stone.

"How much farther do you think it is?" I asked.

"I don't know," Ty said. "Do you want to turn back?"

"No," I said without hesitation. "That's not an option. If Malakan is in here somewhere, we're going to find him. I'm not giving up on Ashe. And I'm not going to accept just rotting away."

"What Darien said didn't bother you?" Ty asked.

"I haven't gone more than a few hours in the last few days without a fight, I traveled through a shadow without having any idea what was happening, I'm apparently a visitor to the Niagara Falls of suicides, and I'm a couple of days away from my dick corroding and falling off. Do you seriously think I'm going to let one pissy bloodsucker scare me because he doesn't want his little girl shacking up with me?"

Ty was silent for several more steps.

"You should write greeting cards," he finally said.

As we walked, I busied my mind by trying to remember all of the twists and turns, but it was impossible. Finally, the closeness of the walls around us started to lessen. The tunnel grew larger and Ty was able to speed up and walk beside me.

Ahead of us I saw a faint light shimmering in the distance. Our speed picked up a little as we got closer to it, and I saw it was another door. It was standing slightly open, allowing light from the room beyond into the tunnel. I took hold of the latch and pulled it open. The bright light from inside felt as though it was stabbing into my eyes, and I had to squeeze my eyelids shut for a few seconds to let them adjust. When I opened them again, I looked around. We were in another entryway, but this one was larger. Lamps of different sizes and shapes added to the glow of torches along the walls. The different types of light bounced off of the stone floor. The surface of the floor itself was strange. It was shimmering, almost metallic. It looked like rocks had been chipped away at to reveal the layers of mica inside and then set into the ground. As soon as I thought that, I wondered if this room, like the tunnel, had been carved out of the cliff itself and left exactly as it was.

I walked out into the middle of the room.

"Malakan!" I yelled out.

I heard a rustling sound to one side, and I followed it down another short hallway and into a second room. This one was much smaller, and torches lining the walls were the only source of light. A figure stood in the center of the room.

"Who are you?" he asked.

It sounded different than the many other times I'd been asked that question recently. Rather than demanding or angry, or even afraid, it sounded like one of the riddles that the Dragon asked. Like he was asking me more than just my name, or even my station.

"Hayden," I said. "And this is Ty. I've come because…"

"I know why you're here," he said. "I've been expecting you. Aurora told me I'd be having a visitor soon."

I stepped closer to him.

"Are you Malakan?"

"Yes," he said.

"Did Aurora tell you why I was coming here?" I asked.

"She told me there was a question you needed to ask me," Malakan said. "And that it was a question she already asked of you."

"Yes," I said. "She says there's something about me that's different, that's special, and I don't know what it is. But I have to know. It's quite literally a matter of life and death. Can you tell me what she wants to know?"

Malakan took several slow steps toward me. His robes rustled against the floor as he approached. Wise pale blue eyes stared back at me from a weathered face.

"I can tell you what you need to know to answer Aurora's question," he said. "But it will require you to relinquish some of your blood."

"My blood?" I asked. "Haven't I already done that?"

"That was for Aurora," he said. "She drew your blood to begin the process of transforming you into a vampire. This is for another ritual. It will reveal your past, so it can be reconciled with the present and the future. After that, you'll have everything you need to know."

"What about Ashe?" I asked. "Do you know where she is?"

He tilted his head slightly.

"I thought you came here to get the answer for Aurora's question," he said. "Isn't that the most important information you seek?"

"I do need to be able to answer her question, but Ashe was taken. I was asking about you, and she was kidnapped as payment by the Dragon. I need to know where she is and how to get her back."

He drew even closer, so close I could smell a strong scent of herbs and smoke coming from him.

"There is something unusual about you," he said.

Suddenly his eyes flashed over to Ty. The bouncer hadn't said anything since we'd been inside. Malakan looked at him with knowing eyes and gave an almost imperceptible nod.

"I'm pleased to see you have embraced your failures so completely," he said.

I saw Ty's spine stiffen and his jaw tighten. He didn't respond.

"When do we start the ritual?" I asked, not wanting to waste time asking what he'd meant.

"I'll need to prepare. Come with me and I'll show you where you can wait until I'm ready."

Without waiting for either of us to respond, Malakan turned and strode out of the room. We caught up with him and followed him down another hallway that led to a short flight of steps. We climbed the steps and he pointed to a room to one side.

"Ty, this will be your room. Wait until I return."

"Why are you putting us in different rooms?" I asked.

"You'll get better rest alone," he said.

"I don't need to rest," I told him. "I need to get this done as soon as possible."

"Your mind will be at its clearest if you rest."

Ty walked into the room, and Malakan continued down the hallway. There was another short flight of steps that brought us up to another door. He opened it and gestured inside.

"Wait here. I will let you know when I'm ready for you."

I wanted to argue with him, but I knew it wasn't going to do me any good. The sooner he did whatever it was that he needed to prepare for the ritual, the better. The longer it took him, the more danger Ashe was in. If she was considered payment, then she was a commodity. She was disposable. I hadn't known her for very long, but I knew enough of her to know that she would not simply submit to being kept as a slave or as a possession. They would have to kill her, or let her die trying to escape. If I was going to have any chance of saving her, I needed to know where she was as soon as possible.

Malakan closed the door behind me as soon as

I walked into the room. I immediately grabbed the handle and tugged to make sure he hadn't locked me inside. Fortunately, the door creaked open, and I was able to take a step out and look down the hall. It had been only a matter of seconds since Malakan left me in the room. He should have been only a couple of steps away, but the staircase was empty. I listened for the sound of his robes rustling on the floor, but it was silent. Part of me wanted to go down to Ty's room. I wanted to ask him about what the old warlock had said to him. What were his failures? And why was him showing up here a sign of him embracing them? Tempting though it was, I forced myself back inside the room. Malakan had told me to wait here until he was ready. As much as I didn't like the idea of following his instructions, I didn't want to risk angering him. It was possible this was some sort of test, and if I left the room before he wanted me to, he would refuse the ritual and both Ashe and I would be screwed.

Turning around, I scanned the room. It was a sparse bedroom with only a bed, a small table, and a lamp. The walls were roughly carved out of stone in an uneven, circular shape that reminded me of an ant colony. There was nowhere to store any clothing or any other belongings. Malakan didn't expect whoever used this room to stay here for long. I didn't know if that was reassuring or frightening.

I paced around the room for a while. There wasn't really anything else for me to do. I briefly thought about the cell phone shoved deep in my pocket. A critical fixture of life before walking into Solomon's that night, it had become far less important since. I thought about digging it out and... what? What was I going to do with it? Even though I got perfectly fine service in Solan City, I doubted I was going to get very good reception in the middle of a cliff. Even if I did, there wasn't really anything I could do. It's not like I was going to scroll through my social media and do a check in at Final View. I suddenly wondered what would show up as my location if somebody decided to look. The thought made me laugh. It really sank in then that no matter what kind of ridiculousness I was dealing with here, I already liked this so much more than my previous life. I felt physically better, but it wasn't just that. It didn't make sense, but I felt more myself than I had in as long as I could remember. Maybe ever.

After I had gotten sick of pacing, I flopped

down onto the bed. It was surprisingly comfortable, and I considered catching a few winks while I waited. Maybe Malakan was right and some rest would clear my mind and make me stronger for the ritual.

"Stupid rituals," I muttered as I turned around to rest my head on the pillow.

"Do you have a problem with our way of life?"

The sound of the voice startled me, and I sat up straight. I looked toward the door and saw Aurora standing just inside the room, a smile on her soft pink lips.

25

"What are you doing here?" I asked.

Aurora stepped further into the room and closed the door.

"You didn't seem to have a problem with the first ritual I put you through," she said.

There was a hint of teasing in her voice, but her eyes still held some of the chill and hardness I had seen earlier.

"I didn't know that was a ritual," I said. "At the time, I didn't realize there could be anything ritualistic about a quickie with a stranger in the back of a bar."

She stuck out her plush bottom lip like she was pouting.

"A stranger?" she asked. "Is that really all I am?"

"That night? Pretty much. I think we've gone beyond stranger at this point."

"So what are we?"

She was walking slowly across the room toward me, untying the knot in the ties of her cloak as she moved.

"I don't really know how to define it, exactly," I said, some of the anger and frustration I had been feeling coming out in my words. "If I interpreted it correctly, we are either about to be bonded for life, or we're a dead dude and the woman who killed him. It's kind of a grey area right now."

Aurora laughed.

"At least you can take comfort in knowing, no matter what, it will all be over soon."

"Forgive me if I don't find that to be a particularly warm and fuzzy thought. Especially considering I have no idea how long it's going to take your friend Malakan to get ready for whatever ritual he's going to put me through. Which brings me back to what are you doing here? Didn't I see you leave with your father? Who is *super* pleasant, by the way."

She waved her hand as though she was brushing away my words.

"Don't mind him," she said. "He's just protective. He wants to make sure I've made the right decision."

"That's funny, because it seemed more to me like he wanted to make sure you leave me to rot. Did he decide to come back here and discourage Malakan from helping me?"

Aurora shook her head.

"No," she said. "Father and the guards are heading back to town. I decided I didn't want to go back with them. So I came back here instead."

I watched her fingers work down the buttons along the front of the dress she was wearing. My mouth was watering at the thought of seeing her body again, but the burn in my thigh was getting almost unbearable.

"Why'd you come back here?" I tried again.

"I wanted to see you," she said. "I thought maybe you could use a visitor."

"Where's your friend?" I asked. "The big dude who tried to take me out while I was in your office."

"You mean Jaxxim? My personal bodyguard

who protected me, and stopped you from stealing my blood against my will?"

"I like how you can just turn it around on me like that," I said.

By now she had undone all of the buttons and was peeling her dress away. It slipped down her body and pooled at her feet.

"He's with everyone else," she said.

"Not a very good bodyguard," I commented.

"Oh, he's very good," she said. "The best. That's why he was assigned to me. But he also has to do what I tell him, and I said I wanted some time alone. I told him I was going to take a walk."

"Why didn't you just tell him what you were actually doing?"

"I did. I walked all the way here, didn't I?" I narrowed my eyes at her, and Aurora laughed. "Don't look at me like that," she said. "You're just my little secret. I don't have to answer to anybody. Especially when it comes to getting what I want. And I always get what I want."

She hooked her thumbs in the waistband of her panties and bent over to slide them off. I felt like my cock was going to burst out of my pants right then. It didn't matter what else she might have to say. I jumped to my feet and tore at my belt, casting my pants aside as fast as I could. Not bothering to take off my shirt, I grabbed Aurora around the waist and drew her up against me. Our mouths crashed together, and she let out a little gasp before wrapping her arms around my neck. I grabbed onto her ass and held it tight so I could grind my cock against her. I felt the heat radiating from between her thighs, and I needed to be inside her. Forgoing all pretense, I walked Aurora over to the side of the bed and turned her around so her back was to me. I leaned down and licked from the base of her spine up her back, then pushed her forward so she landed with her hánds flat on the mattress.

She kept her hands where they were but took two steps back and spread her feet. Arching her back slightly, she presented herself to me. I felt a growl rise out of my chest. Grasping her hips, I plunged into her. Aurora threw her head back as I buried my cock deep inside her. Her hot, slick walls felt so good, I almost came right there. I held tight and pounded into her. It felt like I was going even deeper than I had before, I like I was discovering more of her. Only a few strokes would have been enough, but before I could finish, she pulled away and stood up. She faced me and sat down on the bed. Bending one knee, she propped her foot up on the mattress beside her and spread the other knee out to the side. This opened her up and I was able to get a full, beautiful view of her glistening folds. Her fingers played through them for a second, then she beckoned me closer.

"Taste me," she said.

I dropped to my knees on the floor and tucked my arms under her legs. Yanking her toward me, I buried my face between her thighs and swept my tongue up through her in one long lick. She groaned, digging her fingers into my hair. I swirled the tip of my tongue around her clit, drawing it out from under its hood. The pain coursing through my leg worsened, and an idea ran through my mind. I ran my mouth to the side, then ran my lips over the soft inside of one of her thighs. Kissing it, I moved on to the other thigh and repeated the movement.

How was I supposed to do this? Fighting back the sick feeling rolling through my stomach, I opened my mouth and my teeth grazed her skin. In an instant, Aurora pulled my head back.

"Don't even try it," she said.

Still holding me by the hair, she pulled me in to kiss me. I pushed her back against the bed, guiding her down so her head rested on the pillows. Spreading her thighs with my knees, I lifted her hips onto my lap and sank into her again. I slammed into her as hard as I could, drawing little cries of pleasure out of her with every thrust of my body against hers. Feeling the pressure build through my body, I pulled her up so she straddled my hips, and kissed her hard as I spilled into her. The feeling of me filling her was enough to push Aurora over her own edge, and she came hard around me. Her fingernails dug into my back and she kissed me back hungrily while her hips rolled and ground against my lap.

When both of us were completely spent, Aurora climbed off of my lap and got dressed again.

"Malakan said something really strange when I first got here," I said.

"What was that?" she asked.

"Ty is here with me. I think you know him. He said he used to be one of the Shades. He said he had never met him before, but when we got here, Malakan looked at him like he knew exactly who Ty was. Then he told Ty he was glad to see him embracing his failures. Do you have any idea what that means?"

"No," she said. "But that's not really unusual. I've known Malakan for longer than I can possibly tell you, and he still says things I don't understand all the time."

"I don't find it reassuring that the arbitrary deciding factor in whether or not you are going to complete my transformation rests in the hands of somebody you don't understand a significant portion of the time."

"I didn't say it was a significant portion of the time," she said. "Just occasionally. Besides, there's nothing arbitrary about it at all."

She wrapped her cloak around her shoulders again and tied it into place. Leaning down, she gave me one more kiss and walked out of the room. I stretched back out across the bed, but my eyes had barely gotten a chance to close when I heard a knock at my door. I wondered for a minute if it might be Aurora again, but she wouldn't knock. I stood and crossed the room to open the door. Malakan stood on the other side.

"I'm ready to begin your ritual now," he said.

"Where's Ty?" I asked.

Malakan started down the steps.

"This ritual is for you, and only you. Don't worry, he's safe where he is."

"For some reason, ever since I became a part of the Underworld, people reassuring me how safe everybody else is only makes me worry about them more," I told him.

He didn't answer, just continued silently down the steps. I expected him to lead me back into one of the rooms I had already seen, but instead we turned down another hallway and he opened a large wooden door. I was shocked when I saw sunlight.

"Are we back up at the surface?" I asked.

"In a way," he said. "The network of rooms inside the cliff is only one part of my home. That's where most people who know of me will come to see me. I'm bringing you to a far more secluded place."

We walked through the door and out into an open field. Grass several inches high waved in a breeze that fluttered around us. I turned and saw that the door was now embedded in one of several large trees that lined the edge of the field. Malakan had continued on, and I had to jog a few steps to catch up with him. I looked ahead of us and saw a house in the distance. The white paint looked as old and weathered as the warlock himself, and an old-fashioned weathervane twisted lazily back and forth from the peak of the roof. I noticed a swing and several rocking chairs scattered along a wrap-around porch.

"What is this?" I asked. "This definitely doesn't look like any part of New York City I've ever visited."

"That's because it's not," Malakan said. "I created this place for myself. It's somewhere I went a very long time ago. That door we just went through is the only way to access it, and there are very few in existence that even know it's here."

"Why did you make it?" I asked. "Why don't you just stay closer to Final View, since you made the rooms in the cliff there?"

"I was exiled from my people, torn away from everything I've ever known and much of what mattered to me the most. I came to Solan City because I knew I'd find protection here. Darien ensured I was safe, to an extent. But I was an outcast. I still am an outcast. I created this place to be my home, because it's exactly what I need it to be."

I didn't fully understand the explanation, but he wasn't going to give me any more. He pulled his robes up over his ankles and pressed on through the tall grass toward the house. We went inside, and he led me into a large room. It was nearly empty except for shelves that lined the walls. Each of the shelves held countless books, bottles, and unrecognizable objects with purposes I probably didn't want to know. The only other furniture was in the center of the room. What looked like an elaborate carved wood recliner sat in the center of a dark blue rug. Three glass orbs, one clear, one blue, and one green, sat on a table beside the chair. On the other side was a pedestal holding up a white bowl. I hesitated at the door.

"Go in," Malakan said. "It's time to begin."

26

I willed my feet to move and walked the rest of the way into the room. Malakan gestured at the chair.

"Sit down," he said.

I sat on the chair, leaning my head back against the wood. I had my arms in my lap, but he walked up to me and moved them so they were on the armrests on either side of the chair.

"You know," I said, wiggling a little to settle further into the chair. "When I first saw this, I didn't think it was going to be very comfortable. But it's actually not that bad."

Malakan had turned his back to me, and when he turned around to face me again, I noticed a long, curved dagger in his hand.

"Getting less comfortable," I said.

"I told you the ritual would require you to relinquish some of your blood," he said.

I nodded.

"I remember. Just not looking forward to it."

"Hold out your arm," he said.

I held out one arm, my wrist turned to the ceiling the way Ashe had held hers when she paid the blood price for us to pass through the portal. Malakan walked up beside me and spread a thick substance across the skin of my inner arm. He muttered something as he rubbed it in, then took the dagger and in one swift movement used the tip to slash me open. I gritted my teeth against the pain and turned my head so I wouldn't have to see the blood. Ashe's voice reverberated in my mind, telling me I needed to get over being squeamish about blood. I forced myself to look back. I watched the dark red stream bead up, then drip down along my skin toward my wrist. Malakan let it flow for a moment before gathering it onto the blade of the dagger.

Holding the blade out in front of him, Malakan carried it over to the pedestal. He dipped it down into the bowl and stirred. White steam started billowing up out of the bowl and he gathered some of it into his palms. The steam seemed almost solid as he held it kept in his hands and carried it over to the table with the glass orbs. Malakan draped the steam over the clear orb, then picked the orb up and rolled it back and forth between his hands. He was still muttering, but I couldn't understand any of the words he was saying. Finally, he held the orb out to me.

"Take it," he said. "Hold it in your hand and look into it."

He settled the glass orb into my palm and I brought it closer, so I could stare into it. I didn't know what I was supposed to be seeing. It looked like a bigger version of the glass paperweight my football coach used to have on his desk. The longer I stared into it, though, the more I noticed something strange about it. Rather than looking still and solid like crystal, the inside of the orb appeared to bubble and swirl. I leaned slightly closer, and saw an image forming. It was small and unclear, but soon the edges of the figures started to become more definite. I closed my eyes for only a second, nothing more than a blink, but when I opened them, I wasn't looking into the orb anymore. I was standing in a dark room I didn't recognize, and I felt the hairs stand up on the back of my neck.

Something was wrong. An anxious feeling settled over me. I looked around, trying to figure out where I was, and I saw someone approaching. A man rushed toward me, but he didn't see me. His head was down as he hunched over something in his arms.

"Hey!" I called out to him. "Hey, where am I?"

The man didn't respond. He didn't even lift his head as he continued the rest of the way across the room to the far wall. I stepped closer to him.

"Can you hear me?" I asked.

"You're going to be all right," the man said, but I knew he wasn't talking to me.

He'd lifted his head just enough that I could see his face. It was Ty. There was something different about his face. He shifted what was in his arms, and I looked down at it. It was a baby, a tiny, dark haired baby wrapped in a blue blanket. It was sleeping, but I could see the remnants of tears on its little cheeks.

"Don't worry," Ty said. "You're going to be fine. I promise."

He adjusted his hold so he could take one hand out from under the blanket.

"What are you doing?" I asked. "Whose baby is that?"

Again, he didn't respond, and it sunk in that he couldn't hear me. He didn't know I was there. I watched as he ran his fingers along the wall, and a piece of it disappeared beneath his touch. He looked into the baby's face for only a brief moment more before I saw him plunge it through the wall.

"No!" I shouted. "What are you doing?"

The words weren't even out of my mouth when the whole image in front of me changed. I was no longer in the room with Ty. Instead, I was in another dark, unrecognizable place, and a woman was standing in front of me. She looked around, sharp green eyes seeming to cut into the corners and shadows. Her brown hair was wound onto the back of her head. It exposed her neck in a way that let me see a dark necklace against her pale skin. Curious, I got closer.

"Hello?" I said, wondering if this would be any different.

Her eyes flashed to the side again, but it seemed like they saw right through me. I looked at her chest and saw a pendant hanging from the chain. On it was a silver dragon holding the moon in its claw. Her attention snapped back to the wall in front of her as it trembled slightly. It paused for just a second, then melted away. Hands came through toward her, and I saw the same little baby pass through into her arms. She didn't say anything but clutched the baby to her chest and turned to run from the wall. As it became solid again, I heard the distant sound of a wolf's howl.

I felt like I was being sucked backwards, and suddenly I was sitting in the chair in Malakan's house again. My breath was hard and jagged, and I realized I was gripping the orb so tightly my fingers ached.

"What was that?" I asked. "Where was I? Why couldn't they hear me?"

"That was the past," Malakan said. "They couldn't hear you because you weren't really there. What you saw has already happened."

"To who? I wasn't even there. I saw Ty, but I didn't know the woman, and I've never seen that baby. I didn't recognize the place. I couldn't even really see where we were. It just looked like two dark rooms."

"The place may not be important," he said. "I can't tell you what it means. The ritual is meant to open the past and show a critical moment that has already happened. Why that moment was chosen for you to see, and what it means is something you have to find out."

I didn't like that answer. It felt like another riddle I would have to try to solve. I had come here for answers, and instead I was just getting more questions.

"What's next?" I asked, wanting to get the rest of the ritual over with as soon as I could.

Malakan took the clear glass orb from my hand and put it back in its place on the table. He turned my arm over again and gathered more blood to put into the bowl. This time, the smoke that billowed out was blue. Just as he had before, Malakan gathered some of the smoke in his hands and carried it over to the table. He took up the blue glass orb this time and set it into my hand. I watched as the inside of the orb began to swirl and bubble like the first one had, and an image began to appear. I leaned into it, waiting for the moment when I would flash into the scene. Even though I was expecting it, it was still a shock to find myself standing on an expanse of hard gray stone. Unlike the first vision, I could see my surroundings now. I was standing on a cliff that jetted out over the water. In the distance, I could see the lights of the city.

This time, I also saw myself. It was shocking and disorienting to see myself standing a few yards away, completely unaware that anyone, especially me, was there. I was looking at my back as the figure of myself stood at the edge of a cliff overlooking the city. I jogged over so I could look more closely at myself. As I approached, I realized the figure was holding something. It took a few more steps to realize what I was holding was the limp, broken body of Aurora. She was draped across my arms, not responding, seemingly unaware of anything. I couldn't bear to let myself think she was dead. The longer I stood there, the more I was aware of tremendous heat and the smell of smoke. There was also something less tangible. As I looked down at Aurora, I could feel the heavy, crushing presence of deep sorrow. I noticed something glint on Aurora's chest, a sliver of something that caught the moonlight. I stepped up closer and saw she was wearing a pendant around her neck, resting between her breasts. It was the same silver pendant from the first vision I'd had, a fearsome dragon clutching the moon as it flew.

Coming back into reality was less jarring this time than the first, and my eyes snapped open to look at Malakan.

"What was that?" I asked. "Why would you show me something like that?"

Malakan shook his head, his face serious.

"I didn't show you anything," he said. "I told you, those images are not my choice. I'm just here to perform the ritual. What you see and experience is up to the spirits."

"The spirits?" I asked.

"The essence of magic," Malakan said. "The energy within everything. What lingers after someone is taken from the earth. There are many different types of spirits, and warlocks are able to summon them, to channel them, and to utilize them. That's the gift of our species. All I can do is bring the right spirits together here with you, so they can show you what you need to see. You saw the past, and now you've seen the future."

I shook my head vehemently.

"No," I said. "That can't be the future. Something like that can't be what's ahead of me. I was just standing there. I had her in my arms, but I wasn't even looking at her. I was just standing there holding her while I looked out over the city like I was lost. It felt like something horrible had happened, and like it was my fault. I can't let something like that happen to Aurora."

"That is, in this moment, your future. Whatever happened to lead to that moment is something that's ahead of you."

"So, you're telling me there's nothing I can do about it? I just have to accept that whoever or whatever these spirits are decided what I needed to see was Aurora dead in my arms after a fire?"

"Like I said, that moment, as of right now, is ahead of you. It is the future of this very moment you are living. Maybe it won't be the future of the next moment if you can change it. But for now, what matters is this moment, and the time has come for that. You've seen the past, and the future. Now it's time for you to see the present."

"I don't want to," I said. "That was awful. It felt so completely real, like I really was just standing there next to myself on the cliff. But there was nothing I could do. I had to just stand there and look at Aurora lying dead in my own arms. I was completely helpless, and that's not something I deal well with. I don't ever accept being helpless."

"There's no other way, Hayden. This is what must be done. If you want the answer to your question, and to be able to witness life even at the end of next week, you don't have a choice. You have to go through this ritual, all of it, and only then will I be able to give you the answer you need."

"There has to be another way," I said. "We're just wasting our time here."

"We're not wasting our time, and there is no other way. You agreed to the terms of the arrangement with Aurora, and then with me. You can't change them now."

"What terms?" I asked. "What agreement? She called me to meet her at an office building and told me if she decides to complete the transformation, will be bonded to each other for the rest of existence. If she didn't, I'd be dead within a week. She said in order for me to get the blood I need from her , I had to have her question answered by you. I didn't agree to any of that. Everyone around me has made it extremely clear that I had absolutely no choice in the matter. Whether I liked it or not, she'd already started the process."

"Did you end your life?" Malakan asked.

The question felt like a punch to the chest.

"Did I do what?" I asked.

"Did you end your life?" he asked again.

"No, but from the stories told by your neighbors under the bridge, I probably could have found my way here a hell of a lot easier if I had tried to."

"And when I told you the only way for you to get the answer you needed was to go through this ritual, and to give up some of your own blood for it, did you then end your life?"

"What are you asking me?" I asked.

"You found yourself in these situations, and the expectations and terms were clearly given to you. Aurora told you exactly what you needed to do in order for her to trade you the blood you need to complete your transformation. She offered you all you needed, as long as you brought her back the answer to her question. When you came here, I told you I would give you your answer, but you first needed to give your own blood and submit to the ritual. In both situations you were told exactly what was to happen. In neither did you choose to end your life, and thereby avoid having to follow through with those expectations. You accepted the terms, Hayden. You no longer have a choice. You have to continue."

Gritting my teeth, I held my arm out for a final time. My hand closed around the green orb Malakan placed in my palm. I hesitated to look into it, but I forced myself to watch the change at its core and allow it to take me in. It happened faster this time, and in an instant, I was standing on a smooth polished floor in a room filled with the flickering light of dozens of candles. Ahead of me was a platform. Dangling over it, bound by her wrists above her head, was Ashe. She was hanging from the ceiling and her head was sagging toward her chest. Fear rushed through me, and I ran toward her. She drew in a ragged breath as I approached. I knew she couldn't see me, but the fact that she was breathing was reassuring. At least she was alive.

I looked more closely at the platform and saw she was hanging above a shallow pool of red. The blood beneath her had spread across the stone of the platform thinly enough that I could see a carving beneath it. It was the same image I had seen in each of my visions, a dragon with the moon clutched in its claws.

Even though I knew I wasn't really there, I reached for Ashe. I tried to grab onto her so I could get her down. My hands moved right through her. I wanted to be back in Malakan's house, but I didn't know how to will myself there. I continued to linger. There must have been something more I was supposed to see. He had told me these visions were designed to show me specifically what I needed know, and obviously there was something more I needed from this place. Not wanting to leave Ashe's side, I reluctantly climbed down off the platform and looked around the space. Just like with the vision of the future, I could see my surroundings this time. They were even more clear than in this vision, but I didn't recognize where I was. It looked like a huge old church, but I knew I'd never been there before. I tried to take in every detail I possibly could. The rows of pews on either side of the long aisle. The elaborate stained-glass windows stretching nearly from floor to ceiling every few feet along the walls. The smell, something sharp and yet dusty at the same time.

Before I could venture any further into the room, I blinked and opened my eyes, finding myself back in the chair. Malakan was in front of me, watching my face. The expression on it confirmed to me for the first time that he could see what I was seeing. I put the orb back in place on the table and jumped to my feet.

"Where is she?" I demanded. "She's still alive right now, but she's hurt, and I need to find her. Tell me where she is. Now."

27

"Ask me what you want to know," Malakan said. "What the visions didn't tell you."

"All the visions told me is that Ashe is in serious danger. I need to get to her. I've gone through the ritual. I did my part. Now you need to do yours. What is so special about me that Aurora sent me here? What do you need to tell her about me? Where is Ashe? And what does the Dragon have to do with all of this? In each of those visions, I saw the image of a dragon holding the moon. That has to represent Lunaris, and the Dragon. What does it mean?"

Malakan shook his head slowly.

"I can only answer one question for you," he said.

"What do you mean you can only answer one question for me?" I asked. "You didn't tell me that before."

"It is customary," Malakan said. "The magic of the ritual lets me answer one question, and one question only. It's up to you to decide which you ask. You can either ask me where you can find Ashe, or you can ask to give you the answer to Aurora's question, the answer that will save your life. You cannot have both."

Hesitation didn't even cross my mind. I knew immediately which question I wanted answered.

"Where is Ashe?" I asked.

Fear for her life was making my heart pound in my chest. The seconds were ticking past, and felt like each one was bringing her closer and closer to destruction. I knew if the blood under her was her own, it wouldn't kill her, but it would make her weak. She wouldn't be able to fight and protect herself. I needed to get her away from the Dragon, and I didn't have time to search for her myself. The emotion on Malakan's face was indecipherable. He nodded once and leaned slightly closer as if to make sure I would hear him.

"The Dragon have taken her to a temple across the city. She is there under the protection of mages.

She is guarded, but only by a few. They believe they are too well hidden and too strong to be defeated, and there is no need to guard her any further than that. You, Hayden, can find her. And you can defeat them. Ashe can be saved, but it has to be done before the sun rises. If not, she will die at first light."

"That's all you can tell me?" I asked.

He nodded again.

"That's all," he said. "It's all I know."

"It's going to have to be enough."

I ran out of the house and across the field toward the door in the tree. I opened it and ducked back into the network of halls and rooms within the cliff. Knowing it was far too risky for me to try to go alone, I went directly to the room where Malakan had left Ty earlier. Part of me worried he wouldn't be there anymore. I didn't know what might have happened during the time I was alone in the other room. Malakan could have sent him away. I pounded on the door as soon as I got to it.

"Ty! We need to go. Now."

The door opened, and he stared out at me.

"What's going on? Did you do the ritual?"

"Yes," I said. "And we need to get out of here. Ashe is in serious danger."

"What happened?" he asked, coming out of the room.

I started down the hallway before answering.

"The Dragon took her. They have her at a temple across town. She only has until sunrise."

"Where is Malakan? Did he tell you how to answer Aurora's question?"

I shook my head but didn't look at him.

"No," I said.

"Why not? He said he'd tell you after you went through the ritual."

"I was able to ask one question. I asked him how to find Ashe."

Ty's steps faltered.

"Tomorrow is the third day, Hayden."

"I know."

"You're running out of time."

I stopped and turned to him.

"I know. She has been there for me throughout all this. She's the first person I met in the Underworld, and even though she didn't have to, she helped me. She could have just tossed me out of the bar the morning I woke up after Aurora bit me. She didn't have to tell me what happened or explain any of it. But she did. She's been there to try to help me understand. She has fought beside me when the battles haven't even been hers. I don't know what's going to happen to me, but whatever it is, it's going to happen. I'm not going to let Ashe die because of me."

I started moving again and headed for the door that led us into the brightly lit room at the entrance to the tunnel. Each of us grabbed one of the torches off the wall before delving back into the dark tunnel. I reminded myself what we went through on our first journey through the tunnel, and the knowledge that it would end eventually helped me stay calmer as the walls closed in around us. I knew we just needed to get back out under the bridge, then we could find our way to the temple. I tried to decide whether I should tell Ty about the vision of the past I had seen. I wanted to understand it, but at the same time, I didn't know if I really wanted to hear it. If what I had seen really was a look into the past, it might be something I don't want to know.

"Do you have any idea where the temple might be?" I asked.

I was moving down the tunnel as fast as I could, the torch held high above my head to shed as much light as possible. The way had narrowed again to the point that Ty was forced behind me, but he was close enough I could feel the heat of his torch on the back of my neck. It reminded me of the vision of the future I'd seen, and Aurora lying in my arms as I turned my back to the searing heat behind me. My stomach churned, and I forced my thoughts away from the image.

"There are a lot of churches and temples in Solan City, just like in New York. He didn't tell you which one it was?"

"No," I said. "And I couldn't see the outside."

"What do you mean you couldn't see the outside?"

"The ritual gave me a vision of the past, the present, and the future. I saw her in the temple. It was like I was right there. But I couldn't get out of the room, so I could only see where she was."

"What did it look like?" he asked.

"There were pews. The floor was stone. And stained-glass windows. Huge stained-glass windows." Something suddenly occurred to me. "There was a cross in one of them."

"So it's a church and not a synagogue or a mosque. That narrows it down. Not a lot, but some."

"Anything helps," I said.

The trip back through the tunnel felt longer

than when we had been making our way up to Malakan's house, but I knew it only felt that way because of my worry about Ashe. Finally, we were in the small entryway again, and we set the torches into the metal brackets in the walls before I opened the door. Night had fallen over Final View, and the flames in the trash cans stood out brightly against the darkness of the world beyond the bridge. I wondered how long we'd been with Malakan. Though each of the visions only felt like moments, I knew hours could have passed.

"They're back," someone said.

Several people rushed toward us, gathering around and blocking our way.

"Did you see him?"

"What happened?"

"What's in the cliff?"

"Get out of our way," I said. "We need to leave."

A cackle reminded me of the man who had laughed at us when we first arrived, but this sounded more threatening. My eyes locked on the man laughing and I saw it wasn't the same person. This man appeared older and was better dressed than many of the others. I had the impression this community operated like a smaller version of the world around it, and within the hierarchy that controlled it, this man was toward the top.

"Don't be afraid," the laughing man said. "Night is no different here in Final View than anywhere else in Solan City. In fact, you might be safer."

He laughed again, and I took one long stride toward him, so I was within inches of his face. Though the expression on his face didn't change, he took a step back.

"I am not afraid of you or anything else I might find here," I said in a low, controlled tone. "You saw what we did to the men who confronted us when we first got here. It wasn't the first time, and I won't hesitate to do it again. Get. Out. Of. My. Way."

The man stepped aside, and I pushed through the others. Ty and I broke into a jog as soon as we emerged from under the bridge and didn't slow until we jumped into his car. We roared back down the road.

"Tell me anything else you can think of about the church," Ty said. "Did it look familiar to you at all? Remember, Solan City is just a mirror of New York. The buildings are the same. Is there anything you noticed about where Ashe is that you've seen back in New York?"

I tried to think of something specific about the space that would give me some clue as to which church it might be. Seeing only the inside made it harder to pinpoint.

"I'm not exactly one to frequent churches," I said.

"But you've seen them," Ty said. "You've noticed them when going around the city."

I nodded.

"I have," I said. "When I was in high school, my history teacher brought us on what he called a field trip, and what we all knew was just an excuse to walk around the city and ramble because he didn't feel like being in the classroom that day. Not that we minded. It was way better than sitting at desks and listening to him ramble. We still had to listen to him ramble, but at least we were outdoors and could look at things other than the backs of people's heads. While we were walking, he started pointing out all the churches. He told us a long time ago if a place wanted to be considered a town, it had to have three things. A jail, a tavern, and a church."

"Is that actually true?" Ty asked.

"I don't know. It sounded like he made it up. But it's pretty telling if it is. The one that really stuck with me was the church. If that really was the case, and a place had to have a church in order to be considered a real town, that was a pretty major function. It made me feel like each of the churches was anchoring the area around it and starting its own tiny town. I really started to notice them after that. They stood out to me for how they seemed to exist both as a part of the world around them, and away from it at the same time."

"Just like the Underworld," Ty said.

I nodded. "Where Ashe is isn't a fluke. The Dragon didn't just take her there because it was convenient."

"What do you mean?" Ty asked.

"There are a lot of churches and temples throughout Solan City, just like in New York, right?"

"Yes. Like I said, the buildings are the same," he said.

"But, and correct me if I'm wrong, there probably isn't exactly a thriving religious community? At least not the same types of religion?"

"There are some," Ty said. "But not many. The

different species all tend to have their own lore and histories."

I nodded.

"So, what are the buildings used for?" I asked.

"Most have been converted into different things. Some are hotels or clubs. Some are stores. There are even a few that were turned into houses. A lot of them are just abandoned."

"That's what we're looking for," I said.

"Why do you say that?" he asked.

"There was a crest on the altar."

"A dragon with a moon in its claws," Ty said.

"How did you know?"

"I told you, I've had dealings with the Dragon before. That's their symbol."

"And it was carved into the altar," I repeated. "The Dragon is a secretive organization, right? They literally travel by shadow."

"Right."

"Then they wouldn't want anyone to know where they're doing their work. If they're going to have something so blatant as their crest carved into the middle of the floor, they must feel confident people won't be able to stumble across it. They'll want a building that isn't frequently used."

"A church."

"That everyone thinks is abandoned," I add. "No one will think twice about a church building that isn't used. But it has to be one big enough to conceal the areas they actually use. They'd want it to look abandoned inside, too. Just in case someone decided to make a visit, they'd want it to seem like it wasn't being used. There has to be enough space for them to have one section be empty, and another big enough for their purposes. Wherever it is, she's being guarded by mages and only has until sunrise to be rescued."

"Mages?" Ty asked.

"That's what Malakan told me. He said she was being guarded by just a few mages who don't think anyone will find them, and who believe they are too strong to be defeated."

Ty thought for a few seconds, then made a sharp turn.

"I think I might know where she is."

28

"Where are we going?" I asked.

"You said there are mages guarding Ashe."

"Right."

"Even the Dragon isn't so arrogant to just have a group of mages in the middle of the city. Especially a group of mages willing to imprison a vampire. Things might not be as violent and volatile as they were years ago, but people haven't forgotten. The tensions between the vampires and the warlocks are intense. There are still places in the city where people have been dragged out of their homes and killed in the middle of the street just because they were suspected of being warlock sympathizers. It's brutal and unpredictable. Most people won't even consider touching Aurora or

Darien because of their power, so they'll mutter rumors about Malakan, and not do anything. Everybody else, though, is fair game."

"The Dragon didn't seem afraid of anything when they had me in that room," I told him. "They said that they exist in spite of the vampire rule."

Ty shook his head.

"They can say that all they want. It doesn't change reality, and that is that anytime there's a gathering of warlocks in the city, even for a short time, it draws attention and causes waves of violence. That's exactly what they wouldn't want if they were trying to keep their organization, and the place where they meet, protected. Just like the shadows themselves, the Dragon is always there, but often go unnoticed. People encounter the Dragon and lesser members of Lunaris all the time and never know. Of everyone who went into The Foundry last night, you are likely the only one who even noticed that door, much less considered going through it. The people on the other side the second time we went in got in there through another entrance from the main dance floor. What Aurora is trying to figure out about you, what makes you so different, is what drew you there. You were supposed to find the door, and you were supposed to be transported into the meeting room by the Dragon. It was all intentional."

"What does that have to do with where the church is?"

"They would want to establish their main meeting place somewhere the mages could easily access. It would have to be somewhere near the outskirts of the city, but in an area where unusual amounts of people coming and going wouldn't draw unwanted attention."

"They're warlocks," I said. "Why don't they just snap themselves to wherever they want to go?"

"Snap themselves?" Ty asked.

I nodded and snapped my fingers.

"Snap themselves. Show up wherever they want to go in an instant?"

"It doesn't work that way," Ty said. "Some have the ability to move instantly short distances, but that's more of a fighting tactic than a traveling one. The mages taught the Dragon to use magic to travel through the shadows, but they still have to travel. They still have to get to the location. There's a church near the edge of the city that has been abandoned for more than a century. The last time it was used was for its original purpose. Eventually, the congregation died out or moved on. The building has been exactly the way they left it ever since, including the lock on the front door."

"They locked it?"

Ty nodded.

"Chained it, in fact. The last person of the congregation to leave, the pastor, according to the story, was devastated when he closed the doors for the last time. He loved the church and the people who had gone there, and it upset him deeply to have to walk away from it. Obviously, being familiar with Solan City, he knew people would likely come along and want to get inside and wreak havoc or try to turn it into something else. He didn't want that to happen, so he put heavy chains around the front door and locked it with an enchanted lock. It's supposed to keep anyone out who doesn't have the right to be there."

"Does it?" I asked.

Ty made another turn and I felt the car bump. I looked up and realized we'd left the main part of the city and were now in the outskirts. A large, white stone building rose up ahead of us and Ty turned into an overgrown parking lot. He stopped the car near a small porch that was gradually being reclaimed by vines and grass.

"Let's find out," he said.

We got out of the car and ran directly for the crumbling front steps. At the top of the steps there were two huge wooden doors, with crosses embossed in the center of each. Just like Ty had said, a heavy chain was looped between the handles of the doors to hold them together. In the center hung a huge lock. I reached forward and took the lock into my hands.

"It's not old," I said.

"What do you mean?" Ty asked.

"The lock. It isn't old. You said the congregation who used this church abandoned it many years ago, but this lock couldn't have been put on that long ago. It looks old, but I think the rust and dents were put there on purpose."

"Why would you say that?"

"When I got hurt and had to wrap my head around the fact that I was not going to have a football career, I did a lot of jobs. Some of them I'm not terribly proud of. One I actually didn't mind was being a locksmith. It didn't last terribly long, but something I did learn while I was working for the company was the difference between the types of locks. You'd be surprised at just how many there actually are, and the little details that set them apart from each other."

"As fascinating as that all sounds, you're going to want to get to the point soon," Ty said.

"Sorry," I said. "The point is, I learned how to tell the difference between locks made a hundred years ago versus locks made a few decades ago versus locks made just recently. It's not always as obvious as people would think it is. This lock looks really old, and somebody went to some serious effort to bang the hell out of it and make it look like it's been on these chains nonstop for years, but it hasn't been. It's probably been made within the last few years."

Ty was staring at me like he couldn't figure out how to process what I had just said.

He took the lock from my hand and tugged hard on the chain. It didn't move.

"So, what does it mean? The lock isn't actually as old as it looks. Why would someone go to all of that trouble?"

"To make it look like no one uses the building. If the parking lot looks like a jungle and the lock on the door is old and rusted, anybody walking up to this building is just going to assume it's an abandoned church. It keeps whatever's inside safe.

We need to get in there and figure out what that is."

Ty examined the lock and chains again. He pulled on them, trying to break them.

"What did your locksmith experience teach you about enchanted locks?" he asked.

"Absolutely nothing," I said. "What have you got?"

He shook his head.

"I don't know. It doesn't look any different than any other lock, and I haven't seen anything that tells me it's protected by magic. I think by now it would have responded to us in some way."

"It doesn't matter. We're wasting time. We need to get inside the building now."

The doors were obviously solid, heavy wood. We weren't going to be able to kick them down. We had to find a different way to get into the building. I ran around the side , scanning the stone walls to try to find any breach that might let me in. There weren't even any windows within reach that weren't sealed over.

"What about the stained glass?" Ty asked, on the same train of thought as I was.

I stepped back from the building and looked up, shaking my head.

"In the vision, it looked like the windows were close to the ground because they were floor to ceiling, but they're not. They're at least two floors up."

"Could this be the wrong church? I really thought this was it, but if it doesn't fit with what you saw, and if what I've heard about the magic protecting it is wrong…"

I made an angry sound. If Ashe was inside that building, I was too close to just give up. If we were wrong, and this wasn't the church, we were back at the beginning, and the chances of us finding her were cut to almost nothing. Either way, she was clinging to life, and every minute we couldn't get to her was another minute closer to the sun coming up and her dying. The moon was providing just enough light for us to see the doors and lock and the sealed windows, but it was shadowy and dark around the corners of the building. It made it harder to see anything that might get us in.

"I'm trying, Ashe," I thought. *"I'm trying to get to you."*

"Help me." It was so faint at first, I didn't know whether I had actually heard the words in my mind, or if I was imagining things. *"Find me."*

It was Ashe. I could hear her thoughts. I had connected in with her, and she was reaching out to me from wherever she was. It gave me a boost, filling me with new energy and urgency. She was alive and calling out for me.

"Did you see where they brought you?" I asked. *"Is it a church?"*

"Yes. On the outskirts of the city. Please hurry."

"She's in there," I told Ty. "I know she is. This is the place."

"How do you know?"

"I can hear her," I said.

He tilted his head closer to the building, as if straining to listen.

"I don't hear her," he said.

"No," I said. "I don't hear her voice. Not like that."

I realized I hadn't explained this connection to anyone but Ashe. I remembered her telling me it wasn't a normal ability for a vampire, and I wondered how Ty might react. At that point, though, it didn't matter.

"What do you mean you don't hear her voice like that? How can you hear her?"

"I don't hear her with my ears," I said. I was up against the wall, running my hands across the stones. Maybe one of them would be out of place, or there was a hidden door I would be able to find if only I could feel the edge. "I can hear her thoughts."

Ty fell silent. Several beats passed while I continued to examine the wall. Finally, I turned around to look at him. He was staring at me with an expression on his face that blended confusion, disbelief, and questions.

"When did you find out you could do that?" he asked.

"Yesterday," I said. "I thought she was saying something, and it turned out she was thinking it. Neither of us realized she can hear me too. I was just thinking that I was trying to find her, and she called back to me. She saw where they took her. She's here."

"*We can't get inside,*" I directed at Ashe.

It felt so strange trying to communicate with her this way. I hadn't yet figured out how to hear her thoughts or talk to her silently on purpose. I'd heard both her and Aurora when they obviously weren't trying to let me hear their thoughts, and as far as I knew, this was the first time one of them had been able to hear me. Just like my strength and speed, I was still developing this ability, and controlling it seemed to still be just beyond my grasp.

I ran toward the back of the building and into what looked like a row of trees separating the parking lot and front of the building from the grounds behind it. It was dark enough that I couldn't see clearly, and my body hit something solid. I grunted as I fell back onto the ground. The back of my head throbbed as I sat up. Ty rushed over to me and grabbed me by my shoulder to lift me back to my feet.

"What happened?" he asked.

"I ran into something," I said. "I think it was a tree."

Ty walked over to the trees and reached into them.

"It's a fence," he said. "It's overgrown, but it looks stable. It's tall. A couple feet taller than me. Whoever built this didn't want anyone going over it."

"What's behind it?" I asked as I brushed myself off and walked toward him.

"I can't tell," Ty said. "But we're at a church, so I'm assuming a graveyard."

"An underworld graveyard behind an abandoned church that's no longer abandoned? Fuck that. We'll figure out something else."

"*Windows.*"

The sound of Ashe's voice came into my mind again, and I glanced up. The moonlight made the stained-glass glow. A few feet beneath the huge, elaborate plate of glass I noticed something I hadn't seen before: a small clear glass window.

"How good is your balance?" I asked.

"My balance?" Ty asked.

"Yes."

"I guess we'll find out."

I tore the vines and plants away from a section of the fence and grabbed the top. Confirming its stability by shaking it, I tucked my foot into the chain-link and climbed to the top. I crouched down and held onto the fence as Ty climbed up in front of me.

"I need you to trust me," I said. Ty nodded. "When I tell you to, put your hands out. Catch my foot and give me a boost."

"What are you doing?" he asked.

"Getting inside."

Using the trees to balance, I walked several feet along the top of the fence. I didn't know if the plan was going to work, but there was no other option. I had to try. Taking a deep breath, I ducked my head so it wouldn't hit the trees, tightened my core, and ran.

"Now!" I shouted.

My foot hit Ty's palms and I felt him force all of his strength up. Keeping the image of Ashe bounding off the trash can in the alley in my mind, I launched myself toward the window. My fingertips grasped the windowsill and I gripped it as hard as I could. I felt myself slip, and I dug down harder. Swinging my legs forward, I planted my feet on the white stone wall and braced myself long enough to smash through the glass. Shards of it showered down over me, and I felt the sharp edges bite into my skin, but I didn't care. I was too focused on pushing myself up the rest of the way and climbing inside.

I couldn't see what was beyond the broken glass, so I tucked my head down and rolled. More of the glass dug into my back as I hit the floor, but I jumped to my feet as soon as I stopped moving. Around me, the building was silent. I could hear my own breath rasping in and out of my lungs.

"Hayden!" I heard Ty hiss from beneath the window.

The window was too high off the floor for me to look down at him.

"Go to the door," I called out as quietly as I could.

I heard the metallic sound of the fence shake as Ty climbed back down to the ground, and I headed away from the window further into the room. I could barely see, but I thought of how the building looked from the outside and used that to orient myself. I found a door and turned the knob, pausing before pulling it open. When I didn't hear anything, I opened the door and rushed out. Somewhere deep in the building I thought I heard the rumble of voices, but I didn't hesitate. I followed a narrow hallway and found myself in almost complete darkness as I moved away from the windows and into the center of the building.

All I had left was instinct. Holding my hands out in front of me, I made my way as quickly as I could down another hall and to the top of a set of steps. I followed them down, turned at a landing, and saw a hint of light below me. The double doors were right ahead, only a few more steps to go. I'd made it to the landing and started for the entrance when the door beside me opened.

29

I SCRAMBLED BACK up the steps as quickly as I could and pressed myself to the wall, trying to stay out of sight. I hoped whoever was coming through the door hadn't seen or heard me. My heart was in my throat as I waited. Footsteps started up the stairs and I sank further back into the darkness of the hallway. The shape of someone wearing long robes was barely perceptible at the top of the steps as it paused. I held my breath and pushed even further back against the wall, doing my best to will myself invisible. The figure started walking again, and I listed to the sound of their footsteps to track where in the building they were headed. When the sound faded, I slipped back to the stairs and started toward the front doors again.

My feet had just landed on the floor of the entryway when the door to the side burst open and another figure rushed out at me. I didn't even have a chance to brace myself before it hit me. The person latched their arms around me and slammed me into the ground. I pushed back, jumping to my feet ready to fight. The light from the room gave just enough illumination for me to see who I was fighting. It was a man in long robes similar to what Malakan wore. He didn't say anything as he lunged at me again. I felt like he'd been waiting for me. This was one of the mages here to guard Ashe. That meant he had powers and abilities I didn't and would have the advantage of knowing the building. All I had was my strength and my speed, but it would be enough. It had to be. Grasping the man by the front of his robes, I dropped down onto the floor and rolled back, flipping him onto the floor behind me. I moved to the opposite side of the entryway, then ran directly toward him with a burst of speed. He reached for me as I approached, but I ducked out of the way, causing him to stumble.

Apparently deciding the physical fight wasn't going in his favor, he held up one hand and a ball of white and blue light appeared in it. It swirled like the inside of the orbs from the ritual, and I tore my eyes away from it so I wouldn't get lost in whatever might be pulsating within the glow. The light shot out from the mage's hand and hit me in the stomach. The impact was like a gunshot and I fell back against the wall. My body slid down to the floor, and I hadn't even begun to recover from the pain before I felt myself being pulled up. My back dragged against the wall, and in seconds my feet were hanging above the floor. The mage was holding me up with his magic, and I was completely at his mercy.

I wasn't going to accept that. Focusing as hard as I could, I willed the magic away from me. I knew it was something I couldn't fight with my physical strength, but I called that intensity that lurked inside me forward and pushed it out against the force holding me up. In seconds, I felt it lessening. I started to slip down the wall. The mage made an angry sound and stepped up closer. The pressure felt like a hard piece of steel trying to impale my stomach and I started to rise up again. I had to fight harder. I had to use whatever it was he was doing against him. Releasing some of my strength,

I let the mage lift me up slightly higher. Then I planted my feet on the wall behind me and kicked out with a burst of power. It was enough to break through his hold and propel me through the air toward him. I hit him in the center of the chest and we crashed to the floor.

"Hayden!" I heard Ty shout from outside the doors.

"Be ready!" I yelled back.

The mage and I grappled a few seconds more before I ducked away and ran for the doors. They opened outward, so they couldn't be kicked in from the outside, but from the inside they were vulnerable, and all it took was the force of my boots at the juncture of where the two doors met for them to splinter. The chains resisted, but the wood was destroyed enough for Ty to break through and come into the building.

We faced off against the mage. He lifted his hand again, but Ty grabbed him from behind to prevent him from moving and locked him in a chokehold. Soon the mage lay unconscious at my feet. I took off my belt and looped it tightly around the man's wrists to bind them behind his back. Ty kicked him to the side so he lay in the shadows beyond the light of the room.

"Thanks," I said.

"Where do we go now?" he asked.

"Upstairs," I told him. "I saw another one of them go up there. They were probably going to where they have Ashe."

We ran up the stairs and followed in the direction I had heard the footsteps go. I wanted to take my phone out of my pocket and use the flashlight, but I didn't want to call any more attention to ourselves than we already had. The hallway wasn't as tight as the tunnels going through the cliff had been, but somehow, they felt even more suffocating. I kept my hands to the sides to feel the walls as we went, and when they dipped into the recess of a door, we tried it. The latch was locked.

"Should we break it?" Ty asked.

"No," I said. "It's too small. Ashe is in a sanctuary. The doors will be bigger."

We continued on until Ty stopped.

"I think I found it," he said.

I felt the wall in front of where he was standing. I could tell there were two large doors. Knowing there was no way we were going to get out of this without the mage guards noticing anyway, I pulled out my phone. The light showed dark wooden double doors, but there didn't appear to be a lock or anything to keep them closed. I glanced at Ty, and we each grabbed onto a handle. I had expected to see the elaborate sanctuary when the doors opened, but I hadn't expected it to be completely empty. Dark and almost oppressively quiet, the space didn't have anything like what I'd seen in the vision except for the rows of pews. They hunkered like corpses. There were no candles burning along the walls, and the altar stretched cold and empty at the end of the room.

"She's not here," I said. "How is that possible? This is the place. I know it is. But she's not here."

"Could they have moved her?" Ty asked.

"No," I said. "I don't think so. The way they had her hanging wasn't temporary. It looked like a rig they had built into the ceiling." I ran down the aisle toward the altar. It was a platform, just like I'd seen in my vision, but the moonlight filtering through the stained-glass windows showed a thick layer of dust on the top. "There's no carving," I said. "The dragon with the moon. The crest was carved into the altar underneath Ashe." Something suddenly occurred to me. "The stained glass," I said.

"What about it?" Ty asked.

"The vision was supposed to be the present,

right? That means it was happening at the same time I was seeing it. It was already dark when I went through the ritual, which means it should have been dark when I was seeing Ashe. But it wasn't. It was light enough to see the patterns in the windows and the details of the sanctuary. I thought it was because of all the candles, but that wouldn't be enough to light up the windows all the way to the top. There was light on the other side of the glass."

"There has to be another sanctuary," Ty said. "This one is here to throw people off. If anyone happened to get through the door and into the church, they would find this and it would still look abandoned."

"Right. The Dragon left this one just as it was when they took over the building, and then added their own somewhere. If they are working closely with the mages, it's possible there's one that's been mirrored, but it would have to be inside another room in order for the light to shine through like that."

"How are we going to find it?"

"The Dragon aren't humble people," I said. "You know that."

"Yes," Ty said.

There was more bitterness in that word than I'd ever heard put into a single word before.

"I can't see them going to extremes to put protections on their temple. They wouldn't just leave it unguarded and accessible by anyone who happened to wander by, but they are just arrogant enough to believe their simple protections were enough. They need a lot of space for their private gatherings and rituals. They aren't going to waste all of it with false rooms and traps."

"What are you thinking?"

I walked across the altar toward what looked like a large cabinet at the back of the room.

"I don't know how many churches you've been inside or what details you paid attention to, but for me it's about three, and almost none of them. One time when I was trying to date a girl who went to church a lot, she brought me along. Anyway, I totally checked out during the talking, but I got really fixated on the thing at the back of the altar." I gestured toward the cabinet. "It looked like this. After the service, I asked her what it was, and she explained it was where the clergy kept the relics and the items used for the church rituals. She pointed out that in some churches the cabinet actually connects to a room or even a series of rooms in the back of the building where elders or members of the clergy meet, work, and sometimes even live. I'd never heard of that. I thought she might be making it up."

"But what if she wasn't?"

"Now you're following me. Should we see?"

A tiny hook secured the doors and I flipped it open. I was pulling the doors forward when a crash made us turn. Three more mages ran into the sanctuary toward us. Ty rushed onto the altar and I threw the doors open, running in before I even looked to see what waited for me inside. At first, I thought I might have horribly miscalculated and we really had just climbed into a cabinet. Then I noticed another narrow door in the wall. I opened it and we squeezed through. We found ourselves in a short hall with two doors, one on either side, and a third at the end. Hearing the shouts and heavy footsteps of the mages behind us, I ran for the one at the end of the hall and grabbed the handle. It was hot enough to sear my skin and I hissed as I pulled my hand away.

"I guess they did use one more protection," I said through gritted teeth.

The mages were already in the cabinet passage, and I grabbed the handle again. Forcing myself through the pain, I opened the door and ran into the room. Ty slammed the door shut behind me and slid a large piece of wood that acted as a brace into place. It wouldn't hold them forever, but it was enough for now.

The room glowed with the light of the candles and I saw the stained-glass windows rising up on either side. Soft light was coming through them. I'd been right. The mages had used this space to mirror the sanctuary.

"Ashe," I said, gasping when my eyes found her.

Just like I'd seen in my vision, she was dangling above the altar. Her hands were gripping a chain and leather straps wrapped around her wrists. I could see that her grip wasn't as strong as it had been when I had seen the vision. I ran to her, afraid of what I'd find when I got there. The sound of my footsteps joined the pounding of the mages against the door, and Ashe groaned weakly. She was still alive.

"I'm here," I said. "I'm going to get you out of here."

"Hayden," she murmured.

She was hanging high above the platform. I would need to get up higher to be able to release the strap from her wrists. Ty ran down the aisle and was nearly knocked to the ground by the doors splintering as they burst open. He dropped to his knees, but rebounded, and jumped onto the altar with us.

"We need to get her down," I said, grabbing her around the legs to support her and provide some relief for her wrists.

Ty looked around, then ran to a podium that was pushed to the side of the altar. He brought it over, and I climbed onto it. The wood was barely strong enough to support me, but it only needed to last until I got her down.

"What do you think you're doing?" one of the mages demanded as they approached.

"Take care of them," I said to Ty.

He climbed down from the altar and grabbed up a large piece of wood from the splintered door to use as a weapon. My fingers worked at the hooks that secured the leather around Ashe's wrists as I tried to ignore the brutal sounds of the fight below me. Finally, I got the strap loose and she collapsed onto me. A flash of bright red light burst around us, and the podium exploded under my feet. I held

Ashe tightly to me to protect her as we fell. She landed on top of me. I heard her let out a slightly strained laugh.

"Haven't we been in this position before?" she asked.

I grinned at her.

"I'm glad you still have your sense of humor," I said.

Ty ran up onto the altar with us again, and I noticed his clothes were torn. A gash along his side was starting to heal, but one on his leg looked fresh.

"How are we going to get out of here?" he asked.

"Take care of Ashe," I said. "As soon as you see the chance to run, go. Don't wait for me."

"Hayden," Ashe started to protest.

"Just get out as fast as you can. Get into Ty's car. I'll be right behind you."

I got down off the altar and looked toward the mages. One was on the ground between two pews, but was shifting around, trying to get up. The other two closed in on me, and I knew what was coming. One didn't even lift his hand before the jolts of magic came toward me. They felt like bands of steel wrapping around me, tightening until I couldn't breathe. I squeezed my eyes closed and focused on my strength. I imagined it surrounding me and blocking the magic from getting to me. It was all I could think of to do in that moment, and as I did it, I realized it seemed to be working. The mages started groaning and grunting as they forced more of their magic toward me, and I continued to fight to hold it at bay. When it felt like they had relented enough, I opened my eyes and ran for the nearest candelabra. Several feet tall, it had six arms, each holding a flaming ivory pillar. I took hold of the stand and threw it at the men. The stumbled back, but the flames had caught their robes. Their screams rose up in the sanctuary and I checked over my shoulder to make sure Ty and Ashe were gone as I crawled over the first several pews. When I was past the mages, I jumped into the aisle and ran back through the first sanctuary, through the church, and out into the thin night air. Ashe threw open the back door to Ty's car and I leapt in beside her. The door was barely closed behind me when the tires squealed and spun, and Ty sped out of the parking lot.

"Are you alright?" I asked Ashe.

I brushed her hair back from her face and

searched her eyes. She looked tired and worn, but stable.

"I'll be fine," she said.

I gave her a fierce kiss, then gathered her into a tight hug. I held her to me as I watched the first hints of morning light touch the horizon ahead.

30

"What happened?" Ty asked. "How did you end up there?"

"I don't really know," Ashe said." I was at The Foundry with Hayden and we were waiting for you. We'd been sitting at the bar, watching everybody dance. I decided to order a drink, but the bartender wasn't paying any attention to us. He looked our way twice the entire time we were sitting there and wouldn't even come over to me so I could order anything. I told Hayden I would be right back, got up, and walked over to bartender. That's where things start to get a little fuzzy."

"What do you mean fuzzy?" I asked.

"I'm just not sure. I know I ordered the drink. I remember, because the bartender was trying to hit on me using the names of various cocktails. I guess he thought it would make him seem funny and charming."

"When I went and asked the bartender where you were, he said he brought you your drink, but you weren't there," I said. "He told me you ordered, but then he said he came back with it and you were gone. So, he put it on the bar and you just never came back. What do you remember after you ordered the drink?"

"I turned back around to say something to you," Ashe said. "But you weren't there, either."

"The Dragon came for me," I said. "I tried to get them to wait for you, so you could come with me, but they wouldn't."

"Come with you where? Through that door?"

I explained about moving through the shadows to the octagonal room and my conversation with the Dragon.

"When they decided they were done with me, they sent me out to the alley. That's when I found out you were gone."

"The shadow," she said. "That's what happened. I had just ordered my drink, and I looked over to where we'd been sitting at the bar. You weren't there, but I walked over to wait for you. I figured if I could make the effort to go over to the bartender because he was ignoring me, then he could come over to me once he made my drink. When I got there, I looked at the door, thinking you might have decided to try to battle the guard to get through again. It was darker over there than it had been. The shadows were even deeper. Something moved, and I thought it was you. I thought you were trying to get me to come back there to you. I walked over to them, then everything went dark."

"They grabbed you," I said.

"They must have done something to knock me out. Everything else is just flashes. I remember being in a car. I remember seeing the outside of the church, but I wasn't even sure I was actually seeing it. It seemed like a dream. Then I was out again for a while, and when I was aware again, they were hoisting me up over the altar. I have no idea what they did to me. There was blood all over the floor, and I felt horrible. Like I could barely breathe, I had so little energy. I don't even know if they realized I was awake. I wanted to fight them off and try to escape, but they already had the leather around my wrists and there was no way I was going to be strong enough to break free. Whatever they did to me, it took so much out of me. All I could do was hang in there. I drifted in and out consciousness, and I tried to take in as much as I could, so I could try to escape if I got the chance, but there was nothing I could do."

"Were you alone the whole time?" I asked. "Did the mages stay with you?"

"For some of the time," she said. "There were times when I opened my eyes and they were there in the sanctuary, talking. I couldn't understand what they were talking about, but it didn't sound good. Other times I woke up and I was alone. That's when I would try to figure out how to free myself. If I had just been close enough to something that I could use to support myself with my feet, I would have been able to get enough leverage to release the strap."

"Did it hurt?" I asked, taking her hands in mine.

She nodded, and I turned her hands over to kiss her wrists.

"Yes," she said.

"I'll make it up to you later," I said, nuzzling the side of her neck.

She moaned a little and pressed her thigh closer to me.

"Yes, you will," she said.

"You didn't understand anything they said?" Ty asked, dragging us back into the conversation.

"No," Ashe said. "Why?"

"I know there have always been hybrids in Lunaris that had mage in them. There have even been a few warlocks in the organization from time to time. But I've never known an established link between the mages and the Dragon. If they are aligned, it's for a reason. What's happening that they're both a part of? And what does it have to do with you, Hayden?"

"Why do you think it has to do with Hayden?" Ashe asked.

"They knew I was coming," I told her. "I don't know how, but they did. They said they wanted to see me. But it's also why they took you. They said you were payment for the council they gave me."

"What council?" she asked.

"I asked where to find Malakan," I said. "I thought they might know."

"Did they tell you?" she asked.

"They gave me a riddle to figure out and dumped my ass out in the back alley, is what they did," I said.

"And that was enough to make them take me?"

she asked. "Wow. I'd hoped I'd have a little higher value than that."

"I think their pricing structure is way off," I said with a teasing smile. "They could have at least included a taxi service if they were going to do that."

"Thanks," she said with mock offense in her voice.

"I don't think they'll be too happy when they find out I gave myself a refund."

"They know by now," Ty said. "The mages will have already been in touch with the Dragon."

"If they got out of the church," I said.

Ty's eyes appeared in the rearview mirror.

"What did you do?" he asked.

The thought of the fire consuming the men flashed through my mind, quickly followed by the image of Aurora draped in my arms and the smell of smoke in my nose. I shook my head.

"Whatever you did," Ashe said. "I don't think it killed them. The mages are powerful. It would be difficult to kill them at all, and nearly impossible without some sort of magic or weapon."

"I don't care what happened to them," I said. "Nothing justifies what they did to you."

There was an angry grumble in my voice, and

despite being up all night, I felt adrenaline pumping through me. I should have been exhausted, but I wasn't. All I wanted to do was keep going and bring this all to an end.

"It's over," Ashe said. "You rescued me."

"I want to see Malakan again," I told Ty. "Bring me back to Final View."

"You went to see him?" Ashe asked.

I nodded.

"It's how I was able to find you. He put me through a ritual that showed me visions of the past, the future, and the present. It showed you hanging in the church. He was able to tell me the church was across town, but we had to figure out the rest. Ty figured out where you really were."

"Thank you," she said to Ty. He gave a slight nod. "Where did you find Malakan? What's Final View?"

We described the community under the bridge to her.

"When we got there, Aurora and Darien were coming out of the cliff. They had just been to see Malakan. When we got in to talk to him, he said he knew I was coming. Aurora told him she sent me to find him. He was waiting."

"Really?" Ashe asked. She sounded excited.

"Did he tell you? Did he answer the question Aurora asked?"

I shook my head.

"No, he didn't. But he's going to now. I'm tired of this. I'm tired of the games and getting the runaround. I'm tired of the riddles and the rituals and everyone expecting me to jump through hoops. I'm not doing it anymore."

"What are you going to do?" Ashe asked.

"I'm going back to his house and I'm going to demand he answer the question Aurora asked. She asked me to get the answer to a question, so I can exchange it for her blood. And that's exactly what I'm going to do."

"What if he won't answer you?" Ty asked. "Remember, he's the one in control. He could have told you the answer whenever he wanted, and he decided not to. What happens if you go back to his house, and he doesn't want to answer you, or he says in order to answer you, he has to put you through the ritual again?"

I shook my head.

"What was the ritual?" she asked. "What was the point?"

"He didn't tell me exactly, but it seemed like he had to do it in order to figure out what it is about me that's so different, and what Aurora needs to know. He said the images I saw were going to be the ones I needed to see, and that no one else would really know what they were."

"You really saw your past, present, and future?" she asked.

"Well, I said I saw *the* past. It wasn't mine."

My eyes slid over to Ty, but I didn't say anything more. Now didn't feel like the time to ask him about the event involving the baby I had seen in my vision.

"What did you see?" she asked.

I shook my head.

"I don't want to talk about it right now," I said. "I just want to go and see him."

"I don't think we should," Ty said. "I think I've had enough of mages today. You have no idea how he'd react to you showing up and demanding the answer to the same question again. You're running out of time. I doubt he would be willing to help you any more than he already did."

I considered what Ty was saying. "You're right," I said. "Going back to Malakan would just be a waste of time. There's nothing impactful for him to tell me. Aurora sent me to see him on a whim. That was all. It was just to amuse her and give her some sort of reassurance, because for once she's actually being held accountable for the things she did. She enjoyed being privileged and special because she is a princess, and she thinks she can dictate everyone's lives. That might have worked for her before, but it's not working anymore. I'm done being a plaything for her. Today is the third day. I don't have any options left. I'm done with this. I'm going to take what I need from Aurora."

"What if there are consequences?" Ashe asked.

"Consequences be damned," I said. "If I don't, I'm looking at a slow, miserable death. There is nothing she could do to punish me that would even come close to watching my own dick rot off."

Ashe put her hand on the inside of my thigh and ran it up to cup my crotch through my pants.

"No one wants that," she whispered into my ear.

Ty's phone buzzed on the passenger seat and he reached over for it. A smile crossed his lips as he turned the car toward the center of the city.

"Speak of the devil," he said, tossing the phone back onto the seat.

"Was that Aurora?" I asked.

"No," Ty said. "But it was my contact.

Remember I told you someone had told me Aurora was at Nakatomi Tower?"

"Yes," I answered.

"Seems she's made a return visit."

"Let's go," I said. "With any luck, tonight will be a celebration. My new birthday."

31

I WAS RELIEVED when there was no blood price to get back through the portal, even though I was getting better about the whole blood thing. Not that I really had a choice. I'd seen and shed more of it over the last three days than I had in a long time. Just being able to pass through into the basement of Solomon's without bleeding for it felt like a nice break. Ty went first, moving the tapestry aside as he passed through, then holding it out of the way so Ashe and I could follow. Even though it had only been a few days since the first time I had walked into the bar, the surroundings felt familiar and comforting. Coming back into the basement almost felt like coming home. I wondered if I'd ever feel that way about the Underworld. When this was all over, and I had completed the transition and begun my life as a vampire, I'd have to decide where to go and what to do. They were the same types of decisions I had to make when I realized my injury was bad enough to keep me from ever having the career I had wanted. I'd had my entire life mapped out for me, and grand ideas of everything I was going to do. That day, as I stared up at the ceiling of the hospital room and listened to the drone of the doctor's voice explain the extent of the damage I'd done, I had known none of it was going to happen. The injury had cast me right back to the beginning and I had to rethink everything ahead of me. I had to come up with a completely new concept of who I was and what I was going to do with my life, and it had been overwhelming.

It didn't feel like that this time. Now it felt like freedom.

I led the way as we moved through the basement to the stairs leading up into the bar. It was still early in the day, and I didn't expect anybody to be there when we went in. As soon as I opened the door, though, I noticed several figures in the dim room. Ashe, Ty, and I paused just beyond the door to the basement. The lights in the bar were still off, and the dark drapery hanging from the windows only let a tiny bit of light filter in, enough to show shadowy forms but nothing more. I felt the burn in my thigh, and my defensive instincts tingled. I looked at Ashe and she gave a slight nod. Backing up a few steps, she hit the light switch to flood the space with an even brighter light than I had seen the morning I woke up here. As soon as the lights flashed on, the figures turned to face us. Exactly as I expected them to, each wore crimson colored sunglasses.

"Darien sent them to stop us," Ty said. "He wasn't kidding when he said he wasn't going to let you get near his daughter."

"Too bad for them he doesn't have a choice," I said.

None of the guards had moved from their original positions. I expected them to run at us when they saw us, but their stillness was somehow even more unnerving. I felt like they were daring us to move, knowing the instant we did, they would attack. If there was ever a time for me to be able to communicate without speaking, now was it. I glanced at Ashe to get her attention, hoping it would create the connection we needed.

"We need to split up. We will have better chances if we get them away from each other."

Her eyes slid over to the bar, and I knew she could hear me. I nodded my agreement. Ty and I met each other's eyes. I couldn't communicate with him the same way, but I hoped he would understand. I drew in a breath and burst forward into the room. Immediately, three of the Shades swarmed me. Behind me I heard Ashe jump over the side of the bar, and Ty ran to the other side of the room. A guard followed each of them, leaving me in the center of the bar with the three guards surrounding me.

"Three now?" I asked, staring down the man in front of me. "Did you hear about my little encounter in the Underworld? Or did you bring a friend because two just didn't cut it last time?"

One guard swung at me, but I easily avoided the punch and pushed him to the ground by slamming into his thighs with one shoulder. Another of the men grabbed me by the back of my shirt to yank me away. I threw my elbow back and heard it come into crushing contact with his nose. I punched the third Shade in the stomach and took the opportunity to step away from them.

"What are you doing here?" I demanded.

"You aren't to go to Nakatomi Tower," one of the men said.

"So, you speak now. That's new."

Out of the corner of my eye, I saw one of the men trying to sneak toward me. I spun and planted a kick on the side of his head, then directed another kick backward to take out the guard I had sensed coming up behind me. I faced off against the man in front of me again.

"Get out of my way," I said.

"You aren't to go to Nakatomi Tower," he said again.

"I heard you the first time caveman, but I still disagree."

He lunged at me, and I caught him with my hands around his neck. I pressed in with my thumbs and he began to struggle, gurgling as he fought for breath. Beside me the other guard grabbed onto me and tried to pull me away, while the third yanked me from the other side. I heard a crash from the other side of the bar and in an instant the pressure of one of the guard's hands released and he pulled away from me. The man I was choking was clawing at my hands, but it wasn't long before he crumpled to the floor. In one movement I released him and swung around to land a blow in the middle of the third guard's throat. Turning around, I saw Ty standing over the Shade he'd pulled away. Behind him, the man who had first attacked him was climbing out from the wreckage of a table they had broken.

"Watch out, Ty!" I shouted.

He heeded my warning and turned in time to catch the man's fist. The sound of shattering glass dragged my attention over to the bar. Ashe was leaning back against the rail, fending off the Shade who was trying to overtake her. They had knocked almost all the bottles of liquor onto the floor, but I could see Ashe's fingers creeping over to one that was left. She managed to grab hold of the neck of the heavy square bottle and smash it across the man's head. He dropped down to the floor in a heap. She stepped over him and opened a drawer beneath the bar. Sifting through what was inside, she snatched out a ring of keys.

"Hayden!" she called.

I looked over to Ty. He was still grappling with the Shade.

"Go!" he yelled. "I'll take care of things here. You do what you need to do. I'll meet you there. If I don't, come back for me."

I nodded my acknowledgement and ran after

Ashe out of the bar. She tossed me the keys, and I followed her as she ran to a car parked across the street. The sound of the bar door slamming back open told me at least one of the guards was after us again. I jumped into the car and waited as Ashe got in beside me.

"Whose car is this?" I asked.

"One of the Shades'," she said with a laugh.

The engine roared as I turned the key.

"How do you have keys to a Shade's car?" I asked.

"When you've been around as long as I have, you learn to collect things. During the war with the warlocks, I found out Darien provides cars to all of his Shade guards. Custom made cars that all have the same key."

"Efficient," I said, pulling away from the curb.

"Efficient, and very easy to take advantage of," she said. She looked in the rearview mirror. "Two of them are chasing us," she said.

"How did you get them?" I asked.

"I'd been thinking about the cars ever since I found out about them. Whenever really bad shit goes down around the vampires, the Shades are not far. They're there to protect the Prime and the royal family, which means they're the safest ones to be around."

The Shade driving the car behind us revved his engine and drove up closer. I glanced in the mirror and saw the car was an exact match to the one I was driving, just like Ashe had said.

"Unless you're the one pissing them off," I pointed out.

"Which is why you find a way to look like them."

"Like being able to drive one of their cars," I said, impressed by the plan.

"Aurora came in with several guards a few years back. Usually she just has Jaxxim with her, but something must have been happening that night because she came in with a group of them. I managed to smuggle them off of one when they weren't paying attention. I was pretty proud of myself, to be honest."

I laughed.

"You should be. I'd loved to have seen his reaction when he realized he didn't have them. Or Darien's when he found out."

Ahead of me the traffic was picking up. I took a sharp turn down a side street to avoid it, the Shade close behind me. He drove even faster and bumped into us.

"What the fuck?" I shouted.

I tightened my grip on the steering wheel and sped up. People jumped out of the way, but I didn't care. I was too focused on staying far enough away from the Shade that he couldn't ram us and send us spinning out of control.

"Take the alley!" Ashe said, pointing to an alley that cut behind several buildings.

The car scraped the side of one of the buildings as we took the sharp turn, but we leveled out and shot down the narrow passage and out onto the road. I oriented myself and headed in the direction of the business district.

"Are they still behind us?" I asked.

Ashe turned around in her seat and scanned the road.

"No," she said. "You lost them."

"For now. They still know where we're going. They'll find us. We just have to make sure we get there first."

"I have to admit," she said, sliding across the seat toward me. "I'm very impressed by your driving."

"Oh, really?" I asked.

"You are very good at it." Her hand found my lap and cupped my crotch. She massaged it and I was instantly hard. "I knew your dick was pretty exceptional, but how does it help with your steering?"

I laughed and cupped the back of her head. Kissing her hard, I guided her head down toward my lap.

"I bet it would steer even better from inside your mouth."

Ashe laughed.

"Now, that's something I'm going to have to see."

Ahead of us I saw the Shades turn from a side road into our path.

"Then you better get started, because they just found us."

She stretched out across the seat and released my button and fly. The Shade car slowed and spun so it was diagonal across the road. They were trying to block us, but I wasn't going to be trapped that easy. My cock sprang out of my pants and into Ashe's hand as I slammed the car into reverse and zipped backwards down a short stretch of the road. Hopping over a corner, I got onto the closest road and sped toward the tower. Ashe's mouth slid down over my cock and her hand worked my shaft in tight, twisting strokes as she sucked. The feeling of her mouth gliding over me spiked my adrenaline and stirred the intensity and strength inside me. The lust fed me, empowering me to push even harder.

Ashe met every turn and lane change with a twist of her mouth or flick of her tongue. When I sped up, she did too, until I was spiraling out of control. The Shade fell away, and I exploded into her mouth as we pulled up to Nakatomi Tower. I paused, my head back against the seat, long enough for her to lick me clean, then zipped and buttoned my pants.

"You were right," she said with a mischievous smile. "It was truly a masterful driver from in there."

"Maybe afterward we can try out it's skills from inside other places," I said.

I opened the door and launched myself out onto the sidewalk. Ashe ran up beside me and we rushed toward the revolving door leading into Nakatomi Tower.

32

I could already see the Shades waiting for us in the lobby of the Tower by the time the glass revolving door was halfway around. They knew we were coming, but the fact that they were standing there didn't scare me. It made me laugh, and I swaggered into the lobby as soon as the door opened out onto the polished marble floor. Ashe had been right that the sexual encounter would embolden me and increase my strength. The guard closest to me tilted his head and stared at me as if he couldn't figure out my reaction. I opened my arms out to indicate the swarm of them.

"So many of you," I said. "Didn't trust the friends of yours Darien sent to Solomon's? You knew we were going to get past them without any trouble. That's the only reason you're here."

"You do not go into Nakatomi Tower," the man said.

I rolled my eyes and gave an exasperated sigh. Looking over my shoulder at Ashe, I gestured toward the Shade who had just spoken.

"Seriously?" I said out loud. I looked back at him. "I don't remember pulling your string. But as impressive as it is that you can apparently all say the same phrase in the exact same monotone, it's not going to stop me. I'm already here. And I'm going to find Aurora no matter what you've been told. You aren't going to get in my way."

"Ashe, figure out which one has the access card. We need it to get up to the fortieth floor."

"I will."

The Shade lunged at me, but I was ready for him. My hands clenched on either side of his head, and I gave it a sharp turn. The sound of his neck cracking accompanied his body going limp in my grip. I dropped him unceremoniously to the floor and stepped over him to prepare to face the next man. Ashe was headed to the other side of the lobby, and I saw several of the guards move to follow her. I wasn't worried about her. I knew she could hold her own long enough for me to take care of the other guards, then we would be able to go up the tower to find Aurora.

"Where is everyone else who works in the building?" I demanded. None of the guards answered. "I know Darien doesn't control this entire building, and he wouldn't be so stupid as to let a fight go down when there were hundreds, if not thousands, of other people inside. What did he do to them?"

"They've been removed," one of the Shades said.

"New words. Congratulations. Where are they?"

"It's none of your concern. You need to leave. The Prime doesn't want you here."

"That would have a hell of a lot more impact on me if I actually gave a fuck about what he thought of anything I do. That's the interesting thing about me. Up until about three days ago, I thought vampires were the really pale dudes in books or the guy on the front of delicious chocolate Halloween cereal. I had no idea there was a whole community out there, much less some Prime leading it Now that I know what's really at stake, I'm going to do whatever I want to do, and right now, that's making sure I live to see next week."

I made a move to walk around the Shade, and he stepped back in front of me.

"Not without the Prime's permission," he said.

"You are seriously starting to piss me off," I said.

I rammed the heel of my hand up into the bottom of his chin. It knocked him off balance, and he dropped back. Ahead of me, another of the Shades reached under his jacket and withdrew a long sword. The blade seemed to sparkle in the sunlight streaming through the glass doors.

"Getting fancy now, are we?" I asked.

I had only ever seen the Shades fight hand-to-hand, and the shift from that traditional form of fighting to using weapons seemed significant. They were serious now. This wasn't just trying to discourage me or scare me away. It was obvious now that the Shades had been instructed to do whatever it took to keep me away from Aurora. Darien seriously wanted to keep me away from her, and to stop her from completing my transformation. I didn't understand what I possibly could have done to make the Prime so adamantly against me. I've heard of fathers being overly protective of their daughters when they started dating someone, but calling out uniformed, armed guards to destroy the guy seemed a little extreme. Whatever the reason, no matter how determined he was to force me to run out of time and be condemned to death, I was even more determined to overcome him.

Calling up every bit of my strength I could, I plunged into the fight. I grasped the hilt of the sword and wrestled with it, trying to wrench it out of the Shade's grasp. My hand slid down the blade, but I didn't feel anything. With a hard sweep around the back of his knee, I brought the guard down. The sword fell from his grip, and I picked it up. In a swift movement, I plunged the tip of the blade into the front of his throat. I knew it wouldn't kill him, but it was enough to weaken him for a while. All I needed was the time for Ashe and me to get up to the fortieth floor of the building.

I turned my attention to the next Shade, then the next. Four more lay on the ground when I heard Ashe's cry from across the room.

"Hayden! Watch out!"

The words were no more out of her mouth than I heard a blast. I immediately recognized it as a gunshot. Burning pain seared into my back, and I gritted my teeth as I spun around to face the man who'd shot me. He held a handgun pointed directly at me. In a flash of speed, I crossed the lobby to him. Another bullet tore into my chest, but I grabbed the gun out of his hand and emptied it into him. Gripping the gun in my fist, I bashed it against the side of another Shade's head. One by one, Ashe and I battled the men as we worked our way across the lobby toward the elevators. We were steps away when another blast of gunfire shattered the call buttons for the elevators, sending a cascade of sparks onto the floor.

Ashe grabbed my arm and pulled me toward a narrow hallway leading off the lobby. I ran after her and we dove into the stairwell. We made our way up the stairs as fast as we could, but soon heard footsteps coming down toward us.

"Go out onto that floor," Ashe said, pointing at the door behind me.

I opened the door and was greeted by the surprised face of a Shade, his mouth opened slightly, and his eyebrows lifted above his sunglasses. I wasted no time and swung my fist into his nose, hearing the crack of it beneath my fingers as he crumpled to the ground. I barely had time to think before I heard the second one, to his left, swinging for me. I leaned backward and nearly knocked into Ashe. The man's fist missed me, and it crunched into the doorframe. Without thinking, I grabbed his arm and swung his entire body into the wall. He landed with a thud and spun toward me, but I was already swinging. I connected with my right hand and felt his consciousness leave him as my fist landed on his jaw.

"Take this," Ashe said, coming up to me.

I took the short sword in my hand and experimented with it, slashing the air a few times, before turning back to the doorway. I could hear footsteps pounding toward us from the other end of the long hallway, and one of the Shades from the previous round of fighting was already trying to stand. I lunged forward with the sword and he moved to the side, the blade slicing his arm as he turned. He yelped in pain and I spun behind him, just in time to hear several shots ring out. The man in front of me jerked a few times as the bullets went into him, and I tossed him aside when they stopped. The man with the gun wasn't prepared for me when I leapt out at him, swinging my left fist into his jaw and then swiping at his hand with the sword.

"Ashe! Get the gun. If I get in trouble, take a couple out."

"How many bullets has it got?"

"I think that clip holds nine. He shot four. You've got five shots, Ashe. Make them count."

She picked up the gun and cocked it, a grin on her face that made me temporarily forget the imminent danger we were in.

"I'll try not to hit you."

"Thanks," I said.

At that moment I saw her eyes widen and she ducked back through the doorway. I turned to see three more Shades, one a hulking brute of a thing, come barreling in the door and stop cold, surveying the scene. They had no weapons on them but came charging down the narrow hallway in single file toward me like a train of fury.

I ducked a punch from the first one and stuck my sword in the second, using his own momentum to send it all the way in. I dropped to the ground, letting go of my weapon, and rolled forward, taking the legs out from the largest of them and sending him barreling into the first and second guards. The first Shade stood quickly and charged back at me, but I met him with an elbow that cracked his jaw and shoved him face first into the wall.

"Hey, dickhead," I heard from beside me and both me and the Shade looked up.

Ashe stood in the doorway, the gun leveled and the same smirk on her lips. An explosion of sound filled the room as she sent a bullet directly between his eyes. For a moment he swayed where he stood and then he turned to look at me. I saw the expression of his face fade and his features grow slack before he fell backward like a great oak. His body hit the ground with such force I felt it shake, and I stood wincing, my hand against the wall as I wheezed in a few breaths before forcing my breathing to settle down.

"Four left," Ashe said. "Are you okay?"

I realized I was feeling better already. My body felt like it had only had a few punches thrown at it, and I was ready to go again. I nodded to her, and we turned back to the end of the hall. As we walked forward, I grabbed the sword from the chest of the downed Shade, who was now coughing up blood and trying to sit up. I kicked him hard in the chest and he fell backward, the sword sliding out easily. The sight of the blood everywhere was still a lot for me, but I tried to steel myself and press on. I could hear more footsteps coming from higher on the stairs, and knew the stairwell was the only way up from our floor. I needed to be ready.

I looked over to Ashe, who smiled and reached up to kiss me on the cheek. I swung the door open and we walked through, but the stairwell was still empty on our level. I could hear them coming from floors above us, and I looked around to find something to barricade the door with. I didn't think the Shades we had just beat would be up any time soon, but I wanted to be sure. I found a crowbar and jammed it into the door hinge so that it wouldn't open from the outside and motioned for Ashe to take cover under the stairs. I fell back into a shadow in the corner of the poorly lit landing and waited.

Two Shades came down the stairs and onto the landing moments later. They reached the door we had just come through and paused when I jumped out from the shadow I had hidden in. I buried the sword deep into the neck of the shorter one and immediately kicked forward into the back of the other. He went flying forward into the wall as the first fell to the ground. I lost my grip on the sword, so I left it and rushed forward to meet the now spinning Shade.

I felt him catch my arm at the elbow and land a headbutt into my chest, knocking the wind from me, followed by three quick punches to my face. I reeled backward and moved out of the way just in time for him to miss a kick aimed at my head. As he tried to regain his balance, I lifted my knee to meet his nose. His head flew back and I caught hit in my hands, using his momentum to send the back of his head smashing into the concrete wall. He slumped to the ground, out cold, and I turned my attention to the short one. I had barely noticed the yells of pain he had been bellowing out, and the smell of his blood spraying everywhere made me momentarily sick. I turned my head away from him when I heard Ashe yell out to me.

"Don't look!"

I refrained from watching as I heard her yank the sword from his neck and I heard her grunt as she swung it down. I could no longer hold my curiosity in one, a moment later as I felt something hit my foot. I looked down to see his severed head, blank eyes looking up at me. My stomach lurched, but Ashe pulled me by my shirt to her. She was covered in the Shade's blood, but she met me with a kiss that settled me, and suddenly my focus had returned. I was still breathing heavily, and my body was healing more slowly now, but I felt good enough to barrel up the steps. As we reached the landing for the next floor, the door to it burst open and a Shade came flying out at me. He throttled me and we tumbled back down the steps, each one smashing into my back. When we finally hit the bottom of the steps, I saw him look down and see the severed head before turning back to me. I didn't hesitate.

I leapt at him with my fist, missing by inches and he lifted his knee into my ribs. I stumbled into the wall and felt him crash punches into my kidneys before attempting to lock my head into a choke. I snapped my hips backward into him and rolled forward, sending him flying over me and into the wall. Before he could move, I dove at him, sending my knee into his face and feeling a crack in his neck. His body went still, and I stopped to catch my breath again. From above I saw Ashe looking down at me and I found the energy again to stand. I ran up the steps to her and past her as we bolted up several flights of stairs. As we reached the fifth floor, I could hear what sounded like an army of Shades coming down the stairs several floors ahead.

"We have to go in here, now," I said to Ashe, and we ducked inside the hallway.

There were doors to empty offices lining the walls of this hall, but what interested me was at the very end. An elevator stood, with a flashing number five above it. The elevator was on our floor. I grabbed Ashe's hand and we tore off toward it. We had gotten within feet of it when one of the office doors opened and a Shade came flying through it. Ashe ran forward and pressed the elevator button as the Shade and I tumbled around on the ground. I kicked him hard in his chest and he went backward a few feet. I scrambled up and dove into the elevator. Ashe had pressed the button for the thirtieth floor when the Shade dove into the elevator with us.

Ashe screamed and aimed the gun toward us, but the Shade and I were rolling around too much for her to get an accurate shot. I could hear her thoughts running through my head, as she screamed at herself not to miss. I was not interested in feeling another bullet go through me. Just as she pulled the trigger, I lifted my hand toward her. The bullets exploded from the gun, but stopped halfway between the barrel and the palm of my hand. They hovered in the air for a brief second, then tumbled to the floor of the elevator. I lifted the Shade's head and smashed it into the floor, knocking him out. My eyes snapped to Ashe, who was staring at the bullets with an open mouth.

"How did you do that?" she asked.

"What do you mean?"

"How did you stop those bullets?"

"I just…did. I didn't want them to hit me, so I lifted my hand, and they stopped."

"We don't do that," Ashe said. "That's not just something vampires do. We don't just stop bullets."

I rolled over onto my back to catch my breath and process what she told me, when I felt the elevator slow down.

"Oh, shit," Ashe said.

I looked up at the light above the door. It said twenty-seven.

Someone else wanted on the elevator.

A bell sounded, and I could hear the door begin to open as I scrambled to my feet.

33

The door opened slowly and I exploded through it, smashing the face of the first Shade I saw with my fist. He crumpled to the ground below me and I dove into the body of a second man behind him. We stumbled into a wall and his elbow smashed a hole in it enough to see through to the piping inside. Ashe ran out behind me, swinging the butt of the gun into the first Shade's face as he tried to regain his footing and sending him back down again.

Watching her was too much of a distraction, though, and the one I was fighting caught me with a right cross on the jaw. I reeled back but didn't let go of his shirt and thrust my knee into his crotch. I heard him cry out in pain as I lifted the same knee to make contact with his chest and repeated the move a couple of times. I shoved him down as the door to the stairwell opened and three more Shades barreled out toward me.

A shot rang out and the first one went down in a bloody heap as the bullet tore through his neck. The second Shade charged me and I ducked his punch, running ahead to meet the third one as he crossed into the hall. I swung my elbow into his face and then backhanded him, sending him to the ground. The second Shade had now turned to face me, and he kicked me in the chest, sending me into the wall. Dazed and winded, I couldn't stop a few punches from landing on my face. Finally, I regained my footing in time to feel the third Shade stand up behind me. He grabbed me in a choke hold and I gripped his forearms tightly. I pushed him back into the wall and lifted my feet to kick forward into the Shade charging me. It was enough to knock him off his feet, and I swung the one off my back in a violent motion that had him land on top of the Shade who had been shot in the throat.

I coughed and looked up to see Ashe readying the gun, but I mentally told her to stop and she slowly lowered it. Only three more shots left. We needed to make them count.

Now both of the Shades were standing, and for a moment we stood still, waiting for someone to make the first move. I decided to press the advantage and charged at one of them, tackling him to the ground. We landed hard and I heard Ashe speak to me in my mind again.

"The sword! Take the sword!"

I looked up to see her tossing it toward me, and I reached up to grab it. As I did, I felt the other guard charging me from behind. As soon as the sword was in my hand, I swung it around, slashing from the shoulder down to the hip of the one coming up at me. He fell to the ground, screaming in pain, and I looked down at the one I had tackled. There was a moment's realization that he too could have his head removed before I thrust the sword down into his chest. I yanked it back up as I saw him curl up in a ball below me.

"We need to get to the top floor. Let's go," I said.

Ashe nodded, and we made for the stairwell again. As we opened the door, we could hear the sounds below us of several of the Shade's making their way up and others above us making their way down. We ran up the stairs as fast as we could, reaching the twenty-ninth floor before encountering one Shade, who leapt at me. I grabbed him in mid-air and tossed him down the center of the stairway. As he fell, his screams alerted the ones below us. We had to move faster.

I struggled for breath from my now aching, but healing, ribs. Their ability to regenerate still seemed somewhat random, but it felt like I had gained some measure of control over it. We reached the thirtieth floor and saw that the stairwell ended. I opened the door and poked my head out of the doorway.

A shot rang out through the hall and I ducked back inside. The bullet missed my head by inches, and I tried to calm my nerves. Ashe cocked the gun and poked her head out. Another bullet ripped into the door and Ashe fired twice into the room, then ducked back in to me.

"Come on," she said.

We opened the door and I saw two Shades lying on the ground, bullets in their heads. Ashe was one hell of a shot. At the end of the hallway we saw another elevator, but this one had an ornate door that made it look far older than the building itself Before I could get halfway down the hall, another door opened, and another Shade came out. I ran right into him, tearing the door off its hinges as we grappled to the ground. I wrapped his arm in a lock and pulled back as hard as I could, using his own body weight against him, until I heard his elbow shatter.

His arm went limp and I landed a few blows to his head to send him to the ground. I looked behind us and saw that the shot Shades were beginning to move. Noting we didn't have much time, I ran to the elevator and punched the button until the doors opened and Ashe and I were able to slip inside.

The elevator door closed, and a rush of emotion went through me. The buzz of adrenaline from the fight contrasted with the relief of finally being in the elevator, only minutes away from completing what I had come here to do. These feelings blended with anticipation of what I'd find when we got there, and what it would be like in those first few moments after my change was complete.

"Are you ready?" Ashe asked.

I nodded.

"As I ever will be," I said.

She reached into her cleavage and withdrew an access key card. I tried to ignore the streaks of blood across it, and to not think about how it had ended up tucked between her breasts. She'd done exactly what she needed to do. The only way we were going to be able to get above the thirtieth floor in this building was with that key card, and that meant having to take it away from the Shade who carried it.

"Do you think they'll be waiting for us?" I asked.

"Who?" Ashe asked.

"The Shade," I said. "By now, they should be mostly healed. At least the ones who weren't severely hurt. Are they just going to meet us up on the next floor?"

"I doubt it," she said. "Even if they are healed by now, none of them are going to want to keep fighting. They weren't expecting what you have. Remember, these are men who are accustomed to people being afraid of them. The Shade could just be standing there, and people won't get anywhere near them because of who they are and what they represent. Darien isn't exactly known as being a Prime of his people. His life span and his position grant him luxuries and privileges that he takes full advantage of without hesitation. It's not that he doesn't care about what happens to the rest of the vampires. He's very dedicated to the species and what he believes is right for them. But you're not going to see him spending much time with them or foregoing his power and influence for anything. His full abilities are something people still whisper about. He has the Shade so he can avoid fighting unless he specifically wants the battle. Those guards weren't prepared to fight against someone as strong as you are. Beyond that, though, there are only a very few Shade who are allowed above the thirtieth floor. They have to have special authorization, and I'm almost positive only one or two of those men we just encountered have that authorization. Even if they wanted to continue the fight, they couldn't."

She turned to the control panel on the wall of the elevator and pressed the key card to it just like the Shade had when we had come to the tower after Aurora summoned me. The buttons for the top ten floors of the building illuminated, and Ashe pressed the button for the fortieth floor.

"What's it like?" I asked as the elevator started sliding upward.

"What's what like?" Ashe asked.

"Changing. What's it like to have the transformation complete?"

She shrugged.

"I don't really know," she said. "It was so long ago, I don't really remember anything other than being relieved. The sick, tired feeling of going through the transition before it's complete is so miserable that it was amazing just to know I wasn't going to feel like that anymore. But to be honest it's not a huge difference. It's not like you're going to suddenly have an epiphany about your existence or feel like a totally different person."

"I already feel like a totally different person," I said.

"How are you feeling other than that?" she asked. "You took some pretty good blows during that fight. Not to mention a couple of bullets."

Until she'd said that, I'd almost forgotten I'd been shot during the clash with the Shade. The wounds had already healed considerably, and the pain was not much worse than the ache throughout the rest of my body that came from such exertion. It was nowhere near as bad as the pain I remembered from fights when I was younger.

"I'm actually doing all right," I told her. "Speaking of the bullets, though, what do we do about them? Do they just stay in there like really creepy souvenirs?"

"If you want them to. It's not like they're going

to hurt you. They could make going through metal detectors kind of a bitch, though. If you want to get them taken out, I can bring you to an Underworld doctor."

"There are doctors in the Underworld?" I asked.

"Of course," Ashe said. "We all need someone to take care of us. You do not want to be around a lycan with a cold, I promise. Talk about whiny as hell. It's much easier to deal with someone who understands the needs of the different species, and who you don't have to come up with a clever cover story for. If we brought you to a human hospital to deal with those bullets, you would not only have to come up with a way to explain why you've been shot a couple times, but also how you were able to heal as quickly as you did. I can assure you the police would get involved and the doctors would be trying to study you because of your incredible immune system and cellular recovery ability. It's just a big hassle you don't want to have to deal with. Instead, you can go to the Underworld doctor, say you've been shot, and he'll offer to take the bullets out for you."

"That does sound less stressful," I said.

Ashe nodded.

"Considerably."

"How does Darien get to the Underworld when he goes?" I asked.

"You're just full of questions today, aren't you?"

"This is kind of a significant moment for me. I want to be prepared. And since you have yet to produce that manual for me no matter *how* many times I ask, I have to figure it all out myself."

Ashe laughed, glancing at the numbers on the elevator to watch them tick upward. This elevator was much slower than the special one we'd ridden from the lobby during our visit, but the floors were gradually going past.

"What were you asking?"

"How Darien gets to the Underworld."

"Through the portal," she said. "Just like everyone else."

I shook my head.

"No, I mean, when he doesn't use that portal. How does he get there?"

"What do you mean when he doesn't use that portal? That's the only portal in New York that's used."

"And Ty controls it?"

"He's the keeper. He ensures the blood price is paid when an adult passes through, or whenever else it might be required, and he locks the portal to prevent anyone moving through it when he's not there. A portal not given its blood price can become extremely dangerous."

"So it is possible to move through the portal when Ty isn't there?" I asked.

"Only if he hasn't locked it," she said. "He protects it and regulates passage through, but if it's locked, no one can move through it until it's unlocked. He's the only one who can unlock the portal he's been assigned to protect."

"Does he always lock it when he's going into the Underworld?" I asked.

"Why are you asking all these questions?" she asked.

"When Ty and I went to see Malakan, we went through Final View, and Aurora and Darien were coming out of Malakan's cliff."

"I know. You told me that."

"But how could they have been there? Ty was with me. He had been since we met up at The Foundry and I told him you were missing. He'd come through the portal to the Underworld to meet us there, which means he must have locked the portal when he went through. So how did Aurora and her father end up at that cliff?"

"They must have been there before Ty left."

I shook my head.

"No," I said. "He was shocked to see them."

The elevator stopped moving and the doors slid open. The conversation stopped when we looked beyond the doors and saw Darien standing just feet away.

34

"I have to say," Darien said in a low, cold voice. "You are persistent."

"Get out of my way," I said. "I am going to Aurora.

"No," he said. "I've told you already. You will never have her."

I rushed forward, hoping to take him by surprise with my speed, and was shocked at myself at just how fast I was. Even through my exhaustion, my abilities were strengthening. Darien had barely moved before I crashed into him and we went sailing through the air, landing hard on a door that cracked and fell backward. I began swinging punches, but Darien swatted them away and flipped me over him onto my back. As we struggled with each other, we moved down the hallway and into a room. I could see shelves of books on one wall. On the other, the ancient and beautiful desk of a powerful man. A high-backed chair sat behind it and to the left of it stood Aurora. To her side was Jaxxim.

I tried to silently call out to Aurora. Maybe she had changed her mind. Maybe now that it was so close to the end of the time I had left, she would feel the urgency more and would be willing to finish my transformation. If she was, she could call off her father. I couldn't make the connection, and instead of asking her father to stop, Aurora watched, seeming content to wait for what would happen next.

I turned back to Darien in time to see him kick at me, which I blocked and swung a punch that landed near his eye. I tried to follow with another, but Darien swept my feet from under me, and I landed on the ground, hard. Before I could catch my breath, he had grabbed me by my shirt and lifted me, tossing me through the air and into a small table which splintered, sending shards of wood everywhere, and destroying the lamp that sat on it. The broken glass from the lamp dug into my back and arm, and the feeling enraged me.

"She chose me," I said angrily.

"My daughter has to be protected from her mistakes. You were a momentary spell of whimsy. She never really intended to bond with you. And even if she did, it's not enough. You are not enough for her, and you could never be. I won't allow it."

"It's not your choice."

I charged again, but Darien met me with a series of blows that ended with an uppercut that sent me sprawling backward again, careening into the bookshelves and sending several aged volumes to the floor. I wiped my mouth where blood had been flowing with the edge of my sleeve and stood tall before him. He smirked at me and beckoned me to come at him again. I was happy to oblige.

I ran at him and ducked as he swung a few errant punches, using my speed to make him miss, before crashing my fist into his ribs and grabbing him in a face-lock. Jaxxim took a step toward us, but Darien threw me back, sending me into another chair that imploded on impact, and waved him off. Jaxxim stepped back into his place, in front of Aurora, who was watching with a certain glee that was hard to miss.

Darien was suddenly mid-air and hurtling

toward me, so I rolled to the side, causing him to miss. I jumped on his back and swung my arms into either side of his face before wrapping him in another chokehold. He spun sideways and lifted me up before crashing me directly into the ground and making me lose my grip on him. I rolled to my feet, dazed and hurt, trying to catch a moment of rest for my body to regenerate. He was suddenly face to face with me again, swinging wildly, and connecting repeatedly. I was taking a tremendous amount of damage, and my body wasn't recovering from it as quickly as it had from the Shades. I stumbled backward and then lunged forward, catching him by surprise with a kick to his jaw. He sprawled on the ground, and I felt Ashe in the doorway, her hand on the gun.

"No. This is my fight."

Slowly, Ashe put the gun back in her waistband, and I focused on Darien. He was getting to his feet again and brushing himself off. He seemed to be almost laughing. I looked beyond him to Aurora and suddenly an idea popped into my head. As it did, Darien was again rushing at me, but I dodged him at the last moment. My knee caught him in the stomach and sent him flying past me. He landed hard on the ground from the force of the blow and I looked back at Aurora. If I used everything I had left....

I prepared myself, focusing every bit of energy I had, every resource that was trying to heal me, or strengthen me, or detect things with senses I had never known. All of it was now focused on one thing: speed. If I could just get to Aurora. All I needed was to get to her and I could take what I needed.

I took off, running with my full speed to her. Darien was standing between us, but I ran around him before he was able to react. Jaxxim moved to try to block me, but even he was far too late. I blew past him and scooped Auoroa up, carrying her to the far corner of the room before spinning back to look at her father. He was staring back at me in shock.

"There's nothing you can do," I said. "She's mine."

Aurora didn't resist as I leaned down and sank my teeth into her neck. They broke through her skin more easily than I expected, and a rush of warm blood filled my mouth. It tasted sweet and smooth, and I eagerly drank it down. I could hear Ashe gasp somewhere across the office, and I knew she was relieved and happy for me. It was done.

Aurora's hands came up into my hair and ran through it while I remained latched to her neck. When I pulled my mouth away and stood up to look at her, she was smiling.

"Congratulations," she said. "Your transformation is complete. You are now truly a vampire." She took a step forward to close the space between us. Her hands ran up my chest and wrapped around my neck. "And you are my Lord. I belong to you fully and wholly, forever."

Our mouths met, and I put my hands around her waist to pull her closer to me. As we kissed hungrily, I felt all of the remaining hints of grogginess and fog disappear. Everything around me became sharp and clear. The pain from all of my injuries faded, and when I looked down, I saw my arms healing.

"Hayden," Darien said. I moved Aurora behind me as I turned to face her father again. Rather than the expression of fury I expected to see, however, I saw a smile. "Well done," he said. "I believe congratulations are in order."

"Thank you," I said with uncertainty.

The Prime laughed as he walked up to me.

"Don't seem so surprised," he said. "That one decision proved yourself to me more than anything could have. You didn't just wait around for your transformation to be given to you or try to find some easy path to it. I'm pleased to see my new son is strong and willing to take what he wanted rather than to try to make a deal for it." He stepped up to me and clapped me on the back. "Welcome to our family," he said.

Ashe rushed across the room and I opened my arms to her. She jumped into them and hugged me close.

"You did it," she murmured into my ear. "I'm so happy for you."

"Thank you," I said. I stepped back from her and wrapped my arm around Aurora's waist to draw her close to my side. I craved being near her even more now than I had before. "And, Ashe, thank you for everything you did for me. I wouldn't have been able to come this far without you. I don't think I could have made it through the first day without losing my mind if it wasn't for you. I appreciate it."

She nodded, her bright eyes sparkling, happy tears reflected in the grin on her face.

"Absolutely," she said. "You would have been able to do it. I know you would have." We searched each other's faces for a moment, then laughed.

"No, you probably wouldn't have. But, either way, I'm glad I could have been there for you."

"I am too," Aurora said.

I leaned down and kissed her again. It felt like there was something passing back and forth, like our energy was flowing between us.

"Tell me," Darien said when the kiss ended. "Your speed. It's incredible. How do you do it?"

I looked back at him strangely.

"How?" I asked. "It's just something I realized I could do after Aurora bit me. Like my strength."

Darien looked like he was about to say something else, but Aurora stopped him.

"The hour has gotten very late," she said. "I'm going to bring Hayden to the thirty-third floor."

"What's there?" I asked.

"My private rooms," she said. "The space I use when I want to stay on this side of the portal for longer. Tonight, my new Lord has needs to attend to."

She looked at Ashe, but Ashe shook her head.

"No," she said. "Not tonight. As much as I want to." Her eyes roved along my body, and then Aurora's. "And I definitely want to, but tonight should be about the two of you. It's a celebration of the sealing of the blood pact between you. I'm going to go meet Ty. Maybe I'll see how much I can open up the car."

I laughed.

"Without the master driver to guide you?"

"We'll just have to hope for the best." Her grin faded as she glanced over at Darien. "Call off your men," she said.

"I will," he told her. "There will be no more fighting tonight."

"There aren't many left who have much fight in them," she said. "Hayden took them down. You've lost several."

The Prime gave a single nod.

"I will deal with them."

Ashe met my eyes for a second longer, then swept out of the room.

"Come with me," Aurora said, taking my hands.

She guided me out of the room and back toward the elevator. We got inside, and she reached for the control panel. She wasn't holding one of the access cards, but she brushed her thumb over the sensor and the buttons lit up. She was her own authorization. As soon as the doors closed, I put my hands on either side of her waist and pushed her back against the wall. She gasped slightly, then her full, luscious lips curled up into a smile.

"I've been thinking about those lips since you walked out of my room at Malakan's house," I told her.

Ducking my head, I gathered those perfect lips into another deep kiss. Aurora melted into me, and I held her close. Our bodies were speaking to each other, and by the time the elevator door opened, I couldn't resist her anymore. I scooped her up into my arms and carried her into the room she directed me to. Tossing her onto the bed, I stripped off my clothes without taking my eyes off her. She did the same, and soon we were completely bare. I dropped down over her, feeling the heat of her body radiating off of her, and claimed her again.

EPILOGUE

The same man staggered out from under the bridge as I approached Final View.

"You came back," the one wearing one shoe said. "Disappointed you didn't get to witness anyone join our little world?"

"Not exactly," I said. "Tell everyone around here they have a new Prince. Last night, Aurora completed my transformation and I have been bonded to her through a blood pact."

The man bowed down to me.

"I'm happy to share the good news," he said.

"Thank you. Has Malakan come out?"

"No. It's been a very long time since I've seen him. He stays in there."

He nodded toward the door in the cliff. I

walked over to it and opened it without hesitation. The torch on the wall was still burning, and I wondered if it was enchanted so it never burned out, or if the old warlock came down here every so often to relight the flame. There was no nervousness in me as I held the torch high above my head and started down the tunnel. Even without anyone there with me, I had no fear. The world was clear and bright around me, and I felt like I could do anything. But there was a question in the back of my mind I couldn't let go of. I was still thinking about the ritual I had completed with Malakan, and the visions I had during it. The one of Ashe had been completely accurate. Everything about it, down to the most gruesome detail, had been exactly the way I envisioned it when I found her. I was able to save her, but I couldn't stop thinking about the other two visions. I needed to know anything I could to protect Aurora from whatever danger was waiting for her in the future.

Traveling down the tunnel this time didn't feel like it took as long as it did the first time I made the journey. Whether I was moving at a faster pace because I wasn't trying to stay with Ty, or it was simply because I felt accustomed to the tunnel now and knew where I was going, I ended up at the door leading into the first set of chambers in what felt like only minutes. The lamps and torches were burning just like they were before, and I listened closely to hear any sign of Malakan. When I didn't hear him, I called out to him. He didn't answer, and I made my way through the rooms. Several of them I hadn't been in before and I wondered about their purpose. After exploring all of the rooms, I didn't find the warlock. Knowing that must mean he was at the house, I headed for the door.

The air was sweet when I stepped through the door in the tree and out into the tall grass of the field. Everything was as quiet and peaceful as it had been my first time here. I walked across the field, and as I approached the house, I noticed Malakan sitting on one of the swings. He rocked slowly back and forth as he stared out over the grass.

"Hello," I called out to him.

He smiled and waved.

"Hello, Hayden," he said. He stood while I walked up the stairs to the porch, then extended his hand to me. "Darien told me the good news. Your change is complete, and you are now bonded to Aurora?"

"Yes," I told him. "It didn't go as easily as I

might have liked it to, but I did what I needed to do."

"And that's what you should always do," Malakan said. "The easy way is not always the best way. In fact, it very rarely is. If there is something that really deserves to be had or done, the hardships and challenge to achieve it will be well worth it."

"She is," I said.

He searched my face.

"But you haven't come here to give me your news," he said.

"No," I admitted. "I need to talk to you about the ritual."

Malakan drew in a breath.

"You should come inside," he said. We walked toward the door. "Can I get you something to drink?" He glanced over his shoulder. "Or have you forgone that now?"

I smiled.

"I haven't decided yet," I said. "But I don't think so. I enjoy eating and drinking too much to give it up now. Besides, I think Stephana might be on to something with her idea that it has benefits for vampires even after their transition."

"Perhaps," Malakan said.

We walked into the house and he directed me to the room on the opposite side of the entryway from where we'd done the ritual. Unlike the first room, it was well-furnished. Malakan gestured at the large couch and I settled down onto it. He bustled away, giving me a few minutes to look around. I wondered how much of what he had was smuggled from his life before his exile, and what he had acquired in this new existence. On the other hand, if he had mirrored the entire house and not just the outside, it all could have come along with it. Malakan came back into the room carrying a tray with a tall silver tea pot and mismatched cups and saucers. He set it on the table and picked up one of the cups. Adding a large dollop of cream and a drizzle of honey, he nodded toward the other cup.

"Go ahead," he said.

"Maybe later. Thanks. I need to talk about what I saw in those visions."

He took a sip of the tea and let out a breath.

"I thought you would," he said. "You were so focused on saving Ashe and completing your change that you couldn't dwell on it, but I knew when you were finished with those tasks, your mind would come back to them."

"What did they mean?" I asked. "I don't understand either of them. The one from the past I'm sure I'll figure out at some point. I might talk to Ty about later it if it's still bothering me. The other one, though, I need to know what that meant. In that vision, Aurora was dead, and I was holding her. Something horrible had happened. I could feel the heat and smell the smoke. There was nothing but sadness. And she was wearing the pendant of the Dragon. What could that mean?"

"I don't know, Hayden," Malakan said regretfully. "Like I told you before, the visions are meant for you, and they reveal something you need to know. I can't always discern the details."

"Is there any way to know when it might happen? Is there a specific amount of time into the future that those visions show?"

"No," he said again. "It's just a look into what will come. It could be centuries ahead of you, or it could happen in a matter of hours. There's no way to know. All I can tell you is that the glimpses into the future that ritual offers are usually warnings. Sometimes they are just confirmations of what's to come, or reassurances that something will work out in a certain way. Most often, though, they are cautionary. You are meant to know what is coming and to prepare yourself for it. What you do with that is up to you."

I nodded. I'd been hopeful when I came here, but I hadn't honestly expected much more than what he just said. He'd already told me he didn't control the visions and couldn't interpret them with complete certainty. What I'd seen was going to have to act as a reminder for me to always stay vigilant and prepared. Ready to go back to Aurora and Ashe, who had decided to celebrate my first twenty-four hours as a vampire by heading back to where it all began at the bar in Solomon's Fang, I stood.

"Thank you, Malakan," I said. "I appreciate your help."

I started out of the house when I heard his voice again.

"I can't explain the vision of the future for you," he said. "But I can tell you more about the past."

I stopped. There was something in his voice that made my heart beat faster. I turned back around, and he gestured toward the couch again. When I sat back down, he met my eyes.

"I thought you couldn't explain my visions," I said.

"I don't mean your vision," Malakan told me. "That is still for you to figure out yourself. The significance of that will come in time. What I mean is the truth about your past. Who and what you really are. You told me that the Dragon said they wanted to see you because you are a hybrid of two ancient and powerful bloodlines."

"Yeah," I said. "But I wasn't finished with my transformation yet. I figured they just meant the vampire and the human that was still in me."

Malakan shook his head.

"No," he said. "That doesn't make you a hybrid. That just means you're changing. What they were talking about was a true hybrid. You are a vampire, yes, but that's not all. You were not a hybrid at birth. You became a hybrid the moment Aurora bit you and started to change you into a vampire. That's because you are not and have never been truly human. You are, and always have been, of ancient warlock blood. You were taken and raised far away from your birthright. You were long thought dead, Hayden, but now you're back."

His words hit me hard and I couldn't process them.

"What?" I asked.

"You are a warlock," he said again. "You always have been."

"No," I said, shaking my head. "I was raised in the upper world, by completely normal human parents."

"You were taken," he said again. "They raised you because your parents couldn't. Think about it. Think about the fights you've been in. Your speed and your strength."

"Vampire abilities," I pointed out.

"No," Malakan said even more forcefully. "Vampires get abilities when they change, of course, but not like that. Your power, especially your speed, can't be explained by pure vampire blood. That's the sign of a warlock. And I've heard what happened in the church with the mages. Do you truly believe that's something any of the other vampires could have done at all, much less before they completed their transformation?"

"I don't know," I said.

"No," he said. "None of them could have. They were trying to destroy you with their magic, Hayden, and you resisted it."

"I used my strength to protect me," I said.

"You used your own magic," Malakan said. "You didn't realize it, but that's what you were doing. This is your destiny, Hayden. You've always been meant to be here. You are now more powerful than you could ever have imagined. You are the son-in-law of the Prime, Prince of the vampires. But you also have the blood of a warlock. You can master both and be an unstoppable force for what's to come. I can teach you how to access and control the abilities of your warlock blood."

Everything felt like it was sinking in. I nodded.

"Yes," I said.

He smiled.

"Good. But not today. You've had enough. Go home. Go back to Aurora. Enjoy her. Return soon and we will begin."

I shook Malakan's hand and he gazed back at me with tender eyes before guiding me to the door. I walked down the stairs back into the grass and started toward the door that would take me back to the community under the bridge. I was nearly there when an explosion threw me to the ground. I turned around and saw Malakan's house consumed in flames.

SIGN UP FOR UPDATES

For updates about new releases, sign up for the mailing list below. You'll know as soon as I release new books, including my upcoming new series, as well as sequels to *Vampire Mage*.

https://www.subscribepage.com/joshua_king

ABOUT THE AUTHOR

Joshua King is a Sci-Fi, Fantasy, Urban Fantasy writer that loves a killer story mixed with a few ongoing fantasies. Strong gorgeous women, super evil villains, precarious situations, and a normal dude that gets transformed into making it happen are all part of the fun.

When not writing, he's watching movies, traveling the US with his wife and son, or paying homage to the God of War. He's hoping to entertain you and give you a few minutes of heart-racing fun or mind-bending mystery in the various worlds he's created or the ones he plans to create.

Made in the USA
Columbia, SC
21 February 2019